"YOU BLEW IT, SHEA. YOU FAILED THE SIMULATION TEST. BUT THE COMMANDER OVERRULED THE BOARD—YOU GOT A SECOND CHANCE."

Lt. Shea's second chance was to play pilot to a minimal-hassle scientific mission, mapping a chunk of the solar system.

Then the Wolfpack struck, and the space pirates left her defenseless ship a blasted wreckage, stripped of anything of value.

Now Shea and a handful of survivors drift in an interstellar tomb, farther and farther from any hope of rescue.

Until a ship appears. But as it approaches, the survivors realize that no human could have constructed it.

Nicole's second chance is about to become mankind's first contact with alien life . . .

━━━━━ ━━━━━

"Chris Claremont, well-known writer in another medium, makes an impressive debut in novel-length with *FirstFlight*—solid with plausible technical detail and excellent in story—a writer definitely able to sustain a strong start right to the end. I'm really impressed. I give it my enthusiastic recommendation."

—C. J. Cherryh

Ace Books by Chris Claremont

FIRSTFLIGHT
GROUNDED!

CHRIS CLAREMONT
FIRST FLIGHT

ACE BOOKS, NEW YORK

This book is an Ace original edition, and has never been previously published.

FIRSTFLIGHT

An Ace Book/published by arrangement with the author

PRINTING HISTORY
Ace edition/December 1987

ISBN: 0-441-23584-0

Ace Books are published by The Berkley Publishing Group,
200 Madison Avenue, New York, New York 10016.
The name "ACE" and the "A" logo are trademarks belonging to Charter Communications, Inc.

PRINTED IN THE UNITED STATES OF AMERICA

10   9   8   7

To GB—who bought the silly thing!

And to Charley, Scott, Jean, Ororo,
Logan, Peter, Kurt, Sean, Kitty,
Rogue, Betsy, Alex, Ali—
and all the rest—
who helped (and help) pay the rent!

To my Folks
And my Sister Sue
(Who finally got herself
mentioned in a book!)

one

A HUNDRED KILOMETERS ahead of them, invisible in the darkness, *Hightower* swung serenely around the Earth, following a celestial path as old and well-worn as the planet itself. Nicole knew the giant L-5 station was there—her instruments told her so, both the massed scanscreens and telltales that crowded the main control panel and the head-up displays projected onto the canopy directly in front of her—she just wished she could see it. The distance was close to an hour's drive in her car, half that flying her Beech; today, she'd cover it in a matter of minutes.

"O'Neill Approach Control," she said, automatically checking the instruments and trying not to sound as bored as she felt, "this is NASA shuttle one-two-one, out of Kennedy Space Center, vectoring onto Final."

"One-two-one," a voice crackled in her ears, "this is O'Neill Control, standing for course update."

"We copy, O'Neill," Nicole acknowledged. "One-two-one standing by." She looked over at her co-pilot, Paul DaCuhna —like her—a brand-new Second Lieutenant in the United States Air Force, and asked for a status report.

"Couldn't be better, boss," he said cheerily. "That last correction was *perfectemundo,* and all on-board systems register nominal function."

"Except for my fucking air lines," she muttered, squirming

in her seat and wishing she weren't encumbered by the bulky
pressure suit. They'd been in full gear for three days straight,
ever since lift-off, not even allowed to remove gloves and
helmets, except in an emergency, which this certainly was,
since a blocked hose junction had cut off her flow of oxygen.
She hadn't realized how bad she smelled until she cracked the
seal ring on her helmet and took her first breath of cabin air.
She pitied anyone standing nearby when she removed the entire suit; this stench was murder. The realization that Paul was
probably equally ripe didn't help much, and the longer her
helmet was off, the more rotten she felt, painfully conscious
now of an itch down towards the base of her spine where—of
course—she couldn't scratch. Wiggling in her chair only
made things worse. She was ready to kill for a decent bath, or
a wash of any kind—and as if that wasn't torment enough,
ever since breakfast she'd found herself gripped by an irrational yen for a double-dip hot fudge sundae buried under a
mountain of walnuts, cherries and whipped cream. Just thinking about it was more than she could bear.

She turned on the master switch, and grinned triumphantly
as she was rewarded with a faint hiss from the hose held in her
hand and a rush of cool air against her face. A moment later,
the umbilical was locked back on to her suit.

"That's better," she said, mostly to herself, rubbing her
eyes and wishing the flight would hurry up and end so she
could return to at least a semblance of humanity. She felt far
more weary than she'd expected—this last day it had taken an
effort to focus her thoughts—and she realized that it was
mostly due to boredom. Nothing much had happened once
they'd cleared the relatively crowded traffic lanes in low earth
orbit. The computers ran the ship; she and Paul merely sat and
slept and watched the consoles, which dutifully told them
everything was fine. She didn't know how the regular shuttle
crews stood it, she figured she was lucky to last this one flight
without going stir-crazy.

"Better put your helmet on, boss," Paul said. "Remember
the rules."

"In a minute," she told him, while thinking: *screw the
rules*. She knew she was indulging herself and, this once,
didn't care; she was feeling halfway decent for the first time in

days. "They're taking their bloody time with that callback. Paul, gimme our speed and range to the station."

"Forward velocity, 170 meters per second, constant; negative lateral velocity. Range to station, ninety-five kay and closing. All on-board systems still read A-OK."

"'A-OK'?"

"Vintage, boss—like me."

She snorted, but couldn't resist a smile. They'd known each other for six years, as classmates, friends—and for a short while, lovers—and he'd long ago learned which of her buttons to push and when. She reached for her helmet.

"One-two-one, O'Neill." The urgency underlying the controller's professionally calm tone froze Nicole and brought her fully alert. "We register a slight deviation from flight path, a positive yaw of point-two-seven meters per second. Please correct, over."

"We copy, O'Neill; stand by. Paul—?"

He shook his head. "My screens say nothing's wrong. We should have no drift."

"You think they're lying to us? Punch up a tight-scan course display."

The big 35-centimeter screen centered on the main panel between them flared to life, the shuttle's computers painting the schematics of their approach in brilliant strokes of light and color. Alongside the diagram, a constantly shifting array of numbers and letter codes indicated the myriad aspects of their progress.

A glance told Nicole the O'Neill controller was right. "I knew things were too damn good to be true," she told Paul. "Check the engineering systems and run a test sequence on the Command Auto-Pilot; it should have compensated long ago. Better include the primary fault monitors as well. I'll plot the correction." She reached again for her helmet, half listening to Paul's background commentary.

"I can't account for the drift, Nicole. The engines are shut down, we're flying a ballistic trajectory—*whoa!* I've got something! We're losing pressure in propellant tank number three."

Even as he spoke, the full implications of his words struck them both. That tank was part of the network supplying the shuttle's OMS—their Orbital Maneuvering System. As one, their hands leapt for the EMERGENCY JETTISON switches outlined in red candy stripes on the ceiling instrument panel. They never made it.

There was a terrific *bang* from behind them, and their world turned upside down.

Nicole had loosened her shoulder harness to work on her jammed umbilical, so that when the explosion came she found herself thrown forward into the control panel. At the same time, her helmet caromed off her face—she couldn't hold back a sharp cry of pain—and disappeared towards the rear of the flight deck. There was a sudden salt taste in her mouth— she'd bitten her lip—and her nose was bleeding as well; she hoped it wasn't broken. Serve her right. Around her, everything not fastened down was bouncing through the cabin as the shuttle spun out of control. On the main panel, telltales were already flashing orange, the savage torque quickly pushing systems and spacecraft to their limits.

Nicole found herself totally disoriented, seeing black, starflecked sky through the canopy one instant, the Earth the next, only to be flash-blinded by the Sun an instant after that. She was dimly aware of someone calling on the radio, but she shut the voice out of her mind, breathing a silent prayer of thanks for the years she'd spent as a child, sailing the Atlantic in all kinds of weather; she'd long ago developed a cast-iron stomach. She worried, though, about how Paul was doing; he'd be in rough shape if he threw up inside his helmet.

Bracing her feet against the panel, she shoved herself back into her chair. While one hand tightened her harness, the other ripped the safety shield off the JETTISON rack. She flipped the arming studs, then pressed the trigger. Again, there was a loud *bang* from aft. A quick look at the instruments told her the explosive bolts had blown the tank free.

"Paul!" she yelled, her co-pilot wincing as the words boomed into his ears. "Full power! RCS thrusters one, three and five!"

He activated the firing switches, then slapped the throttles all the way forward, the cabin vibrating as the small attitude control rockets gradually slowed the shuttle's madcap spin.

"Range to station, eighty-one kay and closing," he reported. "Forward velocity, 250 meters per second, with a positive Delta-Vee. Estimated contact with *Hightower*: 5.4

minutes. Spacecraft attitude, nose down, forty-one degrees negative pitch."

Nicole tried to speak, only to have her voice choked off by a coughing fit; her throat felt like she'd been swallowing sand. She could sense herself inexorably driven towards panic. Events seemed to be racing beyond her control. Part of her was terrified, screaming that time was running out, that she had to hurry up and do something—do *anything*—or the shuttle was doomed.

Yet she refused. She took a couple of slow, deep, deliberate breaths, and a swallow of water from the dispenser built into her suit. She knew things were serious, but training, and an instinct she was just beginning to realize she possessed, told her to stay calm.

"Auto-pilot?" she asked, surprised to hear how steady her voice was. "Computer Docking System."

"Both dysfunctional. You okay?" Paul made no attempt to hide his concern.

"Disengage. Shift controls to Manual. I'll live." She pressed the heel of her hand against her nose and sniffed hard to make the blood clot faster. Some droplets floated past and away from her face, making her wonder what she looked like to Paul. Probably awful. She twisted around as far as she could, trying for a glimpse of where her helmet had flown, but she couldn't see it.

"One-two-one, O'Neill. We mark a serious deviation from your flight path. . . ."

"No shit."

"Shut up, Paolo," Nicole snapped. "We had a blowout in an OMS fuel cell, O'Neill; I'm aborting our approach and declaring an emergency. Please notify all local traffic and alert rescue units."

"O'Neill copies, One-two-one, anything we can do?"

"Yeah," Paul muttered, "save our ass." To Nicole, he asked, "What now, boss?"

She sighed, irrationally wanting to yank off her communications carrier and scrub her fingers through her close-cropped hair; she did that when she was nervous and trying to settle her thoughts. "The best we better hope for is a clean miss of the station, by as wide a margin as possible. After that, it's simply a matter of buttoning up and sitting tight until the tugs rendez-vous with us."

"We don't have all that much time."

"I'm aware of that. Plot us a gentle vector into a high Terrestrial orbit. The starboard engine's out, but the port looks okay; I'm going to swing us through another quarter-turn so that our tail's facing *Hightower*, then kick in full thrust. . . ."

"D'you think that's wise?"

"We've got good separation. Our exhaust gasses won't even scorch its skin, much less cause a rupture. The time to worry about the Wheel, Paolo, is when we can see it."

Nicole called Approach Control and briefed them as quickly and concisely as she could.

"I'll work the thrusters," she told Paul after O'Neill had approved the plan, "you monitor the boards."

"Gotcha. Four minutes to impact."

"Hang on, hotshot—here we go."

Nicole curled a hand around the pistol grip of the control column and fired the attitude rockets.

"I hate to noodge," Paul said, "but you sure you don't want to speed things up?"

"No hurry. Look at the telemetry—even at ten percent thrust, we're getting some dangerous stress readings aft. We push too hard and this bucket could tear apart on us."

"Coming up on forty degrees of arc."

"I see it. Prime the OMS, I'm initiating retrofire—now!"

Without warning, there was a tremendous explosion. Nicole threw her hands up to protect her face as the rear bulk-head of the flight deck blew out.

"Explosive decompression!" Paul screamed. The two of them were instantly enveloped in a blizzard of loose debris mixed with chafflike snow as the murderous cold of space condensed and froze the water in the shuttle's atmosphere. Nicole yelped, more in surprise than pain, as a clipboard bounced off her forearms, snarled at her own frailty, then clawed at harness and umbilicals, yanking everything loose and letting the wind take her. She had to reach her helmet and don it before this freak hurricane voided all the air in the cabin; otherwise, she was dead. Paul was watching, eyes wide with fear for her. He didn't think she'd make it and it was killing him that there was nothing he could do to help. He was

saying something—probably cursing her stupidity, which was fine with her, she was doing a fair amount of that herself—but she couldn't hear him, she'd broken their comlink when she disconnected her umbilicals. She saw the helmet wedged against a partially ruptured view port back at the aft crew station—her eyes were beginning to burn as their tears were chilled to freezing, she'd be blind in seconds—and threw herself at it. Her hand closed on the seal ring and she braced herself against the bulkhead while she slapped the helmet on her head and locked it into place. Despite the punishment it had taken, she couldn't see even a scratch; the GEC Lexan was like transparent steel, virtually nothing could damage it.

She wasn't safe yet; there was precious little air left in her lungs, none in her suit, she had to reconnect her umbilicals. She caught a ceiling handhold. All she had to do was hold on until the flight deck air pressure dropped to zero and simply pull herself back to her seat. Then, impossibly, she felt the wall under her back give way. Nicole began to slip through the gap. She cried out, desperately clenching her fingers as tight as she could, eyes widening as her body was twisted around and she found herself looking into the cargo bay. Normally, in transit, the bay doors were opened; now, one was completely gone, ripped off its hinges, while the other, anchored to the shuttle, was wrapping itself around the vertical stabilizer. She levered her head and shoulders back inside and, her last breath misting the inside of her helmet, thought she saw Paul reaching out to her. She managed to wrap both hands around the handhold but that was as far as she could go; the wind wouldn't let up, she had no more strength, there was fire in her chest and her mouth gaped in a frantic struggle for air that wasn't there. She was beaten, no question about it, why deny the inevitable? *No*, she screamed silently—*godddammit, no!* —and heaved herself forward, lunging for DaCuhna's outstretched arm. At the same time, the hurricane finally came to an end, so that she shot past him to crash upside down into the console and canopy.

"How the hell did that happen?" Paul demanded furiously, locking Nicole's lines into her suit and settling her into her chair. "We're carrying cargo, not passengers; there should have been a vacuum in the bay! That was Earth-normal pressure, at least! And a helluva lot more exhaust than we had atmosphere in the cabin!"

"You're asking the wrong person, pal," Nicole told him between gasps, once she'd recovered enough to talk; she was drenched with sweat and her head pounded—but in her opinion she'd never felt better. "I'm as confused as you are. What's our status?"

"Lousy. You had a negative retrofire on the verniers. We're still spinning and still on a collision course with *Hightower*. A hundred seventy seconds to impact." He changed channels on the primary scanscreen. "We've suffered a major hull fracture from frames 38 to 51. Zero atmospheric pressure in the cargo bay, zero pascals on the flight deck. Port OMS still reads in the green." He turned towards Nicole. "Your plan's busted, boss. By the time we set up the right thrust vectors, assuming that's even possible anymore, we'll be too close."

She groped for coherent thoughts. "Okay, let's go for a miss. I'll try to cancel this damn spin, but you work on the assumption I can't. I want a firing window that'll punch us past the station."

"You sure you're up to it?" She gave him a look. "As good as done."

Precious seconds passed as the two young officers worked to save what remained of their crippled spacecraft. In her aching mind's eye, Nicole saw them crashing into the gleaming doughnut-shaped station, the shuttle's fuel cells exploding, fire cascading across *Hightower*'s artificial sky. At the same time, kilometer-long cracks spread outward from their impact point, the pressure of the colony's atmosphere completing the job the collision had begun, shattering the torus and hurling people, livestock, buildings—the work of a lifetime—into oblivion.

Angrily, Nicole thrust the images away and entered the coordinates Paul read into the computer. With a final look at the main panel, she was about to fire when her arm was suddenly grabbed.

"Nicole, *don't!*" Paul cried. "Something's up!"

"What are you talking about?"

"The computer's numbers don't mesh right. I want to go over 'em again."

"Paul, there isn't time."

"Give me one more spin. Please, Nicole! I know what I'm talking about!"

Paul took a spin and a half to review the figures with his own personal PortaComp, cursing as his bulky suit gloves gave him trouble with the tiny keys.

"These are good, boss," he said finally, passing her the results. They were different from those plotted on the main screen. Without hesitation, Nicole changed the settings and, on his cue, pressed the firing stud.

Nothing happened.

"Ter*rif*ic," she said softly.

Then, the lights went out.

It was an eerie feeling, to be plunged so completely into darkness and silence. The only illumination was sunlight spraying briefly through the cabin to mark the passage of another spin. There was no background susurrus through her com headset, either, no equipment noise. No sound at all save the hiss of her own breath and the thundering beat of her heart.

Nicole spoke, and jumped in surprise. She thought she'd whispered, but her mind registered it as a shout. Remembering her training, she fumbled at the umbilicals and snapped them free. If the systems failure was as total as she feared, the only air she had left was that inside her suit; disconnecting the lines prevented any of it from leaking away, as well as protecting her from any unhealthy gasses. For the moment, she was all right. Without power, she had no heaters, but the suit was well insulated. With a grim chuckle, she realized she'd suffocate long before she froze. And crash into *Hightower* long before that.

Something jarred her. It was Paul, canted across the center console, touching his helmet to hers.

"Everything's out," he reported, his voice echoing hollowly.

"No foolin'."

"Want to see a helluva sight?"

"Sure, why not."

He pointed through the canopy and she caught her breath in a gasp of astonishment and awe. Ahead of them, looming seemingly out of nowhere, *Hightower* filled the sky, a monstrous wheel five kilometers across, as wide as Manhattan

Island, with a skeletal framework already extending from the central spoke to form a companion ring beside it. Nicole had seen pictures and holos of the great L-5 colony, but not even her wildest imaginings were the equal of this reality. It seemed impossible that their shuttle—the size of a domestic airliner—could do it any real damage; she knew different. For all its size, there was little extraneous space. The station as a whole would survive the impact, but the local consequences, whether to agriculture, industry or, worst of all, the habitats, would be catastrophic.

"We're not done yet, hotshot," she said, mind racing furiously, searching for the means to save them. "The OMS fuel supply is a hypergolic mixture. When I give the word, open the manual release valves."

He nodded, "It could work. The separate elements will ignite the moment they come into contact. But without throttles, we've no way of controlling the burn."

"At this stage, anything less than full power won't do us any good."

"How're you going to time the ignition?"

"Have to eyeball it."

"That's crazy, it can't be done!"

"You got a better idea?" When Paul said nothing, Nicole continued, "Watch for my signal, I mean to cut loose on the next spin."

She was staring so intently out the canopy, attempting to gauge the precise moment to cue Paul, that she didn't realize he was set until his PortaComp bumped her helmet. She tucked it into a thigh pocket of her suit and, when a crease of light appeared below the shuttle's bulbous nose, waved her lantern frantically.

To Nicole, time seemed to be both standing still and moving faster than ever. She knew Paul was opening the fuel flow valves, that centrifugal force was pushing reactants into the firing chamber, that any split second the whole mixture would ignite—why then was it taking so long? Without pumps to regulate the flow, she knew, the mix would be uneven, generating a rough start and a rougher ride. The blast might even backfire into the tanks themselves, causing an explosion that would destroy the shuttle. *Who knows,* she thought morbidly, *maybe that would be best—for the station, at any rate.* Once they got a fair burn, however, inertia from their forward motion would continue forcing fuel into the engine until the tanks ran dry.

"Hold on," she called to Paul, forgetting that their suit radios had failed with the rest of the on-board systems, "it's starting!"

She could feel a faint vibration beneath her gloved fingers. As the tremors increased, a gentle pressure began forcing her into her seat. An arm brushed hers—Paul climbing into his own chair, strain evident on his face. His exertion had cost him a lot of irreplaceable oxygen.

Was it her imagination, Nicole wondered, or was their spin slowing? The shuttle was visibly shaking, and she thought she could hear the basso rumble of the engine vibrating up through her suit from the deck. There was another sound, something that made no sense—until she realized it was herself, humming, half singing, half chanting *Starbourne,* a classic by her favorite rockstar, England's Lila Cheney. She shook her head in bemusement, but didn't stop. They were so close to *Hightower* that she could no longer see the stars, and yet their trajectory was still taking them straight for the ring.

Then, as she watched, the station began moving aside. With agonizing slowness, it slid off to the right; already, she could see a line of darkness below the shuttle's nose. It would be a terrifyingly close call but Nicole didn't care; she'd be satisfied if they missed by a millimeter.

"We're gonna make it," she breathed, "sonofabitch, we're gonna *make it!*"

There was a small *click*-sound as Paul's helmet touched hers. He'd unfastened his harness and was leaning across the console. Nicole guessed they were pulling over three Gs; Paul was using his remaining strength, and air, to hold himself in that awkward position.

"It's no good," he said quietly.

"What?" Nicole protested.

"I guesstimated our trajectory. We were too close when we fired. We're not going to clear."

Nicole tried to compute the angles in her head, but she couldn't keep the three-dimensional mathematical model straight. That was Paul's special gift.

She grabbed once more for the JETTISON switches—they

had their own independent power source, batteries designed to keep them functioning even when all else failed—and pressed three of them in sequence. There was a faint shudder from off to the right and the deck tilted beneath her.

"What'd you do?" Paul asked.

"Starboard verniers. I blew their tanks! We're yawing belly up to the station hull. If we're lucky, this way, it won't be as sharp an impact. We'll probably total the shuttle, no matter what, but we won't do anywhere near as much damage to *Hightower*."

Nicole looked at the station, at the steadily growing strip of ebony below them—she could even see a few stars, despite the glare—and finally at her co-pilot's face. This section was new construction; she could see workers scrambling frantically to get out of the way, those inside the pressurized skin running like ants for the safety of airlocks they'd never live to reach. The shuttle was so close, she could make out the individual beams that formed the lattice-work support of the giant torus. They were only seconds from impact. She racked her brain, searching for something—anything—she might have missed, one last procedure to try, barely aware of Paul as he reached out for her hand.

An instant before they struck, a massive bar of steel swinging straight for the canopy, the L-5 station vanished, to be replaced by the soft glow of a hologram field, in the center of which floated the legend:

CONGRATULATIONS, ASTRONAUTS, YOU HAVE JUST CRASHED.

two

HER HEAD STILL ached around her eye—after two days, the bruise was a wonder to behold—as she sank down into a chair across the desk from NASA's Chief Astronaut, Dr. David Elias. Paul chose the couch behind her; she hadn't, out of fear that she'd simply collapse full-length onto it and fall asleep. She couldn't remember feeling so exhausted, not even that first miserable summer at the Academy. She hadn't done more than catnap since they'd crawled out of the simulator, to face medical exams, a murderously thorough debriefing and a final session in front of the Evaluation Board, before they'd been put on a flight from *Hightower* to the Moon. The hearing had been the worst of it; the longer it went, the more convinced Nicole became that she'd failed, that her nascent career was ruined. In full view before her now was a thick pile of computer print-outs. The hardcopy critique, she assumed, of their performance, together with the Board's recommendations. She didn't know what it said, but she could guess. And that didn't make her feel any better.

Elias—her height but broader in the body, with balding, sandy-red hair and a deceptively open face; Nicole had heard he was a deadly poker player, unmatched at running a bluff and utterly ruthless in exploiting an opponent's weakness—stepped away from a sideboard and handed Nicole a glass of amber liquid. "Hail the conquering heroes," he announced with a slight smile and more than a touch of irony, emphasizing his native Georgia drawl as he held a similar glass out to Paul before pouring a final one for himself. "You look like you could use this."

She took a cautious sip; it was pure malt whiskey that went down her throat like fire. Imported, too. She recognized the taste. It must have been brought up on the supply shuttle from Florida. This was a rare, singular treat, but at the moment it was far more than she could handle, and so, she set the glass aside.

"How's your nose?" Elias asked her.

"Better, I'm told. Those docs should try things from my end, they wouldn't sound so damn cheery. I'm supposed to be grateful it isn't broken."

"No, you're supposed to be grateful you didn't lose an eye," Elias countered calmly. "That was a pretty close call."

"If she had been seriously hurt, sir," Paul challenged, "whose fault would it have been?" Nicole tried to signal him to shut up—she was perfectly prepared to fight her own battles, thank you—but he ignored her. "Everything that happened in that simulator was a contrived event. It was done deliberately."

"True, mister, to a point. Circumstances were established to force one of you to violate suit integrity. Luck of the draw made it you, Shea; for what it's worth it could just have easily been DaCuhna. But she had plenty of time to put the helmet back on. As a matter of fact," Elias dropped his stout form into his chair and leaned way back, resting his drink on his chest, "the explosive decompression was an improvised addition to the test, as a direct response to Ms. Shea's predicament."

"Suppose I'd been voided out of the bay?"

"The test would have been over."

"And I'd have flunked," she finished for him.

"Who says you haven't?" Elias said, straightening up.

"No one," she answered, looking away from him to the print-outs, painfully conscious of how small and quiet her voice sounded.

"It wasn't a fair test," Paul protested.

"It wasn't meant to be, Lieutenant."

"In a real situation, things wouldn't happen like that!"

"On the other hand, you're both still alive. We put pilots through simulator runs in the *Hightower* facility for precisely the same reason we do on Earth—to expose you to impossible situations, to teach you how to handle yourselves and your vehicles in life and death crises, *without* the death, and the mess. Of course you crashed, you were meant to crash, nothing you did would have made the slightest bit of difference in the end. We wanted to see what you'd do and, more important, how you'd behave. What you endured was not primarily a test of skill—my God, d'you think, after six years at the Academy, after flight training, after astronaut training, we don't know how good you are?—it was to gauge your character."

"*My* character," Nicole said, because Elias had been looking at her as he spoke and she sensed he meant her alone, not Paul.

"That's right, Shea. You flew left seat, you were SPACOM—spacecraft commander—you had authority and responsibility. And," he finished, eyes flashing as he let his anger show, "you fuckin' blew it! You, darlin', screwed the pooch."

"I made a mistake, is that a crime?"

"You made a *stupid* mistake. You got careless. And that *is* a crime." Elias drained his glass and added a finger more whiskey before continuing. Nicole wanted to argue, to defend herself, to beg forgiveness and promise she'd never do it again—anything, so long as it would save her—but she sat silent and still. He was right. She could already see herself on the DownSide shuttle, the Moon getting smaller and smaller behind her, sentenced to a career and a life that would never again take her outside Earth's atmosphere except as a passenger. All her work, all her dreams, shattered in a moment. With a start, she realized Elias was talking.

"You throttle-jock a high-performance aircraft, Lieutenant, you're talking absolute control over ten million dollars' worth of hardware; the bigger the plane, the more the bucks. Well, up here, the price tag starts at a billion—the pressure suits alone cost more than you'll earn in your entire military career—and we've discovered enough ways to wreck 'em without throwing in the human element. You took things for granted, Nicole, and we burned you. If the fuel cell program hadn't already been running, we'd have blown out your canopy."

"Would it help to say I've learned my lesson?"

"Would 'I'm sorry' make any difference if all that had been for real?"

"No." Her voice was barely a whisper.

"Take the elevator up to the surface, find an airlock, step outside—you're dead. It's that simple. Five meters, five million, five light-years, doesn't matter. All the excuses in the world won't help. This is an environment, we're building a way of life, where perfection is the rule and mistakes kill. Your ass, I could care less about. But others'll be depending on you, what about them?"

"So I'm a washout?"

"We bounce you, it'll go on your record. You're still on probation, you have the option of calling it quits—you'd be surprised how many hotshot pilots, even top astronaut trainees, can't hack life up here. Resign from the program, and you go home with no black marks."

"Don't do it, Nicole."

"I'd watch your mouth, mister, your ass isn't exactly safe and sound."

Nicole shook her head. "You can fire me, Dr. Elias—and maybe with good reason—"

"No 'maybe' about it."

"—but I'm sorry, I won't quit." She looked him in the eye and braced herself for the blow to fall.

"You know you're the best fuckin' pilot to come off the ramp in twenty years."

"No, sir, I didn't."

"Don't bullshit me, Shea, anyone as good as you has to be aware of it. With a record like yours, the hearing board was ready to bounce you straight home from *Hightower;* they didn't see any point in letting you back to the Moon."

"Why," Paul demanded, "I'd've thought they'd be desperate to keep someone like that?"

"Arrogance?" Nicole wondered aloud. "Complacency? I was bored. I figured because nothing had happened, nothing was going to happen."

"Precisely. And who's to say it won't happen again. You say you've learned your lesson. Perhaps you have. But should I risk Lord knows how many lives and how much money to prove it?"

She fought to keep her face an expressionless mask and blinked back tears. It was over, she was beaten. "What happens next? Where do I go from here?"

"Dinner."

"I beg your pardon?"

"Canfield, she wants to meet you."

"The Commandant of DaVinci Base wants to see *us?!*"

"So I'm told, Mr. DaCuhna, and she doesn't like to be kept waiting."

"Hold it," Nicole cried, "what about me, what did the Board decide? Am I in or out?!"

"The boss overruled the Board," Elias said flatly. "You got a second chance."

Judith Canfield stood to greet them as the *maître d'* led them to her table beneath one of the young trees that gave the Oak Room its name. She was a tall woman, matching Nicole's meter-eighty, and lean as a dancer. Hers was a strong, handsome face, skin tanned almost as dark as Paul's, with lines formed as much by a generous sense of humor as her years spent working in pure, blinding sunlight. Her left eye was a rich jade green, her right covered by a black patch, and like most spacers she wore her ash-blond hair cut short. Although she preferred casual civilian dress, tonight she was in full uniform—short-sleeved royal blue tunic and slacks, with the four stars of a full General on her shoulder epaulets. Below the Command Astronaut wings on her left breast was a single ribbon, the white stars on blue field of the Congressional Medal of Honor.

Everyone in the service knew her story. It was required reading at the Air Force Academy. She was a trail-blazing astronaut, a hero a dozen times over, before a midair collision during shuttle re-entry to Earth seemingly destroyed her career and, very nearly, her life.

The medics wrote her off. The crash had smashed much of her body to a pulp. It was a miracle she hadn't been killed outright. But that was merely the beginning of her ordeal. She spent two full years in hospitals—first on Earth and then, as soon as she was fit to travel, in orbit—while teams of surgeons tried to salvage what they could and replaced the rest. When she was finally released, the Pentagon offered her a

medical discharge; she was told, by both the Air Force and
NASA, that, for all the doctors' work, she would never again
be the person she was, never again be as good an officer or
astronaut, or woman.

She set out to prove them wrong.

It was a long, grueling fight that culminated in a landmark
ruling by the Supreme Court, but in the end Judith Canfield
was reinstated.

All that had happened before Nicole and Paul were even
born. For the past eleven years, in the dual role as Commander of the largest American base on the Moon and
NASA's Director of Manned Spaceflight, she'd become responsible for an ever-expanding sphere of operations that included the entire Solar System, as well as the stars in the
immediate galactic neighborhood.

"At ease," she told them, her voice low like Nicole's but
not as husky, "have a seat. Our other guests will be joining us
shortly but before they do, I wanted us to have a private chat."
Nicole wondered if it was her imagination, but Canfield
seemed to look a fraction longer and harder at her than Paul.
She met the gaze without flinching and, after a second of eye
contact, the General looked away, a hint of a smile on her lips.

Canfield sat at the head of the table, Paul and Nicole on her
left, David Elias on her right. Nicole counted settings for
nine. While a waiter brought their drinks, the General told
them: "There are really only two times we insist on ceremony
up here—when someone gets a medal, or they get buried.
Regrettably, those often go together." She raised her glass in a
toast. "Let us hope, Ms. Shea, Mr. DaCuhna, that your careers turn out to be both uneventful and long.

"DaVinci is a comparatively young community," she continued, "and very much a frontier one; however, we've begun
a few traditions. Among the nicer ones is dinner here, to celebrate the assignment of an astronaut's First Flight." As the
realization of what Canfield was telling them sank in, Nicole
sagged in her chair, she didn't know whether to grin or trem-
ble and found, to her surprise, that she was doing both.

"It doesn't seem possible," she murmured.

"You mean, in light of the Evaluation Board's recommendation?" Canfield asked. Nicole flushed. *I can't have spoken
that loudly,* she thought desperately, *can I?!*

"Dr. Elias said they bounced me."

Canfield nodded. "One of the problems of being among the best is that you're held to a higher standard than most. As a matter of fact, Nicole, your performance in that simulation astounded the examiners. And rightly so. You came as close as anyone—perhaps as close as humanly possible—to beating the computer."

"Way to go, boss," Paul grinned. She wished she could share his good cheer, but all she could think about were the mistakes she made.

"The Board and David recommend, but *I* decide," Canfield finished, with a deliberately pointed glance at Elias. "I trust my people, but I trust my instincts more."

"I won't let you down, ma'am," Nicole said softly.

"Just do your best, Lieutenant." She smiled. "It's the least we ever ask.

"We're giving you a 'milkrun,' a minimal hassle, minimal risk profile—but also a mission of maximum importance—from DaVinci to Cocytus Station on Pluto and back again. En route, you'll lay a series of marker beacons—navigational benchmarks—essentially, mapping a chunk of the Solar System. On board will be a NASA science team, who you'll assist in the execution of various research experiments. Transit time should be eighteen weeks Outbound, two weeks in Pluto orbit while your passengers pull the data packs from the automatic monitors at Cocytus, another eighteen Inbound."

"Plenty of time to get bored," Elias noted almost absently, allowing himself the smallest of smiles as Nicole glared at him.

"That isn't a joke," Canfield said. "More than one mission has been lost due to crew incompatibility and the mistakes that come from a small number of people living in a comparatively confined space for an extended period of time. It's all very well to speak of traveling in hibernation but someone has to be conscious to deal with the unexpected. You do get bored, you do get cabin fever, you do get squirrely. And yet, as I'm sure David has told you, your life depends on never losing your edge."

"Excuse me, ma'am," Paul asked, a slight hesitation in his voice, "but it sounds like you're trying to get us to pull out."

"We offer every opportunity to withdraw from the program," Elias replied, "without prejudice to your career, Mr. DaCuhna, right up to the moment of primary ignition."

"People have flaked at launch?"

"Yup. It's a shitload cheaper having it happen there than a megaklick into the mission. Once you go, there's no practical way we can bring you back quickly; if anything goes wrong, with personnel or equipment, you're on your own. That amuses you, Miss Shea?" he questioned sharply, making his words an accusation.

"We've got starships that can fly to Alpha Centauri in a couple of weeks . . ."

". . . but in our own back yard," Elias finished, nodding his head in agreement, "we're essentially fucked, that's right. Only two kinds of vehicles on our road: Ferraris and Volkswagens. That's why the *Wanderer* missions are so important. You're building a highway and traffic-control system that can handle both."

"Before the turn of the century," Canfield said, "it was assumed that a century, or more, would pass before we spread out across the galaxy and, at that, only aboard sublight starcraft such as Bussard RamScoops. Nobody foresaw Jean-Claude Baumier stumbling across a practical, efficient, feasible means of traveling faster than light, or that Manny Cobri would then figure out how to build the damn thing. As a direct consequence, here we are, today, barely three generations after Neil Armstrong first set foot on Tranquility Base, exploring neighboring star systems. Literally overnight, we made a quantum leap in our ability to move about the Cosmos.

"Unfortunately, we lacked a technological infrastructure capable of supporting that new and marvelous potential. We were charting the galaxy, while we still knew virtually nothing about our home system. We learned very quickly and . . . not without cost—" Nicole wondered if the General's slight hesitation had to do with memories of her own tragedy or whether they involved someone she knew. "—that traveling to Faraway was child's play compared to a trip from Earth to Mars or the Outer Planets. A fair analogy would be to take a modern, hydrogen-powered, hypersonic jumbo jet and dump it into the air traffic environment of a hundred years ago. In 1960, the fastest commercial airliners flew at five hundred

knots and ten thousand meters, carrying perhaps a hundred
passengers. Most aircraft didn't even achieve those performance levels. Now, introduce a Boeing triple-seven, cruising
at Mach 4—almost two thousand knots—and fifty thousand
meters, with six hundred people aboard. How does Air Traffic
Control cope with that? In those days, most civil radar didn't
reach that high and if the HST was traveling at full throttle, it
would be on and off the scope before the controller knew it
was there. How would airports handle the logistics? It would
be chaos."

"That fantasy's come true, for us," Elias said. "The Baumier starships are just too friggin' efficient for their own
good. We want, desperately, to use 'em, but we're hamstrung
because we can't maneuver with similar ease through our own
system. Or any system, till it's fully plotted. Your benchmarks, your sighting reports on whatever astral bodies you
come across, added to data already gathered, are enabling us
to evolve the workable inertial plot we need."

"David," Canfield interrupted, "our other guests . . ."

For the next few minutes, greetings were exchanged, seats
taken, drink and meal orders given. Nicole found herself sitting across from a short, raven-haired, olive-skinned woman
whose eyes flicked over Paul once before locking on to her.
She was a Major and the star mounted on her wings marked
her as a Senior Pilot. The General introduced them: "Catherine Garcia, your Mission Commander," she said, the Major
acknowledging this with a slight bow of the head. "Her responsibility relates to the strategic, overall aspects of the mission; she won't interfere in the day-to-day function of the
vessel unless she deems it necessary for the continued safety
of it and the crew.

"You, Nicole, are Spacecraft Commander. As the term im-
plies, you're in complete charge of the spacecraft, with full
authority and responsibility." *Even after I fucked up,* Nicole
thought desperately, *they're not only giving me a mission but
pretty near the top slot! Only this won't be a simulator, this is
for* real!

Caught up in her own apprehensions, she was only vaguely
aware of Canfield stating that Paul would wear two hats as
Astrogator and Electronics Systems Officer. His job would be
looking after the hardware and laying the benchmarks. They'd

be carrying a trio of Mission Specialists: two men and a woman. The woman who took the seat beside Nicole's was Japanese, the same age as her, a fraction taller, and staggeringly beautiful.

"You're staring," she said quietly, with a smile, and Nicole grabbed for her wine in embarrassment.

"Jesus," she muttered, straightening in her chair, eyes widening and tearing as the massive gulp she'd taken roared down her throat. She let out her breath slowly, taking the roll the other woman offered, desperately scared of what a large amount of liquor might do to her semi-starved, emotionally and physically exhausted system; all she needed—icing on the fucking cake—would be to make a fool of herself in front of the General. Suddenly, she was painfully aware that she hadn't pulled all that far back from the abyss; it still gaped, she could still pitch over the edge. "I'm sorry," she said, afraid to look around to see how many others noticed.

"I'm used to it." She leaned forward and continued in a conspiratorial tone that seemed to Nicole as much a joke as serious. "I think you got away clean, Lieutenant. If there was a *faux pas*, it was just between us, and I'll never tell."

"Thanks. It's just, I've never seen a blue-eyed Japanese before."

"Blame my grandfather." The woman had a great smile, too, and looked like she loved to laugh; Nicole wished she could be so relaxed and easy with strangers. "Your basic man-mountain Swede out of Minnesota, swept my Gran off her feet like a *tsunami*. Just like her gran-dad had a blond and blue-eyed embassy gal, way back. Scandalous, iconoclastic, polyglot bunch'a mongrels, my Japanese family. You think I'm something, though, you should see my Aunt Brigit."

"You're American?"

"Nope. I just speak the language and have a raft of relatives scattered from the Great Lakes to the Rockies."

"I'm East Coast, myself, Massachusetts."

"Really? I did a summer at MIT, working on my doctorate."

They compared notes, and Nicole discovered that had been "Beast" summer, that traditionally murderous introduction to the Air Force Academy. They were reminiscing about pizza parlors they'd known and loved when she shook her head in wonderment and exclaimed, "I feel like an idiot!"

"Okay, how so?"

"We've been talking all this time and I don't even know your name!"

"I was wondering when you'd notice."

Nicole flushed and felt her world tilt ever so slightly. "Where's the fucking food," she muttered. "I wasn't listening," she told her new friend, "when General Canfield made the intros. I was thinking about the mission."

"It's a lot of responsibility."

"Especially for someone who this morning figured she'd flunked out."

"That's the way to inspire confidence in your passengers."

"Christ, I'm drunk."

"Nowhere near, but the shots you're giving me are too tempting to resist. I'm Hanako Murai. Hana, to friends."

"Nicole Shea, but I guess you know that."

"The 'Shea' part, anyway; it's written on your nametag." And Hana tapped the plastic plate pinned to Nicole's tunic. When she groaned in dismay, Hana's smile broadened into a laugh. "Couldn't help it, Shea, you're too easy a mark."

"Who're the guys? I think I'm way over my pratfall quota for the evening: from now on, I want to play things as safe as can be."

"The distinguished scholar is Chagay Shomron, Hebrew University. He's Life Sciences, he'll be running all the biological experiments." The Israeli was built like a blockhouse, solid and unspectacular, but absolutely dependable. He looked more suited to a wilderness *kibbutz*, heaving rocks out of farm fields or engine blocks out of trucks with equal facility. His hair and beard were very closely cropped and much more salt than pepper in color. The first image that came to Nicole's mind when they shook hands was some great, comfortable bear, and she wasn't surprised to learn that was his nickname. "The towering troll next to him is Andrei Mikhailovitch Zhimyanov. . . ."

"'Troll'?"

"As in 'ugly as a . . .'" Nicole looked from Hana to Andrei and back again in utter disbelief.

"You have got to be kidding. You're two of a kind."

Hana's response was a strange look, with a wryly ironic twist to her mouth, hinting at a perception Nicole had clearly missed. "Someone has to keep a sense of proportion about the man," she said.

"Be still my heart." Name and face clinked within Nicole's memory and she asked, "Is he—?"

"Center for the Soviet SpaceForce SkyBall team over at Gagarin, that clobbered you guys last time, that's him."

"I saw the finals, he was impressive."

"A face you'll never forget. And a body to match, damn him."

"Hana! He'll *hear* you, for God's sake, or Canfield will!"

"No problem, he says worse about me. By the way, he seems rather taken with your Mr. DaCuhna, is that likely to be repicrocated?"

"He's gay?" Thinking, with a sigh, *I should have known*.

"Andrei is, I'm asking about Paul."

"I don't think so. I've never asked. Is that likely to be a problem?"

Hana shook her head. "I doubt it. Andrei's been here before; this is his third long-haul. Stands to reason he knows what to expect and how to handle himself. Medically, he's as clean as any of us. Probably more than most, considering how especially careful he has to be."

Nicole looked long and hard at the Russian, easily and naturally the center of conversation on his side of the table. When he flashed her a dazzling smile, she couldn't help responding in kind. But as she did, she also couldn't help thinking of the quarantine regulations that barred male homosexuals from Earth or, possibly worse, from space should any ever decide to return home. In her father's youth, AIDS had cut too deep and terrible a swath through the populace—the after-effects were still being felt today—and no one wanted that virus, or any like it, exported off-planet. The irony was that because of the strictly monitored and controlled medical environment, mores up here were far more relaxed than downside on Earth. She was glad of that.

"Who's he?" Nicole asked, motioning towards the man sitting to Hana's left.

"You really were in another world. That, dear heart, is our hired gun. Law Officer. He's wearing a gold badge, that means he's a Senior Marshal, the best of the breed. Name's Ben Ciari."

"Doesn't look like much." He had a thick moustache and wore his shoulder-length brown hair pulled back into a queue. He slouched deep into his chair as if he was missing half the bones in his spine. His uniform was black and hung loosely on his lean, spare frame, its only decoration the gold badge of office and his nametag. He seemed more asleep than awake, bored with the people around him and uninterested in their conversation. There was silver at his temples and the lines around his eyes and mouth were carved as deeply as Canfield's, prompting Nicole to wonder how old he really was; he wasn't handsome but there was a rugged character to his face that reminded her of old Bama and Remington portraits, and some of the real-life cowhands she met while at the Academy.

Their eyes met for a moment and she smiled, but he didn't respond.

"Helluva guy," she whispered to Hana.

"You know the stories, don't you?"

"C'mon, you can't be serious."

"I don't know, he's the first I've ever met, much less worked with. But I think I'm a lot more of a believer now than I was an hour ago."

Looking at him, Nicole found herself reminded of her introduction to Edwards Air Force Base, where after completing astronaut training, she'd done a brief tour at the Flight Test Center. A hundred years old, it was still Mecca for every hotshot airborne throttle-jock worth the name. The best of the best became test pilots there and some of them still were legends. She remembered Harry Macon, pushing fifty and still able to fly the pants off kids half his age and younger. In many ways, those had been the happiest days of her life; she'd never worked harder, nor had so much fun. One night in particular, a sort of impromptu celebration, they ate steak and drank beer and vintage whiskey and sang under the brilliant high mesa stars and watched the sunrise. Macon asked her to stay and join his command, but her sights were set on reaching those stars they'd seen. He withdrew into himself slightly at that and for a while the party was stiff and awkward, and now Nicole wondered if he'd been one of those pilots who Elias had said had withdrawn from the Space Program "without prejudice," the day before being bounced for cause. Then, four days later, at high-altitude and high-Mach in a Forward Swept Wing vehicle, a computer glitched and in a split second his whole aircraft disintegrated. They never found a piece of wreckage bigger than a hand and so were forced to bury an empty coffin.

"Something the matter, Nicole?"

She let out a breath and finished her glass of water before replying, "Some memories, that's all. Have I missed anything?"

"They're talking about Wolfpacks."

"Ah." From the first, Paul had hoped for a combat assignment and Nicole knew this milkrun wouldn't sit well with him. Evidently, the General had picked up on that because she was telling him, "You'll get your chance at glory, Lieutenant; everybody does, sooner or later, some to their eternal regret. But for now, you're untested. Virgin."

"Shit me, Jud, you come on strong as that, you'll scare these poor wee bairns to death!" All eyes turned towards the man who'd suddenly appeared by Canfield.

"How do, Cat m'love, Davy," he said as he stepped into the light. He was a head taller than Nicole, with red-blond hair and a beard, and, from what she could see, in perfect physical condition. He was elegantly dressed, but didn't carry himself like a civilian or a dirtsider, and despite his drunken air there was an inherent power to him that reminded Nicole of Canfield herself. This was someone used to command, who'd faced the ultimate test. Out of the corner of her eye, Nicole saw Marshal Ciari tense slightly. Anything could happen, none of it good.

"Been a while, General," the man brayed, waving his arm over the table as he attempted a bow. His drink spilled, some of it hitting Canfield in the face, the rest splattering across her tunic. The General said nothing, freezing Nicole in place with a basilisk glare as the young woman rose to protest the obvious insult, but merely wiped her face with a napkin while the civilian looked aghast at what he'd done.

"Oh, Jud, I am so very, very sorry," he said contritely, his apology as deliberate an insult as the spilled drink. "How terribly clumsy of me. *Très gauche!* I'm afraid I'm drunk. But that's no surprise—my normal state when visiting brethren.

Helps me forget what I am..." he paused deliberately. "... and what I was." Nicole saw Cat Garcia wince at the barely concealed fury in his voice.

Canfield rose to her feet, and said to Elias, "I'm going to touch up my uniform, David. I shan't be long. If you'll excuse me, gentlemen, ladies."

There was a stunned silence while she threaded her way through the restaurant, until the stranger broke the mood by flopping into her chair.

"Dear me," he said, finishing his glass with a single gulp, "have I done something wrong?"

"You're not welcome here, Morgan," Elias said quietly.

"You gonna make me leave, Davy?"

"If he doesn't..." Nicole replied, her face set, a dangerous edge to her voice; she'd eased her chair away from the table and was already instinctively gauging where she'd strike and how hard.

"Oho! The l'il lady with fire in her eyes! I'd better pay attention."

"Take the hint, mister..."

"Major, Lieutenant. Daniel Morgan, USAF—retired."

Good riddance, Nicole thought, but said: "You've accomplished your goal. You've wrecked our evening. Why not quit while you're ahead?"

Morgan leaned forward and made a show of reading her ID tag. *If he touches me,* she decided, *I'll break his fucking arms.* He didn't, but the alcohol stench of his breath was enough to make her stomach lurch. "Shea!" he cried in delight and she wondered why he recognized her name; so far as she knew, they'd never met. At the same time, and without quite knowing why, she realized that if a fight started between them, it would be to the death. The look in Morgan's eyes told her he was just as aware of that and even looking forward to it. *What the hell is going on here,* she wondered desperately, *this is crazy!* "I should have recognized you sooner, cutie," he told her. "I am indeed honored to make your acquaintance; the fame of your family name precedes you."

"Really?"

"Ask Canfield, it's her precious little secret." He turned towards Elias, sloppily refilling his glass from the table's bottle of wine. "Naughty little trick you tried to pull this morning, Davy-boy. You think Jud'll appreciate how you tried to con her protégé into a resignation when she'd already said the kid stays? *Tsk-tsk-tsk!* Ought'a be *ashamed* of yourself!" Nicole kept her focus on Morgan, but out of the corner of an eye she saw Elias's face become an emotionless mask; the accusation had struck home, and it had been said loudly enough to be heard at the tables around them. *So much for an environment built on universal trust,* Nicole thought bitterly. *But why? What made him try such a thing? Politics with the General— something,* impossible as that sounded, *to do with me? He'll never tell. I wonder if I'll ever learn?*

Morgan, reading the confused questions on her face, seemed about to elaborate when he noticed that Marshal Ciari had slipped silently around the table to stand behind him.

"I'm not asking, Major." Ciari's voice was as unassuming as his manner, deceptively casual. "Leave. This table, this establishment and, as soon as possible, the Moon."

"Get outta town, huh, Marshal?"

"Precisely."

"That's a violation of my Civil Liberties."

"As you are of ours. Disturbing the peace. Public nuisance. Drunk and Disorderly." A slight pause for emphasis. "Resisting arrest."

"An old favorite, that, with you law-enforcement types." Ciari didn't rise to Morgan's bait and the Major evidently decided he'd pushed the outside of tonight's social envelope far enough. "Well, I don't want to be any bother. . . ." He lumbered to his feet, taking Canfield's wine with him as he reeled towards the door. Nearly there, he staggered, seemed to trip, and careered into General Canfield's Vice-Commander who was just entering the Oak Room with his wife. Admiral Sheridan's face twisted with anger when he saw who'd hit him but, with an effort, he mastered himself, pulled back a step and saluted. Morgan returned it sloppily and continued on his way, his mocking laughter echoing after him.

Nicole sensed Paul's outrage by her side. The young man's eyes shot daggers towards Elias, and she knew he was about to say something that would probably destroy his career. She moved quickly, instinctively, to head him off. "Did you see that?" she whispered, leaning as close as she could to him. "Admiral Sheridan actually saluted that sonofabitch!" At the same time, she caught his eye. *Lay off,* she commanded silently. *Keep your peace.*

"It's customary, Ms. Shea," Cat said tightly. "Officers on active duty, regardless of service or rank, are required to salute holders of the Congressional Medal of Honor."

"With respect, Major, General Canfield wears the medal, too. Why didn't she do something when that bastard insulted her?"

"That 'bastard,' Lieutenant, is an authentic hero!"

"I don't believe it!"

"You have no right to judge," she snapped, the rawness of her emotion making her West Texas accent more pronounced. "In his day, which wasn't all that long ago, Daniel Morgan was the *best!*"

Elias, who, Nicole realized, hadn't missed the exchange between her and Paul in the slightest, told the story: "His cruiser was shepherding a Cobri, Associates freighter Inbound from Titan when they were jumped by a Wolfpack. Textbook ambush. When it was over, the freighter was a gutted hulk, the cruiser not much better. Morgan bundled the survivors into a lifeboat and headed for the Sun. As things turned out, the nearest planetfall was Earth itself. The trip took seven months, but he brought his people home."

"For which feat," Cat Garcia interrupted savagely, "NASA and the Air Force, in their infinite wisdom, gave him a medal —and a medical discharge. He was a hero, but they dumped him!"

"It wasn't quite that simple, Major," Canfield said as she returned to her seat, surprisingly calm and relaxed considering what had occurred. Nicole wondered how much she had seen and what she made of it. "The Medical Board examined Morgan and concluded that his ordeal had left him permanently psychologically unfit for active service as an Astronaut. We offered administrative and teaching assignments, but he refused, preferring retirement with full disability pay. I understand he's done quite well for himself since, as a private spacer."

"But isn't that an indication that the Board may have made a mistake?"

"The criteria and responsibilities are markedly different between civilian and military operations, Cat. And I hardly think this is the time or place for such a discussion."

"I'm sorry, ma'am. But it seems like such a godawful waste; Dan taught me everything I know."

"His gifts were—are—undeniable but they're not enough. I've seen nothing since his hearing to convince me that my decision was wrong."

"I was in that boat, too. I'd be dead if not for him."

"He broke, you didn't. No one else could have done what he did, Catherine, but the wounds cut too deep. I know how close you were, I know what this cost you, but it's done."

Canfield's gaze swept the table, fixing first on Paul, then on Nicole. No one dared say a word. "My apologies for this scene," she said finally, in a tone that made it clear the subject was closed. "Daniel Morgan was a respected and popular officer, deservedly so, and the circumstances of his retirement did not, and do not, sit well with a great many officers. Since I signed the Medical Board's report, approving their recommendations, his feelings for me are something special.

"On this note, I believe I'll say goodnight. Please, stay, finish your meal. *Wanderer* is scheduled to depart Lunar orbit in six weeks. I strongly suggest you get as much rest tomorrow as possible—Ms. Shea and Mr. DaCuhna, especially— because I guarantee it's the last you'll enjoy for a considerable time. Preliminary flight orientation begins at 0700 the morning after, in Dr. Elias's office.

"Heaven help you, if you're late."

three

IT WAS FOUR weeks before they boarded the spacecraft, in her parking orbit a thousand kilometers above the Moon, twenty-eight jam-packed days that began on the mark at seven and, with occasional meal and bathroom breaks, lasted till midnight. In classrooms, they pored over briefing books on the mission and design schematics of the vessel that would be their home—their world—for the better part of a year, learning every aspect of *Wanderer* and her myriad systems. From there, they went into the maintenance facility for hands-on experience with DaVinci's full-size mock-up, picking modules apart, stripping down the main engines—done in full pressure suits and radiation armor, just like in space—tracing wiring for endless miles through the body of the giant cruiser, until it seemed to them that they were as familiar with the spacecraft as the people who'd built her. At the same time, Elias's team put them through their paces in the simulator, beginning with the mundane, an introduction to basic flight operations, but quickly advancing to all manner of problems. Nicole and Paul faced systems failures, equipment malfunctions, natural disasters, combat. Everything from a family of mice in the ventilation ducts to a black hole, from deep-space rescue to planetfall, a feat *Wanderer* was never designed to perform. More often than not, they died.

Finally, a month into training, a fortnight before departure

—to Nicole, it felt like a lifetime either way—they transferred up to *Wanderer* herself. She was huge and built for function rather than aesthetics, yet Nicole thought her the most beautiful thing she'd ever seen and blushed to realize it. *Like a storybook sea captain,* she thought, as the shuttle soared over the Lunar pole towards rendezvous, *and I don't really care how ugly she looks. She's mine!* And yet, with only fourteen days left until their scheduled departure, she wondered how they would get everything ready.

From Command Module to exhaust, *Wanderer* was a long-stemmed toadstool 217 meters long—well over six hundred feet—the forward third the crew's living and working environment, the middle for stores, the rear consisting of fuel and ion-pulse engines. The CM stood at the apex of the central core, a gently pointed dome, with flight deck view ports directly below the nose. *If all else fails,* Nicole figured with a grin that no one else saw, *at least the crew can see where we're going.* Ringing the CM's base were hatchways for the small *Rover* craft, two work, two exploratory and two combat vehicles, for going places and doing things that the far larger and more cumbersome cruiser could not.

Below the Command Module was "Home," two rotating "carousels," roughly thirty meters in diameter and fifteen thick, wherein the astronauts would live and work in a gravity field provided by the rings spinning around the central axis—hence, the nickname. The "carousels" were necessary because of the debilitating effects on the human body of extended periods of weightlessness; their main drawback was that the coriolis effect produced by the spin tended to be rather extreme. The floor was the outer shell of the ring but things dropped or liquids poured within it tended to fall a little sideways, in the direction of that spin, as well as down. It was a strange sensation but you quickly got used to it, or so Nicole had been told.

Living quarters were in the upper stage, labs and the hydroponics greenhouse in the lower. Next along the core were the massive bulk storage modules, which held most of their supplies, followed by the communications and sensor antenna array. This, too, could be rotated around the core, to allow for the most precise possible alignment on target.

Then came the fuel stacks and the engines themselves. Secondary thrusters were mounted on gimbals forward and aft, so that the spacecraft could be shifted along any axis, vertical or horizontal.

Once aboard—the shuttle docked with a vacant *Rover* bay —Nicole was the first to crack her helmet and take a breath of *Wanderer* air. It had a homey, lived-in smell. They'd discovered only too well that she wasn't a new ship, in design or construction. Not what she'd expected but it wasn't bad. For most of the week that followed, she and Paul shared the ship with the training team, putting the finishing touches on their transition from schoolroom to reality. Like any machine, *Wanderer* had her idiosyncrasies, which in turn had to be learned the hard way, through experience. The trick was to make sure you knew how to handle the glitches when you ran into them.

Throughout this shakedown process, Cat Garcia stayed mostly in the background. Some days, they hardly saw her, though she was aware of every move they made. She left Nicole and Paul on their own to make and hopefully discover their own mistakes. Surprisingly, there were few errors and all were caught by the rookies; in spite of herself, Cat was impressed, as was Elias, but they still double- and triple-checked the novices' performance. More than a few good men and women had been killed by overconfidence and Cat had learned the hard way to take nothing for granted.

That same week, the Mission Specialists began loading and stowing their gear, the crew spending as much time aboard the spacecraft as dirtside at DaVinci. They divvied up the cubicles and got to know one another. The first night they were all together, Nicole went eyeball to eyeball with Ciari over a poker deck and learned that, good as she'd been on Earth, she'd met her match. She ruefully figured that in a year's time, if they kept playing, and she was certain they would, assuming the best, she'd owe him somewhere close to the National Debt.

When they tested the "Carousel," running it up to two-thirds Earth-normal gravity, Andrei christened the galley by making *crêpes* and everyone except Cat and Ciari made a mess of the compartment and themselves trying to pour the wine. Nicole had trouble sleeping, too, so much so that she eventually climbed up to the flight deck and curled up in her seat at the control console. She was worried. If she couldn't hack the "Carousel," that would effectively scrub her from the

Mission, and NASA. But the gripes and rude comments at the breakfast table told her the other novices felt pretty much the same. This, too, would pass. Paul handled the computer and marveled to her at the size of its memory banks; then, they started loading programs and wondered how the hell everything would fit. An extraordinary amount of file space was devoted to entertainment—books, music, films, games—because the most dangerous enemy they had to face was boredom and the last thing they could afford was getting on each other's nerves. They couldn't work all the time and yet dared not lose their edge. The "goof" programs were meant to make that a bit easier.

On Wednesday, four days before *Wanderer*'s scheduled departure, the crew was still commuting between the spacecraft and DaVinci; there was a helluva lot left to do but they were on track, the end was in sight. However, a routine check of the primary dish antenna revealed that one of the components had failed; Hana and Paul tinkered with it for an hour before deciding that it was a total wreck. Without the module, there was no way to keep the antenna locked onto the huge communications arrays on Luna and Earth, so it had to be replaced at once. There were three complete sets of spares, but since there was time they decided to grab the new unit from dirtside storage and took the shuttle down, leaving Nicole the only one aboard.

Or so she thought. She was on the flight deck, working through the weapons systems checklist, when a sealed teapak floated past her nose, making her yelp in surprise. She grabbed for it, managing to catch the cup an instant before it splattered against the console.

"Butterfingers," Ciari said as he pushed off the ceiling and eased his long, lanky form into the chair beside her.

"Christ, you scared me! I thought I was on my own for a while."

"Certainly for the night, by the looks of things. I'll wager DaCuhna and Murai have plans." Nicole snorted in mock disgust. It was hard to hide an incandescent smile and each lit up like a nova the moment the other entered the room. "I was on the shuttle," Ciari explained. "I should have reported in. Sorry, I'm too used to operating on my own."

"No harm done, except to my nerves. 'On your own,' in a singleship?" He nodded. "I thought that wasn't allowed."

"We Marshals tend to make our own rules."

"So I've heard."

He leaned towards her to get a better look at the ring-bound notebook clipped to the console. "How's it going?" he asked.

"Page seven," Nicole replied, trying a cautious sip of tea before setting the cup aside to cool. "Only about forty more to go in this chapter, and that just covers the weapons board. The whole bloody book relates to the command console and it's five centimeters thick! There are a dozen like it, dealing with every aspect of spacecraft operations. This one's the *smallest,* and Paul and I had to memorize them all!"

"Life is tough."

"You're a great help." She shook her head. "Somehow, they didn't seem so big, or imposing, in class."

"Nothing to lose in class."

She reached out, hesitantly touching the candy-striped safety shields on the firing switches. "I still find it hard to imagine us ever getting into a fight."

"We certainly have the hardware for one."

"Yah! Missiles and anti-missile laser batteries on *Wanderer* herself, plus two *Rover* strikecraft loaded for bear with mini-missiles, rapid-fire gatling gun cannon, HighPower laser, plus hand weapons of all sizes and shapes. Plus battle armor. Y'know, Marshal, we could wage ourselves a fair-sized war with this lot."

"It's been done."

She looked at Ciari. He wasn't in uniform fatigues, but a sweatsuit that softened his rough edges. He lounged easily in the chair. After weeks of close association Nicole recognized this as a pose. He could go into action anytime, without warning and to deadly effect. His mahogany hair was thinning at the temples, unfashionably long and clipped into a ponytail with a turquoise and silver clasp. His left ear was pierced twice, for a small silver ring and a ruby star, the latter according to rumor a farewell gift from a Russian colleague. There were very few facts known about him—like all Marshals, his personnel file was sealed—and he wasn't given to conversation, friendly or otherwise; indeed, this was the most relaxed and forthcoming she'd ever seen him. From the first, Nicole trusted him implicitly, but she didn't know yet if she liked him. He scared her. He was too much the loner, the hunter. The killer.

Unless those stories were lies.

"Ever been in a firefight, Marshal?"

"In one of these buckets?" He shook his head, making no secret of his contempt.

"But you've seen your share of action?"

"I'm a Senior Marshal, Lieutenant, it comes with the territory."

"Have you killed?"

"None of your fucking business."

She flushed at the flat dismissal in his voice, feeling thirteen years old and the consummate fool. "I'm sorry," she stammered, "I didn't mean to pry."

"Bullshit. You've been dying to ask me since we met, you and DaCuhna both."

"You have to admit, the tales they tell about you people are pretty incredible."

"So?"

"I was curious."

"You'll learn soon enough."

Nicole sipped some tea. "That's what my parents said about sex."

"Probably didn't pay 'em any heed, either."

"Suppose I freeze?"

"You'll die. Or kill someone who's depending on you."

"That's brutal."

"It's the way we live up here."

"I'm asking for help, Marshal!"

"It isn't available, Lieutenant, not the kind you want. The moment, the experience, is unique for everyone who faces it. Yours could come with the press of a button and the detonation of a multi-megaton nuke a million miles away, or hand to hand, popping some bastard's helmet."

"What about when it was your turn?"

"I survived."

"You make it sound like a jungle—kill or be killed."

"Survival of the fittest, that's a fact. This is a frontier, Shea. In some ways, it always will be. The distances are simply too vast, the people too few, the stakes too high. And in the final analysis, we're still too goddamn human, subject to the same old frailties. We get as many crimes committed out of passion as greed. The Marshals, and you blue-suits, are around to ensure things don't get too crazy."

"You a philosopher, too?"

He looked at her strangely and laughed. "Holy Mother, I forgot how cloistered you rookies are."

"What's that supposed to mean?"

"What d'you take me for, Shea, your typical dumb-ass, quick-draw cop? Typical I may be, but I doubt in the way you think. I am, in fact, a philosopher, with the sheepskins and books to prove it. I have a master's in spacecraft engineering and astronomy, I'm a Board-certified medic, and a lawyer. And that's just the official crap."

"Oh."

"'Oh,' she says, in a very small, wee voice. What the hell kind of people you figure you'll be dealing with, woman? The scum of the Earth? The dregs and wretched refuse of a thousand teeming slums? People who couldn't cut life dirtside and fled to space the way men used to join the French Foreign Legion? *Ha!*

"Christ, I'll bet DaCuhna's exactly the same. Too damn much video reality." He shook his head and let his laughter fade. "You know what constitutes a 'dreg' in this neighborhood? A body with only a couple of degrees, in one or two fields. You know why?" Nicole shook her head. "Because it's too bloody expensive to send someone up here and keep him alive! No corporation, no government, is going to invest that kind of money in a clown who won't last long enough to make it worth their while. They send the best and the brightest and of the lot, only the best and brightest—and maybe luckiest—survive. Good and bad, Shea, you'll be dealing with some very hot numbers, products of the ultimate in natural selection. Underestimate them and you're finished. That's why none of the Earth-based syndicates have ever been able to get even a foothold on Luna. Because their people are quite simply no match for ours, crooks or cops. It's also why Luna-based criminals are no real match for Belters and vacuum riders. Different turf, totally different sets of rules."

"I'll remember."

"Mark this, too. Most spacers pass the time when traveling, since it takes so bloody long to get anywhere In-system, by studying. Anything and everything. It keeps the mind honed, and the mind is what keeps you breathing. Never take anyone at face value; chances are, if they're top-notch spacers, they're polymaths, experts in a half-dozen fields and knowledgeable in a score more. At this point, and for a helluva while to come, you're at the disadvantage, in an arena where, as you've no doubt heard often, there's no margin for error."

"So how does anyone manage to survive?"

"Skill and talent. And never making a mistake. Survival of the fittest."

There was a soft *ping* from the panel between them and the main speaker crackled: "DSC *Wanderer* from DaVinci Port Control, how do you copy, over?"

"DaVinci," Nicole replied, after flicking the appropriate switches. "*Wanderer* reads five-by, over."

"Please activate your video comlink, *Wanderer;* we have Major Garcia on-line."

Nicole acknowledged and, a moment later, Cat's face appeared on the fifty-centimeter main screen.

"As you've no doubt guessed," she said with a slight smile, "Lieutenant DaCuhna and Dr. Murai will be spending the night baseside."

"No problem, Major," Nicole grinned. "All on-board systems are nominal, and I've got Marshal Ciari to keep me company. And out of trouble."

"Of the one, I'm sure," Cat murmured. "The latter, less so."

"I think we'll be okay." Nicole kept her tone light, on the assumption that Cat was needling her in fun. But she was sure there was a faint edge of nastiness to Cat's voice, a burr of resentment. Half listening to what the other woman was saying, Nicole cast her thoughts back to dinner in the Oak Room and the way she'd reacted to Nicole's attack on her friend, Morgan. Did she still carry a grudge? What effect would that have on the mission? *Perhaps,* she rationalized, *it's me, my imagination, making this up.*

Cat was looking off-screen. "I'm just scanning your medical telemetry—" Mission Control had them under constant biological monitoring while they were aboard, via remote scanners scattered throughout the spacecraft. "When was the last time you got a decent night's sleep, Shea?"

"Same as everybody else, I suppose, about six weeks back."

"Very funny."

"Sorry, Major. We've been busy."

"That's no excuse. You've been doing far more than your fair share, Nicole, and while that's very laudable, it's catching up with you. You've overtired and starting to make mistakes. You know you missed two items on the weapons checklist?"

With a startled, *"Damn!"*, Nicole jerked forward in her chair, forgetting she was weightless. Her suddenly flailing hand knocked the ring binder off its perch, which in turn sent her teapak tumbling away. She caught both easily, but she also knew she should never have struck them in the first place.

"I rest my case," Cat said. "Go to bed."

"Major . . ."

"Lieutenant, you've already had one lesson in the dangers of overconfidence; I guarantee the second won't be as pleasant. And General Canfield won't save you this time. I'm told you're special, prove it."

"Yes, ma'am."

The screen went dark and Nicole rubbed her face with her hands. "Stupid, stupid, stupid," she told herself, over and over, thinking far fouler and more scathing comments.

"You'll have to shut down the weapons board," Ciari said quietly, "and recycle the command systems over to automatic." She nodded dumbly and he reached for the checklist. "I'll handle the guns," he told her, "you do the rest."

When they finished, Ciari swam through the air towards the core hatch and down to the "Home" Carousel. Nicole stayed behind on the flight deck, sitting in the dark, gazing through the viewports at the stars. There wasn't a sound around her; she had to strain to hear the *shush* of the air cyclers, though their status telltales told her they were functioning perfectly. In the distance, she saw a crease of light along the Lunar horizon, then held her breath as the full Earth slowly, majestically, rose into view, bright and blue and more beautiful than anything she'd ever seen.

It had been five months since she'd last stood on its surface, a little longer since she'd last seen her family. Her folks had celebrated Christmas early, combining it and Thanksgiving, just for her. Because when Christmas actually rolled around, Nicole would be on the Moon.

Everyone had been there. Family, friends, people she'd known and loved all her life, some she hadn't seen in years. A few, like her grandmother, she might never see again.

By Saturday, though, the constant good cheer was beginning to drive Nicole batty. She'd always been a fairly solitary person, more at home in the mountains or on the ocean than amid the hustle and bustle of the big city where she grew up. That ability to endure long stretches by herself was part of what made her a potential spacer. As the weekend wore on, she discovered that what she craved most was some time to herself. It was early morning, pre-dawn, when she slipped out the back door and headed for the beach. She thought no one had seen her leave; she was wrong.

Conal Shea found his eldest child sitting on the crest of a giant dune, overlooking the ocean. It was a favorite spot for both of them, with a panoramic view of the Atlantic. Sighing, he eased down onto the sand beside her, Nicole looking at him in surprise; she'd been so lost in thought that she hadn't heard his approach.

"Dad," was her lame greeting.

"Saw you scoot," he said, answering her unspoken question, "thought you might like some company."

"Not bloody likely," Nicole snorted, with a toss of her head toward the house, the words out of her mouth before she realized what she was saying. "Oh, hey, Dad, I'm sorry, I didn't mean . . ."

"No offense given, hon, none taken. Besides, I didn't mean that kind of company."

They sat in silence for a while. Nicole sensed that her father had something to tell her, yet she was unsure of how to break the ice. She had a lot to say herself, and once again wished she had Paul DaCuhna's gift for conversation. Nicole was all right with people she knew, and had learned to deal with those she didn't, provided she was familiar with the subject under discussion, but whenever things turned personal, she froze. It wasn't that she didn't want to talk about herself —occasionally, the need was desperate—she simply couldn't. Terminal shyness. Which was pretty ironic, considering her father was a lawyer and her mother a world-class journalist-turned-novelist, both of them able to cope marvelously with even the most ticklish social situation. Somehow, Nicole had never picked up the knack. They always assumed that, sooner or later, she would. She knew better.

"Will you miss this place, Nicole?" Conal asked.

"Yeah," she replied wistfully, "more than anything, I think. Nothing like it where I'm going, that's for sure. The latest Lunar Appropriations Bill provides funding to expand the Park System to five acres. Can you believe it, Dad? Five acres, for the entire *Moon!*"

"Don't knock it, sweetheart. When I was a boy, there was no park, period. No DaVinci Base, either; no Copernicus, no people at all higher than low Earth orbit."

"The times, they have a'changed."

"That's for sure. And Dylan lived to see it. Judith Canfield still runs things up there, doesn't she?"

"Uh-huh. And, the way she's built, she'll probably last forever."

"Show some respect, brat."

Nicole chuckled and shook her head. "That was only partly a joke, you know. Her bionics give her a real edge over us purely organic critters."

"Given the choice, Nicole," her father said, with a faint warning edge to his voice, "I'm certain she'd prefer otherwise."

"I'm sorry, Dad. I didn't mean any harm. I didn't know I was hitting any sort of raw nerve. I didn't even know you knew her."

"A very long time ago." He spoke with a finality that meant this was all he intended to say on the subject. "I'm all for the irreverence of youth, Nicole, but in this case you haven't earned the right."

There was another silence, as gulls cavorted overhead, arguing over a scrap of edible garbage one had scooped from the water. It was light enough to see, but the sun hadn't yet appeared, and the dawn breeze made Con wish he'd worn a heavier sweater. Siobhan would cheerfully kill him if he caught cold and spoiled their New Year's vacation.

"Scared, Nicole?"

"Stiff, pops."

"Are you certain this is what you want?"

"Helluva time for second thoughts, isn't it?"

"If you have them, better now than when you're in deep space."

"Y'know, Dad, when NASA first got started, people called space the 'Final Frontier.' Well, that's what it is for me, a frontier. I need to know what's out there—*who's* out there! It's a challenge I have to answer. Crazy as it sounds, that's where I belong. Christ, it does sound crazy!"

"I understand. Look back through our history—both your mother's family and mine—we've always been a footloose, wandering clan."

"Mom cried last night."

"Not for the first time, I'm afraid."

Nicole looked at him in astonishment. "She never let on she was so upset! Not in letters, not on the phone!"

"It's been building, in both of us. Nickle"—he used her childhood nickname, which she hadn't heard from him since she entered high school—"surprising as it sounds, your mother and I, whose stock in trade is words, more often than not find ourselves tongue-tied when dealing with those we love. We're very proud of you—what you've accomplished —but we also don't want to see you go."

"I've been away before. And I'll be back."

He shook his head. "If all goes well for you, the earliest we can hope to see you again—in the flesh, in front of us where we can touch and hold you—is six years from now. And if you're assigned to OutSystem duty, even allowing for the Baumier StarDrive, we may never see you again."

"I . . . never thought of it like that."

"Neither, I confess, did we." Conal took a deep breath and Nicole noticed a slight shudder in his voice that had nothing to do with the chill wind. "Now we think about it far too much.

"This past week, I've become painfully aware of everything I've done for you—and to you—in your life. And also of some things that had nothing to do with you. But perhaps will. All my decisions, good—and bad. And the person they created in you."

"I don't understand, are you disappointed in me?" she asked softly.

"Good Lord, no, quite the opposite!" Conal's mouth twisted in wry amusement as he searched for the precisely proper phrase, the way Nicole had seen him do in court, on the rare occasions she'd been allowed to watch her father argue a case to the jury. "What I mean, Nicole, is that I, and your mother, have become terribly conscious of all the missed opportunities of our lives together. The moments we might have shared, should have shared, but didn't."

"Balanced against those we did," Nicole countered.

Her father smiled. "Very sensible, eminently logical. Unfortunately, I'm talking emotion, which often has very little sense to it, but simply *is*."

Nicole caught sight of a crease of fire along the horizon, so blinding she had to blink; and when her eyes cleared, the sun was fully visible. She heard Conal laugh, almost to himself. He sniffed and she realized he was crying. She was shaken. It was a part of him she'd never seen and, in truth, hadn't thought possible. She didn't know what to say, so she said nothing.

"I'm only human, Nicole," he said at last. "And it's only human to feel sad when one is about to lose something supremely precious. There's an old saying: that you never truly realize how important some things, or people, are until the moment you lose them. I thought I'd learned that lesson, the hard way, years ago. My error."

"Dad . . ." Again, Nicole was too stunned to speak. She'd never heard such naked emotion in her father's voice, seen it on his face. She was all confused inside—privileged that he would open his heart to her like this, yet embarrassed at the exposure. She supposed she'd wanted him to be stronger than that. She'd always tried to pattern herself after him and if he was flawed, what then did that mean for her? And what did his enigmatic references to the past have to do with her future?

She looked up, met his eyes, and suddenly all her questions fled and she was in his arms. They held each other fiercely close, letting tears run free.

"Wherever you go, my heart," Conal told her, "always remember that we love you. With all our hearts."

"I love you guys too, Dad."

"Yo—anyone home up there?" Ciari called from the hatch, yanking Nicole out of her reverie.

"Hmnh?!" Oh, Jesus—sorry, Marshal," she said in a rush, feeling like a total fool. "I was just taking a minute to unwind."

"No problem. And the name's Ben." He flashed a smile, the light from the core DropShaft below giving his face a very sinister cast, and turned back for the Carousel. Nicole called to him.

"Ben, you remember the dinner when we all met."

"Yup."

"That drunk, Morgan, he made a crack about me and the General, you know anything about it?"

"I'm a cop, Shea, we don't traffic in blue-suit gossip."

"Then there is something?"

"I don't know. Strikes me there's only one person who does."

"Right, I'll just phone the General and ask her."

"The man was trying to be hurtful, Nicole, because you represent something he can never be again. Dump his file, he isn't worth the effort."

"I suppose. It bugs me, that's all—especially with Cat making the same kind of crack."

"She likes to needle, that's her way of seeing how good you are. But she's good at her job."

"You've served with her."

"Run a few missions, out in the Belt. I'd trust her with my back."

"I guess that's high praise."

"You'll learn. Face it, Canfield intervened to overrule her trainee evaluations board. That almost never happens. It's made you special. You fail, by implication she fails; some people would like that."

"I didn't ask . . ."

"Irrelevant."

"Is Elias one of them?"

"Of who?"

"You know—the crowd that's after the General. Morgan was right on the mark with him and the stunt he pulled to try to force me to resign."

"He had his reasons."

"Who? What were they? Damn it, Ciari, stop being so elliptical!"

"Morgan wanted to fuck with your head. I assume that much was obvious—" She nodded. "—and to that end, I'd hazard he was prepared to say anything. As for Elias, he trusts his instincts as much as Canfield does hers. He's also proud. It could be he thinks she made a mistake and he was simply doing his best to protect her."

"What do you think?"

"Simulators aren't reality, Nicole. Neither is orbit. I'll reserve judgment."

"Shit."

"It's done, Shea, something you'll have to live with. C'mon, we're overdue for bag-time. You wouldn't be half so crazy about this if you weren't so tired."

She started to speak, but voice and resolution trailed off together and she felt more foolish, more at sea, than she'd been at her first teen-age dance—and that had been an utter disaster. Ciari said nothing, but merely floated in the hatchway, looking at her, expression masked by shadow.

She tried again. "I was, *uh*, wondering . . . I . . . feel sort of nervous. I don't want to spend the night alone." As she spoke, she tried to see his eyes, wondering what he saw, what he was thinking; too late, she wished she'd never said a word.

"Your place or mine," was his reply.

The ship was in nocturnal mode, with a minimum of illumination; Nicole left the cubicle lights off as well, so that all they saw of each other as they undressed were random highlights cast against the darkness of their bodies. She was aware of his closeness, her back so tense it ached, as she slipped under the catchweb beside him, fastening it to the bed to prevent even natural movement during sleep from pushing them all over the place. She wanted to be held, yet found herself afraid of what that contact might bring. She wasn't a virgin and, though she was nowhere near as adventurous as Paul DaCuhna, didn't think of herself as a prude. Yet there was something about Ciari that activated all her defenses. Perhaps a sense that if something started between them, it wouldn't be casual. That thought surprised her.

"Am I so scary, Nicole?"

"Yes," she replied, so softly she was sure he couldn't hear her. And as certain that he had.

Wanderer was silent when she awoke, positive something was wrong. She shook her head to clear it. The motion pressed her up into the catchweb. She discovered Ciari lying snug against her, arms around her waist, hers holding his, their legs slightly tangled. One of his hands covered her breast and as she realized their position, the nipple suddenly hardened against the thin fabric of her T-shirt, prompting a sharp, surprised breath. He stretched, still more asleep than awake, but responding to her physical cues, and she felt his erection between her legs. He nuzzled her ear from behind—the sensation felt delicious—and she turned her face until their lips touched. His eyes opened and she saw the beginning of a smile; to her amazement, he looked a much younger, and gentler, man, and she became aware that she was experiencing a rare privilege, that Ciari was revealing a part of himself ordinarily kept very deeply hidden. She stroked his belly with her nails, glad to hear him gasp as loud as she.

Then, the phone rang.

"Shit!" Nicole cursed, her mood not improved by Ciari's laughter at the timing of the interruption; she slid free of the web and fumbled for the communications board. She found it on the third try, and accepted the call, audio only.

"I trust all concerned are suitably refreshed," an all-too-familiar voice crackled from the speaker. "A new day has dawned and it's past time you were up and about."

"We hear you, Major," Nicole said, stifling a yawn. She gazed blearily at the clock beside the phone and her eyes opened wide in shock. "Twelve hours," she squawked, "we've been out twelve hours!"

"Relax, Nicole," Cat told her. "The Medical Board felt the entire crew needed the extra downtime. The launch window's wide enough to allow such leeway. It's not unusual, on first flights, for novice crews to let their enthusiasm get the better of their judgment. I was no different. More sensible to delay departure a bit and thereby ensure maximum performance from all concerned rather than push to meet an arbitrary schedule and risk someone making an idiot mistake that might punch all our tickets.

"You've an hour to make yourselves presentable, *Wan-*

derer, before the rest of us start shlepping aboard; I trust that's sufficient. Garcia, out."

"Wanderer, out," Nicole acknowledged automatically. She tapped one foot against the headboard and hovered with legs crossed in midair, a little above the bed. Her underpants had rucked down about her hips and she automatically pulled them back into place. "D'you think she knew—I mean, what we were just doing?"

Ciari made an amused growl, stretching every centimeter of his body, like some great jungle cat, and nodded. Nicole buried her face in her hands with a wail, unaware that movement had started a slow forward somersault until Ciari caught her, almost completely upside down.

"Isn't there such a thing as privacy?!"

"In pre-launch, in Lunar orbit, on a novice mission?" he replied, helping her twist herself upright. "I'm sorry, Nicole —truly—I should have warned you."

"What they must think down there. . . ."

"It's nothing they haven't seen before. It's no disaster, either; it's not as if they were filming us, all they were doing was watching our bio-telemetry and making a few smart-ass extrapolations. It could've been worse."

"Yah," Nicole looked at him with a wicked grin and started to chuckle, "Cat could've called five minutes later."

"Or five minutes earlier. I figure she timed it just about right."

"I guess I owe her?"

"No big deal. But crew takes care of its own."

"Another thing to remember."

"That's what you're here for, Red, to learn."

Nicole made a face. *"Ugh.* Good thing we didn't kiss for real, my mouth tastes like somebody died in it."

He hooked a hand around an ankle and pulled her close, until they were barely touching.

"You're tense," he said.

"No fooling."

"I still scare you, Shea?"

"In some ways, more than ever." *But,* she thought, *do I scare you, Ciari, that's the question?*

"What d'you plan to do about it?"

She pushed away and, a moment later, was gone, kicking

off the headboard like a diver and swimming through the air
as she curled out the door and around the curve of the Carousel. Ciari didn't follow. Instead, with a sigh, he reached for a
pack of smokes, muttering in annoyance when he didn't find
them; they were in his cubicle, where he'd left them. He'd
forgotten he'd spent the night at Nicole's. Stuck onto the
mantle were family pictures and he flicked on the reading light
to take a closer look. She was the oldest, with a pair of
brothers; her parents had evidently waited before having children. The father was familiar, he'd seen the face before. He
had a nasty suspicion where. At a glance, there wasn't much
to look at; the only other personal item in view was Nicole's
guitar, a classical acoustic, clipped to the wall. The cubicle
was much like his own—a very private place, a loner's.

A faint hiss from below along the curve told him Nicole
was using the shower. He thought of joining her, but stayed
away, telling himself it was best for both of them.

"Wanderer from DaVinci Port Control, on my mark the count
will be Tango minus three-five minutes and counting. Three
. . . two . . . one . . . *mark!"*

"Roger, DaVinci," Nicole responded into the tiny boom
microphone of her headset. "We copy your mark at Tee minus
thirty-five. All on-board systems read nominal function."

"Affirmative, *Wanderer."*

Nicole shifted uneasily in her seat; over the past weeks,
she'd gotten used to working the main console in shirtsleeves,
rather than the bulky, confining mass of a full pressure suit.
She looked to her right at Paul DaCuhna, who mimed removing his helmet and laying it on the console before him. She
glared and flicked him a finger, and his grin widened. He'd
have laughed out loud if they hadn't been using an open channel, with Cat Garcia listening in from her own console behind
them.

Between Nicole and Paul was the one-meter diameter holographic navigation tank, a new addition to their avionics
systems which would more accurately show their position and
course in a three-dimensional setting, rather than the two-di-
mensional presentation on the scanscreens. The flight deck
hadn't been designed with it in mind, of course, so while no
doubt useful the tank was also very much in the way. Beneath

it, on the lower stage of the compartment, Nicole could see the Mission Specialists at their own consoles. Hana Murai gave her a "good luck" wave, which Nicole returned. In line beside her were Chagay and Andrei, plus Ben Ciari. Unlike the others, Ciari was armed—a nasty-looking flechette missile gun in a hip holster. Another difference was that his suit was black. Outside the ship, he'd be virtually invisible, whereas everyone else's were brightly colored; they wanted to be seen and found, he didn't.

Above and slightly behind the holo tank sat Major Garcia, in what they'd all come to refer to as the "throne," enfolded by a console that monitored every key function aboard the spacecraft as well as those of the crew themselves. If anything went wrong, she'd know about it as soon as they did and the main computer possessed an OVERRIDE program allowing her to take direct and absolute command should Nicole or Paul ever prove unable to cope. From the throne, she could run the entire ship, all by herself.

The countdown had thus far been flawless. *Wanderer* was performing as expected and, although only Cat and the Da-Vinci controllers knew it, so were her two novice pilots. Step by painstaking step, Nicole and Paul covered the master checklist, their actions pacing the calm voice of the flight controller. They were moving quickly, but there was a rhythm to their actions; neither was rushing.

As the countdown shifted from minutes to hundreds of seconds, however, tension began to build. Nicole found she was sweating, despite a perfectly functioning air conditioner, and that her guts had turned to ice. She shook her hands in a vain attempt to relax and grinned sheepishly as she caught Paul's eye. He was mouthing something, but it took a repeat for her to get the message: "Don't worry, boss. I feel the same way!"

"Wanderer, Tango minus one hundred seconds. Stand by for Main Stage Ignition."

"Nicole," Ciari announced from his console, "final medical update. Everyone's simply splendid."

If this is splendid, she thought, *spare me an example of when things are lousy. Come on, come on—what's taking so bloody long, let's get this show on the road!* They hadn't been alone since that night, and Ciari had been as taciturn with her as he was with everyone else. Nicole wondered if she'd imag-

ined what had happened, or had he indeed been scared and
backed off for his own protection?

"*Wanderer,* Tango minus seven-five seconds."

"Paolo?"

"I'm on it, boss. Computer's handling things nicely—
sixty-four . . . sixty-three . . . sixty-two . . . sixty-one . . . sixty—
ignition! I have confirmation of Main Stage Ignition at Tee
minus one minute—by both automatic and manual firing!"

"We copy that, *Wanderer,*" the flight director confirmed
from the ground. "You're looking good."

This is it, Nicole thought, *we're committed.* She knew she
was still afraid, as she felt an almost imperceptible vibration
across her seat and back—the huge engines slowly generating
thrust—but now she felt okay. No ice inside, no shakes,
nothing. She was actually beginning to enjoy herself.

She heard Paul's voice, counting down to zero: ". . . five
. . . four . . . three . . . two . . . one . . ."

"*Lift -off!*" someone yelled; in the sudden burst of excitement, Nicole didn't catch who, couldn't even tell if it was
male or female.

"Forward motion," Paul announced, "right on the mark!"

"*Wanderer,* DaVinci. We copy your departure on schedule.
Initial flight track appears nominal. We'll continue to monitor
your course and systems telemetry until you pass the Outer
Ring at fifty thousand kilometers, where you'll be handed
over to Mission Operations Control for the duration."

"Roger, DaVinci," Nicole acknowledged, "thanks for all
your help. See you next year."

"Been our pleasure, *Wanderer;* have a nice trip. Approaching one-minute mark, active systems review."

Nicole thumbed a toggle on her console, letting Paul handle things while she indulged in a slow, deep breath.

"Well, kiddo," she whispered, "you're on your way."

four

CIARI TOUCHED HER and, seemingly without effort, spun her into the wall. She cursed, tasting blood; she'd bitten her lip.

"That hurt," she hissed.

"Was meant to."

"Bastard!"

He slapped her, hard. She tried to strike back, but he glided away from her flailing arms, always a fraction of an inch out of reach. The few times she did catch him, he broke her grip with contemptuous ease. Too late, she realized he'd lured her into the center of the compartment; in this weightless environment, with nothing at hand to grab on to or push against, she was suddenly virtually helpless.

She sighed and forced her aching body to relax. She hated losing, especially when the cause was her own stupidity.

"Pathetic," Ciari told her, not bothering to hide his disgust.

"I get the message."

"Like hell."

"I'll do better next time."

"That what you're going to say when you're by yourself in the Belt, facing down a rock full of miners, or a Wolfpack? Or am I to assume some belief in reincarnation, the fuck-ups of this life to be rectified in the next?"

"Gimme a break, Ciari! I've never done this before!'"

"You're Air Force, for Christ's sake," he complained in exasperation. "Didn't anyone teach you how to fight?"

"Not the way you do!"

"Let's try it again." He held out his hand and, like a fool, Nicole took it—only to find herself slammed face first against a bulkhead with her right arm yanked high up her back in a brutal hammerlock. She couldn't stop a reflexive cry of pain, or the tears that brimmed in her eyes, so she made an instant decision to turn those reactions to her advantage. She whimpered, as if the fight had gotten too rough for her, hoping Ciari would think he'd pushed things too far. Whether he did or not, however, it made no difference; his grip didn't slacken.

She lunged across her shoulder with her free hand, going for his hair, at the same time hooking a leg behind one of his and kicking sideways, shoving them both away from the wall. Before he could recover, she wrenched free and twisted to face him. Unfortunately, she hadn't escaped unscathed; her right wrist was numb. She had no idea whether it was sprained or broken and, at the moment, didn't care.

She sensed herself closing on the opposite bulkhead and bounced off at an angle, pushing hard this time to gain some speed. Ciari followed suit, staying out of reach, watching, waiting for her mistake, certain it was bound to come. He was a head taller than she, with a longer reach and considerably more muscle, but his greater bulk and strength weren't the advantage in zero-gravity they'd be dirtside or in the Carousels. He had to be careful with his punches, lest they send him spinning out of control, vulnerable to her counter. Speed and agility were far more important; it was only up close that the ability to shift mass became critical.

Of course, he had twenty years' experience on her, that was the big difference between them; she knew intellectually what to do, he'd actually done it.

Sensation returned to her hand, with a throbbing ache that wreaked havoc on her concentration, and she cradled it under her breasts, angling her body so that it was always on the side farthest from Ciari. He was smiling, the cocky bastard, figuring he had the match locked.

She stuck out a leg, pivoting on her sneaker to jam herself into a corner—the junction of two walls and the ceiling—bracing herself in place with her legs while she tore off her sweatshirt. It wasn't easy, one-handed, and for a few seconds, as she dragged the shirt over her head, she was blind. As expected, Ciari came after her, in a bull rush full-tilt across the compartment. Nicole faced him like a matador, flipping the shirt into his face at the last instant and diving under him, grinning wildly as she heard a thump and curse behind her.

She arched her body, snaring both her ankles, and pulled them towards her. Fire streaked up her right arm past her shoulder, but she ignored the pain as her maneuver turned her and Ciari in opposite directions. She flattened out along his back, bending at the waist to bracket his head with her legs. He was jammed into her crotch and she hooked her ankles together, squeezing for all she was worth. He tried to break loose, but she had the leverage; if this had been a combat situation, it wouldn't require much pressure to snap his neck.

He patted her buttock and she heard a muffled exclamation which she decided to assume was his surrender. But to be on the safe side, when she let go, she made sure she was out of reach. He made no move to follow, but floated in a half-crouch, face flushed dark crimson, rubbing his neck with both hands.

"Not too shabby," he conceded finally.

"You mean the exercise, Marshal, or me?"

He smiled, slowly and appreciatively, as if he'd only just noticed she hadn't been wearing anything under the shirt. His expression turned serious, though, when he saw a bruise over her right breast, and he pushed over to her.

"I do that?" he asked.

"Among other things," was her reply. "Careful," she yelped as he touched her injured wrist.

"Sore?"

"Very."

"You were using it pretty well there at the end, so I doubt it's sprained or broken, but we'll X-ray it anyway."

The wrist didn't feel any better when he'd finished taping it in the infirmary and Nicole grumpily told him so. He wasn't very sympathetic.

"No EVAs for a couple of days," he said, scribbling notes on a compad, "no heavy work; in fact, try to use that hand as little as possible. I'd suggest bagging in zero-gee, at least for the next few days, less danger of accidentally rolling over on it in your sleep. If the pain gets too bad, take some aspirin; better yet, soak it in a hot whirlpool."

"Cat's going to love this." When he didn't respond, she asked, "Should I show it to Chagay?"

"If I'm busy or asleep."

"And then what, another lesson in the mat room?"

To her surprise, he took the question seriously. "I'll check the wrist every day," he said. "Directly the swelling settles down, and you can move it without much trouble, we'll pick up where we left off."

"Ter*rific*," she said, as dryly as possible. "That's really something to look forward to, Ciari, y'know—the two of us bashing away at each other until I'm in a full body cast, or maybe a bag."

"You won today, remember?"

Nicole made a face. "Luck."

"No such animal, Lieutenant, and I wasn't holding back."

"Don't bullshit me, Ciari, you weren't going anywhere near flat out."

"If I had, one of us would be dead. I was fighting as hard as I could in a practice duel; the combat edge is something you can't fake." He ushered her out the door towards the weightless core DropShaft. "Next time, we'll try it in pressure suits, minus, for the initial sessions at least, backpacks and helmets."

"Seems like a wasted effort. There are occasions when I'm wearing a suit I think I can barely move. How d'you expect anyone to fight?"

"It's done all the time, Red."

"At the Academy, they told us it wasn't practicable. I mean, so you punch some sod; how the hell is he supposed to feel it through five centimeters of re-enforced cloth and armormesh? And if you're not anchored, the reaction'll send you flying off in the opposite direction." She looked up the DropShaft at the CM hatch twenty-five meters away, then down between her feet at the Stores Modules, slightly closer; the Carousels spun around her but in the core all was still and she stretched lazily, as if she was already on her bed. That was one of the nicest things about zero-gee, you were almost always comfortable, no matter what your position. She could hear singing, far away, muted by walls separating them—Andrei, passing the time while he worked—and, even though she didn't know the tune, not being much of a fan of opera, she smiled at the pure beauty of his voice.

"True," Ciari agreed, "to a point. But generally speaking, if two bods in suits go for each other, it's for keeps. You have to know how to handle yourself. You have to have an edge."

"Which is?"

"Go for the weak point."

"The air, you mean." She stifled a yawn. "Yank the hose?"

Ciari snorted. "That's a novice answer, Shea, I expect better from you. Think this through, if you can." Her eyes snapped angrily open. "You disconnect the suit from the air-pack, then what happens?"

She shrugged. "If the link isn't restored, the bod's dead."

"Time, Shea, that takes time. There could be five minutes of breathable ambient atmosphere inside the suit proper. Anything could happen. If you're in a scrap, you want to end things fast—how?"

"Helmet?"

"Bravo! The body's a magnificent machine; it can sacrifice any extremity to survive, save one. Indeed, suits are designed to do precisely that. If the arm is holed, it'll seal at the shoulder; you'll lose that arm but live to tell the tale. The head, however, is the sole exception. Helmets have to be designed to be locked easily into place by people in bulky pressure gloves; there's no time for delicate fastenings when you're in the middle of an explosive decompression, and you can't depend on magnaseals that might jam open or closed."

"But that means killing?"

"Simplest way there is of resolving a dispute."

"You saying it always comes to that?" She was wide awake now.

"More often than not."

She pulled herself up the railing to the "Home" Carousel access hatch and thumbed it open. "Maybe that lights your torch, Ciari . . ."

"Don't judge what you don't understand, Lieutenant. Ours is the most merciless of environments, we rarely have the luxury of being gentle. And the cost of being wrong, of making a mistake, is usually your life."

"So everyone keeps telling me."

"There's a reason, Nicole."

"I don't think I want any more sessions, Marshal."

"With respect, Lieutenant, you don't have the option of refusing. *A demain.*"

Hana Murai was in the wardroom, masked from sight, as Nicole clambered awkwardly down the ladder from the core, giving full vent to her fury. "Goddamned, arrogant, pig-fucking, buggering, motherless *bastard!*" she cried, her voice building to a roar that boomed through the huge torus.

"I beg your pardon?" Hana asked, poking her head into view.

"Oh, shit, Hana, I'm sorry," Nicole said, instantly ashamed of her outburst. "I didn't realize anyone was here."

"Obviously. I'm making a snack. Want?"

"What'cha got?"

"Nova salmon and cream cheese."

"Yum—Hana, this stuff's *real!*"

"The last of my personal stash," she said with a heartfelt sigh.

"Oh, I couldn't, you should . . ."

"I am, and if I want to share, that's my privilege."

"You are a true friend."

Hana ordered a teapak for Nicole from the meal console; as usual, it tasted stale. But the fish was heavenly. She ate slowly, savoring the taste for as long as she could. Now she was beginning to understand why the restaurants, and even basic DaVinci Base catering, had so high a rep; after months of living on pastes and dehydrated, reconstituted, semi-synthetic "food," astronauts demanded—and deserved—the best of the real thing when they returned home.

"Rough session with the Marshal, Nicole?"

"Scumbelly slime."

"That good?"

"He's teaching me to kill people, Hana."

"And maybe in the process, avoid getting killed yourself?"

"You defending him?!"

"Just remembering what General Canfield told us at dinner, when she announced the mission. We're virgins, Nicole, Novice Astronauts; the lady might know what she was talking about. And the man, what he's doing."

Nicole sighed, wishing her cup would cool enough to safely drink. "It wasn't what I bargained for."

"Really? Then why'd you join the Air Force?"

"I wanted to be an astronaut. I wanted starships. Blue-suits have the inside track. If I'd flunked out of astronaut training, I suppose . . . I'd've become a test pilot. But Ciari's so god-damned cold-blooded, it's as if he's trying to remake me in his image. And I don't like it!"

"You tell him?"

"Kind of. Not that it made any difference. He means to keep at it, regardless of how I feel."

"Appeal to Cat. She's Mission Commander, she could stop him."

Nicole thought long and hard, then shook her head.

"Got a reason?" Hana asked. "You figure she'd side with him?"

"Hell, no! Quite the opposite, in fact. I don't think she likes these training sessions at all. I say the word, they're history. But I don't want to involve her." The flatness of her tone made her lack of trust obvious.

"We've barely begun this trip, Nicole," Hana said seriously. "This is not a healthy attitude."

"I'll work it out." Nicole blinked, as if noticing something for the first time. "Why're you wearing that turban?" Hana had a vibrant, peacock blue silk scarf wrapped tightly around the crown of her head. To Nicole's surprise, the young Japanese looked agitated. Then, with a wry, self-mocking chuckle, Hana unclipped the scarf and swept it away. Nicole couldn't help a gasp of astonishment.

Most of Hana's shoulder-length, raven's wing hair was gone; only a four centimeter wide strip of glossy black running from forehead to the base of her skull remained; the rest of her scalp had been shaved. The "Mohawk" had only been slightly trimmed and as Hana ran her hand back across her head, its natural wave reasserted itself, so that her hair stood straight up for a few centimeters before sweeping elegantly to one side. It had been left longer at the back, and a modest tail fell to her shoulders.

Grinning shyly, Hana asked, "You're the first to see this, outside of Andrei. What do you think?"

Nicole bugged her eyes slightly, grinned like an idiot,

made a silly face that she prayed looked funny. Anything to cover the fact that the only thought to immediately come to mind was envy; she wondered how she'd look, and that fantasy immediately convulsed her with giggles. Hana was looking at her suspiciously, unsure whether she was being made fun of.

"I love it," Nicole assured her. "God Almighty, Andrei, he—?" Hana nodded. "The sly dog, I didn't know he had such talents in him. But, Hana, why—?! Whatever possessed you?!"

Hana shrugged. "I felt like it. I figured, if it doesn't work, I can always shave my head completely and let it grow again. I mean, who's to see—outside of my friends—you are my friends, right—" Nicole nodded enthusiastically, "—before we get back to Luna?"

"You're a braver woman than I."

"You military types have to look all prim 'n' proper."

Nicole closed her teeth and made a wistful, *cluck*-noise with her tongue, shaking her head. Now it was Hana's turn to laugh, because her friend's thoughts had become so painfully transparent. She was really debating whether or not to call Andrei and have him try the same cut with her, or something equally outrageous. But then, Nicole shook her head. *On a later flight,* she told herself, *aboard my own command.*

"I was wondering, Nicole," Hana said, turning serious again, "how *do* you feel about Ciari?"

Nicole looked up, a little surprised, the question—the change of subject—had come out of left field.

"I hate the sod's guts. Don't look at me like that, Hana, I do!"

"I believe you. I was just thinking back to that day before we launched, when you two were . . ."

"Oh, hell, I don't believe this, I'm blushing!"

"It's very becoming."

"Bitch!"

"He still gets to you, *hmnh?*"

Nicole slowly nodded, slumping deep into her chair. "I didn't want anything to happen, or maybe I did," she said, absently munching on a cracker, "because when we woke up, I felt so incredibly horny. It was this primal male/female thing, but it was also that I wanted *him,* Ciari! I've had affairs, but never anything like this, the rush was indescribable."

"Sounds wonderful. How is it nothing's happened since?"

"Are you kidding? Every day, in every way, we try our best to bash each other's brains in. What more traditionally loving, quintessentially American relationship could we have?"

"How clever."

Nicole made a face. Her tea was cold, but she drained the cup. Hana ordered another from the console.

"There wasn't time in orbit; we were all too busy. Since then . . . I dunno. He's been all business and I guess I've been taking my own cues from that. I saw him with his guard down, maybe that scared him; with it up, he scares hell out of me. But what about you? What's the line on you and Paolo?"

"He's nice." Hana smiled at Nicole's nod of agreement, and pointed from one to the other. "You two, *uhh . . . ?*"

"Classmates. Friends. Partners. To hear him tell it, we're the 'Team Supreme.' Shared the sack a couple of nights on a survival test, but nothing earth-shaking. He wasn't my type."

"Don't get me wrong, I like him a lot. . . ."

"He's an eminently 'likeable' fella," Nicole agreed.

". . . and I have to admit, *nobody* ever makes me laugh the way he can. But at rock bottom, it's a casual thing."

"I hope Paul knows that," Nicole said quietly, then asked, "You have anyone back home?"

"Waiting?" Hana paused for a breath, looking anywhere but at Nicole, and faked a grin. "Gracious, no! I couldn't be that cruel." Another pause, longer, the grin fading as her memories wouldn't be danced away. "I had two what I'd call real affairs. One in Japan, undergraduate, the other at Stanford. That was serious. For nearly three years we were inseparable. We went the whole route. Worked together, vacationed together, lived . . . together. I made no secret of my application to NASA. That was why I came to Stanford. But I don't think either of us ever thought seriously about what we'd do if I was accepted."

"And when you were?"

Hana's voice went flat, her eyes hooded, and Nicole wanted to reach out to her. But she held back, sensing rightly that it would be a mistake. "A lot of screaming," Hana said quietly, "a lot of tears. Cops came by one night, a neighbor was really afraid one of us would kill the other. I don't think she was that far wrong. All my life, I'd had this dream about going to space. It was what I wanted, more than anything, where I knew, *I knew,* I was meant to be.

"I couldn't give it up, Nicole, even for love."

Now, Nicole's good hand touched Hana's. The other woman took it, unconsciously holding it as tight as she could. It hurt, but Nicole said nothing as they sat silently for a while, before Hana sniffed and blew her nose.

"Sorry," she said, wiping her eyes and face with her hands.

"S'all right."

"I heard from Beth, just before we left DaVinci." Nicole wondered if she'd heard the name right, if she understood. "She moved East, she's teaching at MIT, still solo. But at least we're speaking again. I really hurt her. I was so afraid she'd never forgive me."

"Would you do things differently, if you had the chance?"

"Would you?"

"The choice never came up."

"Lucky you." Hana sighed and turned away. She tapped the communications panel. "I'm playing MixaMeal, Andrei Mikhailovitch, you guys interested?"

"Chagay is enraptured by his slides and smelly chemicals, as usual, and I fear will not be tearing himself away anytime soon, but I, dear lady, would love a snack."

"Stop babbling about it then and come on up."

Zhimyanov moved through zero-gee with an easy grace that put the rest of the crew, with the possible exception of Ben Ciari, to shame; he was no less impressive in gravity. The tallest of them, he'd barely slipped under the maximum height requirement, but his body possessed a dancer's lean, muscular frame. Nicole considered him one of the most beautiful men she'd ever seen. Unfortunately, he was happily married and while always in a mood to flirt, he showed no interest in going beyond that. His lover was a psychologist at the Russian base at Gagarin, so well regarded that his practice extended across to the American zone. Nicole had met him early on during pre-flight training and had been stunned to discover he was even better looking than Andrei. Her initial reaction had been: *there ain't no justice.* But as time wore on, and she got to know them better, she realized that this was one of those rare relationships where both parties really were made for each other. The bonds between these two men were stronger than among almost any couple she could think of, including she realized with a start, her own parents. If she found something half as rich, she decided, she'd be content.

Andrei looked at their plates and made a sorrowful face: "This is a snack?"

"Suits our needs," Hana told him.

A look told them what he thought of that.

He considered a moment, using a compad to access the computer's recipe and stores file, scribbled some notes, and began entering an order into the main menu.

"Did I ever tell you, Andrei," Nicole said, "I saw your parents skate, when I was a kid."

"So did most of the world. If not their first Olympics, then certainly the second."

"They were wonderful."

"The best."

"You don't skate?"

"Not here, no."

"You know what I mean, dammit!"

He tasted his concoction, then slid it back into the console and programmed a pinch more spice and flavoring. "Not like that," he replied, shaking his head. "I never considered it."

"Why?"

"Why, Nicole, did you not become an attorney, like your father, or a writer? I've read your mother's work — as journalist and novelist — she is superb."

"She has the Pulitzers to prove it."

"Precisely. And in my parents' home, above the mantelpiece, hang three gold medals. For ten years, and those three Olympics, my mother and father were the finest pair figure skaters in the world. No one has ever proved their equal, before or since, and I really had no desire to try. Like them, I have little patience with being second-best. I want to be remembered as Andrei. Not Mikhail and Larisa's boy."

The console *pinged* and he busied himself for a minute with his soup. "Here," he said, holding a spoon out to Nicole, "try this. Careful, though, it's hot."

"It smells delicious!" Hana told him, leaning forward for a taste herself.

"Yum," Nicole groaned. "How do you get that beast to perform such wonders?"

"You forget, I've been this way before."

"Don't rub it in."

"Fyodor and I had the same system installed in our flat, so I could practice and"—he made a fluttery gesture with his hands, coupled with a slyly self-mocking smile—"play a bit. Our way of pushing the outside of the culinary envelope."

"Is there enough for Paul?" Nicole asked. "He's got Watch, up on the flight deck."

"Take this." He sealed the bowl, clipped it to a tray and handed it to her, ignoring her protests. "I'll just make another for myself. The basic recipe is in the menu's permanent memory; you can call it up whenever you like and simply season to taste. Then, if you prefer, you can file that variation and, from that point on, let *Wanderer* do all the work. Actually—" he tapped a command onto his compad—"now that I think of it, I had better take a container down to the Bear. He's so absorbed in his work, if I didn't remember to bring him food, he'd probably starve."

"You two make a pair." Hana grinned. Andrei's response, to both her and Nicole's surprise, was serious.

"The last of a breed, I think," he said, in a slightly musing tone. "Within a generation, this way of life—slowship transport through the Solar System—will be gone. There won't be as much need for people like us." He meant them all, Nicole realized, not merely himself and Chagay.

"What d'you mean?" she asked.

"Loners. Solitary souls who can endure months in these pretentious tin cans. Even in the submarine service, there are opportunities to sail on the ocean's surface, for the crew to stretch their legs, breathe fresh air, take in the view. Not here. The closest analogue would be the Antarctic scientific stations, where the teams are literally housebound for the entire winter, completely cut off from the outside world. That way of life demands a special type of person, as does ours. We're allowed our eccentricities because, for the moment, there's no one else who can do our work. But that will change. It always does. The mountain men had their day in your country's Wild West, Nicole, but days always end. For them. For us."

"Cheerful thought," Hana muttered.

Andrei nodded towards the container Nicole was holding. "I think Paul would prefer that hot, don't you think?"

"Shit, yes! I forgot—! See you guys later. Hana, thanks for the fish!" That last was said over her shoulder as Nicole hauled herself up to the access hatch. She thought better of it halfway and made a brief detour, past the others, to her cubicle, where she grabbed her leather Edwards flight jacket before heading at last to the Command Module at the very nose of the spacecraft.

She heard music as the hatch cycled open and she smiled, recognizing the rich, whiskey-rough contralto at once.

"Since when were you a Lila Cheney fan?" she called.

Paul shrugged from his right-hand seat and turned the volume down a notch. "She ain't bad, but I've heard lots better."

"The hell you say."

"I got a friend in Houston who has a friend in her entourage—a techie, one of the sound engineers—and we worked a deal for some tapes."

"That's *Rollin' Thunder*. I heard crowd noises, is it live?"

Paul smiled more broadly than a cheshire cat. "San Francisco, exactly one calendar week ago."

"Son of a bitch, you're kidding!"

He shook his head. "What you got here are legal, artist sanctioned, friend to friend private stock reproductions of the best of Lila Cheney's Sundowner Tour. And some studio jam sessions that should curl your hair. And as if that wasn't enough . . ."

"There can't be more."

"Christ, you're like a six-year-old at Christmas! I wish I had a camera."

"Thank your lucky stars you don't, bubster."

"Danno tossed in some archive *Nazgûl* tapes as well."

She wanted to say something, to tell him how much this meant to her. Nicole's near-adoration for Lila Cheney had been a running joke between them ever since they met, forever at odds with Paul's equally passionate reverence for classic rock and roll. Instead, she left the soup container to float in midair while she pulled herself onto his chair and gave Paul the biggest, strongest hug she could.

"Well worth the price," he said as she disengaged.

"It must have cost . . ."

"A favor. Nothing monstrous, nothing lasting. Danno and I grew up together. Actually, the way he tells it, Lila thought it was neat. I figure she figures doing you a good turn'll help her get a gig on the Moon."

"Sounds great to me."

"My way of saying thanks for all the kindness you and your folks showed me over the years."

"Goddamn, Paolo, how'm I ever going to repay . . . ?"

"I could be soppy, boss, and say the sparkle in your eyes is more than enough."

"I wouldn't believe it."

"Tough. Someday, someway, the scales will balance, I have faith. What'cha got?"

"A gift from the galley."

"Can I pass? I've eaten there before."

"Give it a shot, you won't be sorry."

He tried a hesitant taste, and wasn't. "How's the bus?" she asked.

"Nominal. Housekeeping traffic, mostly. Assuming the mail is uploaded on schedule, it'll be here in about fifteen minutes. I think the Bear's expecting some results from the experimental data we sent Houston yesterday." He frowned, setting his soup aside, and pointing a thumb towards her bandaged wrist.

. "Ciari?" he asked. And when she nodded. "I'd punch his lights out if I thought I had even a ghost of a chance."

"My knight in shining armor. Better watch yourself; he's teaching me how to kill in full pressure suit."

"Jesus, he's putting you through the wringer."

"No less than you, hotshot."

Paul shook his head. "He's teaching you a lot more, and pushing a lot harder. I wouldn't last a minute against you."

"You never could."

A wry smile. "True enough. Which is why I'm here and you're . . ." He finished with his thumb again, gesturing towards Nicole's left-hand pilot's chair.

"Someday, my son," she responded in mock solemnity, "this, too, shall be yours."

"Not my ambition."

"That's a change. The Paul DaCuhna I remember . . ."

". . . was going to set the stars afire. Imagine my surprise when I learned they were already burning."

"Very funny."

"Not really. Not the way I mean. I'm good, Nicole—real good—but I've learned some limitations. Mostly that I'm lots better with you than without you."

"You're crazy."

"Of course. Look who I take after. Hey, boss, Hana down below?"

"Stuck cleaning up the mess, I suspect."

"Think she'd object to some help?"

"Worth a shot. I'll mind the store. Just don't be too long!"

As Paul left, Nicole turned off the music and rewound the tape, preferring to sit in silence for a while. She'd enjoy Lila later, in private. Automatically, she ran a systems check on *Wanderer*. All readings were precisely where they should be. She snuggled deeper into her chair, cinching the safety harness tighter so she'd stay put. She pulled her jacket close, absently stroking the silver astronaut's wings embossed on its left breast. The temperature hadn't changed—it was as comfortable here as in the Carousel—but she felt a chill. The jacket was a memento of her stay at Edwards, marking her as one of a select band of fliers; it was given by the senior test pilots to those they considered their peers. The honor had nothing to do with rank or seniority, it was a recognition of courage and skill and talent, of all the myriad elements that go into making a great flier. Harry Macon slung it over her shoulders the day after she'd co-piloted the XSR-5 Controlled ReEntry Vehicle —basically a shuttle craft designed to transport passengers and cargo from orbit to a planetary surface and, more important, back up again—through a perfect mission. Her first and the SR-5's as well. A week later, she was flying the Number 4 aircraft of the memorial flight over Harry's grave. In its own way, as signal an honor. Just short of the cemetery, she pulled her fighter into a steep climb, so that, when the flight passed overhead, there was a missing aircraft, symbolic of the lost airman. She waited while the others headed home, watching from on high as the mourners followed in their cars, and then dropped for the deck, pushing her engines beyond their limits. This was her own private tribute, a Valkyrie dive that broke the sound barrier as she crossed his gravesite, thunder whip-cracking across the still, high desert as it had for decades, ever since Yeager's landmark flight. She'd roared towards the setting sun, eyes blinded by its light and her own tears.

So long ago, and yet she still wept.

She wiped her face, and deliberately turned her thoughts to Hana, wondering how deeply Paul felt for her and what implications that might have for the mission. She'd seen Hana's dossier; she'd left Stanford for the NASA training center in Houston over two years ago, but the ache in her voice when she spoke of Beth was eloquent testament to the depth of her feelings. And loss. *What,* Nicole asked herself, *would it be like to care so much for someone? Could I make that kind of sacrifice, the person I loved for a dream? Or for duty? And suppose it happened in reverse? Could I endure being left behind?*

Her thoughts turned to Ciari and she jumped as she heard his voice.

"You wanted me, Cat?"

He was on the deck below, where the Mission Specialist consoles were located; presumably, Major Garcia was with him. They must have believed themselves alone—perhaps because they'd seen Paul descend to the Carousel—because they were speaking freely, and as the conversation progressed Nicole realized that the last thing she wanted to do was reveal her presence.

"What are you playing at with Shea?" Garcia demanded, a hard, angry edge to her voice.

"My job."

"Crap, Ciari, you're teaching her your own personal bag of tricks, moves you wouldn't even show me!"

"Jealous?"

"I want an explanation. She's not Law, she's not Ranger, you're giving her more than she'll ever need."

"Doubtful."

"You're not teaching it to DaCuhna."

"It's wasted on him. And to his credit, the boy knows it."

"Why?"

"He doesn't have the knack."

"Not a born killer, you mean?"

Ciari sighed. "If you like."

"That apply to me?"

"Retrofire, Cat—I'm not in the mood for this scene, I'm too tired."

"Nicole score some points?"

"Not as many as you're trying to."

"How would you rate her?"

"One of the best I've seen."

"That's what they said dirtside at Edwards. And Houston. Yet in the shuttle simulator, she made the most elementary, classically stupid mistake."

"I thought that was what simulators were for."

"What about against me, Ben? Where does she stand?"

There was a pause, and Nicole could sense a flaring anger in Ciari's voice that matched Cat's; she'd pushed him too far. "Your edge is experience," he said, "but she'll live longer."

"Oh?"

"You're careless, Major. You don't always think things through. You react from the gut, emotionally. As you're doing now, goading me."

"I'm getting results."

"Bully for you. I don't know what you feel you have to prove, or why you see Nicole as a threat . . ."

"Come *on*, Ben, you've heard the stories about her and Canfield. And before that, on Earth, with Harry Macon."

Nicole almost gave herself away, a murmur of pain almost escaping her tightened lips as she reflexively clenched her injured hand.

"Are you suggesting it's my turn?"

The woman's silence was her answer.

"You're out of line, Cat. And even if it were true, all the juice in creation doesn't matter a damn now; the kid's on her own, just like the rest of us. And she's given you no reason to doubt her competence."

"I'm not reassured."

"Now that you mention it, Major, neither am I."

"I don't want you giving her special treatment."

"I'm teaching her to the fullest extent of her capabilities, that's part of my job."

"I draw the line, Marshal, when it interferes with ship operations. The Medex says that because of her hand, Nicole will be out of action for the better part of a week; that puts more pressure on the rest of us. I want a perfect mission, and I won't tolerate anything that jeopardizes it. So, Mister Ciari, moderate your enthusiasm for your *protegée*. That's an order."

Ciari didn't reply as Cat stormed out of the compartment. The silence stretched on about Nicole, while she sat quietly, deep in thought: *jesus, where the hell did* that *come from?!*

"You didn't hear a thing," Ciari's voice hissed next to her ear.

"*Jesus!*" she cried — and would have leapt from her chair in surprise had it not been for her harness holding her in place. Her heart was hammering against her ribs and she clenched her teeth to keep them from chattering; he'd caught her completely by surprise. Absurdly, the first thought to pop into her head, once she calmed enough to have coherent thoughts, was, *I guess I do have a lot more to learn; I wonder if I'll get the chance.* And, to her surprise, she realized that she wanted that chance, very badly.

"Not one fucking word," he continued in the same flat tone, as if she hadn't responded. "As far as you're concerned, young lady, you weren't even here, understood?"

She nodded, not trusting herself to speak until he turned to go, and then she called out: "Ciari!"

"Yes?"

"What was that all about?"

"Private business."

"The hell it is. My name came up, that involves me!"

"Let it ride, Nicole."

She loosened her harness, pulled herself up and over the seat to face him. "We've barely started this goddamn mission, how can I be expected to function — how the hell do I even survive — with a commanding officer who hats my guts?"

"She doesn't hat Nicole, not really."

"Cold fucking comfort, Marshal."

He shrugged. "Is there an alternative?"

"Don't patronize me! It's not as if she and I were the only women in the Air Force, or in space, or even on this bucket. Why's she on my case, what makes *me* so frigging special? We could at least stand each other until you started these special training sessions!"

"I know."

"Helluva lot of good that does."

"Depends on your perspective, doesn't it? The transitory

grief and rage you're experiencing now versus permanent death later on. I'm not playing games, Lieutenant. I'm trying to give you an edge that'll save your life. And maybe ours in the bargain."

"First that clown Morgan, back on the Moon, makes a reference to me and Canfield. Now Cat—what's the big secret that everybody seems to know but me?"

"You'll have to ask the General."

"I'm asking *you!*"

"Let it ride, Nicole. Please."

"I don't like being jacked around, Ciari; you have no right to do this!"

He smiled, without humor. "If you want to take your frustrations out on anyone, Nicole, you know where to find me."

"You may regret that."

The console beeped and Nicole accepted the incoming signal from Luna.

"Mail call, people," she announced over the ALL HANDS circuit. "Computer's sorting it now and should have everything distributed to your private datastacks directly." She switched to a local line to the C2 Lab Ring. "Chagay, looks like bad news."

"Damnation bloody hell," he growled. "I shall need time, Miss Shea."

She popped the computer's schedule onto her screen. "Looks pretty light for the next ten hours; can you take what you need from that?"

"It should be sufficient."

"If not, let me know, we'll work things out." She punched access to C-1. "Paolo, old chum, you're needed."

Without waiting for an acknowledgment, she cleared her circuit and glanced over her shoulder. As expected, Ciari was nowhere to be seen. Her wrist was aching and she absently started stroking it—a frown on her face, worry deep in her eyes—trying to wish more than pain away.

———— five ————

FOUR WEEKS OUT of DaVinci, just inside the fringes of the Asteroid Belt, they sighted the derelict. It was morning, Ship-Time, and Nicole was running her before-breakfast laps around the C-1 Carousel. She was still working out with Ciari, though the matches were nowhere near as one-sided as they'd been, and if Cat resented the fact, she masked it well.

"What'cha got?" Nicole asked, as she swam out of the DropShaft and onto the flight deck, in response to Paul's summons.

"Contact," he told her, gesturing towards the holo tank. "Relative bearing zero-three-eight horizontal by three-four-three vertical, ballistic trajectory; range, roughly three hundred thousand kilometers, closing slowly. Forward velocity, a constant one-six-one meters per second."

"Any sort of transponder squawk?"

"Yup," he muttered, gently twisting the gain control of the communications panel. "On the Mayday frequency—probably an automatic distress beacon. Signal's weak, though—hear it?"

"Yah."

"I'm boosting our reception to the max and we're still barely picking it up."

"Hang on, I'll run the numbers for an ident." Almost immediately, the answers flashed on a secondary scanscreen.

"Transponder code identifies her as the DSV *Rockhound*—original name, that—Ceres registry. Miner base ship. Privately owned."

"I know her," Cat Garcia said quietly, startling both Nicole and Paul; they hadn't heard her enter the flight deck. She was floating a little above and behind them, scanning the consoles as intently as they were.

"Wait a minute," Paul said, "something makes no sense." He activated another screen and brought a SKYSCAN program on-line. Halfway down the main frame of the spacecraft, an array of telescopes and sensors swung towards their contact. "There's a regular, radical shift in *Rockhound*'s albedo," he announced, as data flashed before him.

"She's tumbling," Cat told them.

"That fits," Nicole confirmed. "I'm registering no power readings, or fuel residue emissions, and the gross infrared scan says *Rockhound* is cold. No internal heat generation." She pressed the ALL HANDS button on the intercom board. "Duty stations, everyone; we may have some trouble."

When Ben Ciari sleepily acknowledged the alert, Nicole told him: "Prep a Rover for launch, Marshal. Two-man crew, active weaponry. Copy?"

"I copy, skipper. On my way."

Nicole switched circuits to Chagay Shomron, who never seemed to sleep. "Bear, would you prep the sickbay and set up a full medikit for the EVA team? If there are survivors, they'll probably need care; if there are bodies, you and the Marshal will have to perform autopsies."

"I understand, Lieutenant. I shall be ready."

"Thanks." Chagay was the oldest and most experienced spacer aboard; nothing fazed him, nothing took him by surprise. She had a wild feeling that he'd stay awake every moment of the voyage and then dive into a year's hibernation to restore himself the moment they returned to Luna.

She looked towards Cat and asked, "Anything to add, Major?"

"You're doing fine, Nicole. The best thing I can do for the present is stay out of your way. If you need me, I'll be at my console."

"Plot an intercept, Paolo," Nicole told him. "Get us as close as you can for as long as possible."

"Already in the works. But don't hope for much."

"How so?"

He pointed at the holo tank. *"Rockhound*'s cutting across our course at a fairly steep angle; the best I can manage is maybe a seven-hour window. Even then, we'll be cutting things awfully tight. The Rover'll be operating at maximum range, there won't be any room for glitches. To try for a more convenient rendezvous would entail a massive course correction and all the time we spend reorienting this bucket, *Rockhound*'ll be opening the separation between us. We'll have to go virtually dead in space, facing a long chase to catch her. And that, boss, will shoot our mission profile all to hell."

"They'll love that at Copernicus."

"'Specially if we come up empty—if there are no survivors and what happened was no more than an accident."

"Notice the encouragement I'm getting from on high?" she murmured.

"Cat, you mean?" Nicole nodded. "You expected anything else?" She met his eyes and saw minimal sympathy. "Canfield said you're in command, Nicole. I guess this comes under the heading of earning the title, and the pay."

"Sod."

"True, but I'm *your* sod." That got him a smile, to echo his own.

"ETA?"

"Window opens in fifty-three minutes."

"Better start your countdown, then. You have the Con, Paolo; I'm going to change." Nicole couldn't help grinning as she spoke, feeling a little silly giving orders in cut-off Levi shorts, an old, well-worn sweatshirt and running shoes. But within days of their departure from the Moon, none of them, Cat included, were wearing their uniforms. Comfort, as always, among even novice spacers, had become the order of the day.

Before leaving the flight deck, Nicole thumbed the intercom: "Marshal Ciari, Dr. Shomron, we estimate rendezvous with *Rockhound* in approximately fifty minutes."

"All hands," Paul interrupted, "stand by for main engine burn. Five seconds full thrust, plus ten seconds attitude burn —negative pitch, negative yaw." *Wanderer* would be moving down and to the left of her line of flight, as well as increasing her speed slightly. "All hands, we have Ignition."

Nicole felt the deck vibrate fractionally as the huge primary motors flared briefly to life, acceleration nudging her backward and to the right.

"PECO!" Paul announced. "Primary Engine Cut-Off, on its mark. Nominal track, boss," he told Nicole, in answer to her unspoken query, "we're in the groove."

"Nicole," the speaker crackled, Ciari's voice, "d'you want me in combat armor."

Kinky, she thought absurdly, *but I prefer you naked.* And blushed. "You, uh, think there'll be trouble?" The steadiness of her voice surprised her. *How could I have thought such a thing,* she wondered, *and why in hell* now?!

"As my Zen master often said, I expect nothing. Just a thought, was all."

"It won't inhibit your movements?"

"No."

"Then do it. Will you need help dressing?"

"Not necessary, but I'd appreciate it."

"Major—?" Nicole asked, looking toward the center console.

"My pleasure," Cat said, and headed down the DropShaft, while Nicole found herself wishing silently, *I wish it could be mine.* And sighing in annoyance at the ease with which her mind dove into the gutter.

Paul's voice drew her out of herself: "Look at this," he told her, tapping one of the screens. *"Rockhound's* tumbling end over end, a full rotation every two hundred seconds. I think she's rolling as well, positive arc—that is, clockwise."

"Shit."

"This is getting very hairy."

Nicole said nothing as she stared intently at the screen, evaluating the information as it was continually updated.

"Nicole, who flies the mission?"

"That a question, hot shot, or a request?"

"You're the boss, your place is here."

She shook her head. "Cat'll be here; she can handle the command responsibilities. And I'd rather have you back-stopping me while my ass is on the line than sit here helpless worrying about you."

"I'm flattered. I hope you're not making a mistake."

"Don't be so eager to be a hero."

"Look who's talking."

"You'll get your chance, Paolo."

"Just don't fuck up yours."

Nicole shrugged.

"You better get rolling," Paul told her. "You'll need a full two hours to purge your system, so you can handle the pure oxygen atmosphere of your suit. It will come out of your rendezvous window."

"Be just as true for you, Paolo."

"I got a bad feeling, is all."

"About staying or going?"

"I wish to hell I knew."

"If the risks prove unacceptable, I'll abort."

"With respect, O fearless leader, there are occasions when you wouldn't know an 'unacceptable' risk if it bit you."

He looked away, leaving her to float above the hatch, knowing his words had struck home. She made a frustrated, almost angry noise deep in her throat as she searched in vain for an argument to refute him. "I'm not Cat," was what she said, and then, as she sighed and left, "Be seeing you, hotshot."

The rover bays were arranged in a ring around the base of the dome-shaped Command Module—seven in all, holding two general purpose craft, two exploratory, two combat and the lifeboat. The Changing Room—the antechamber that held the crew's pressure suits—ringed the core DropShaft, subdivided into seven completely isolated segments, one for each bay, the idea being that a loss of pressure in one wouldn't necessarily affect the others. Each segment, indeed, each major level of *Wanderer,* contained two basic suits, same-size-fits-all, to provide crew members a decent chance of survival in the event of an emergency no matter where they were. Additionally, the Changing Rooms held suits appropriate to the primary function of their particular Rovers and, finally there were the custom-fitted suits, tailored to the crew's individual specialties. Ciari's was a black hardsuit—combat armor crammed full of hunter sensors, able to withstand laser blasts and solid shot both, with power enhancers that gave him exceptional strength, speed and maneuverability. Nicole's was a Command suit, as was Cat Garcia's, trading off the enhancers and some of the armor in favor of more, and more varied, sensors and communications systems. Wearing it, Nicole could tap into every system aboard *Wanderer* or any of the Rovers, call up data from their computer systems on her helmet head-up displays, and eavesdrop on any conversation, ship to ship or suit to suit; if necessary, she could even remotely control those vessels as well.

She broke her suit out of its cocoon, which automatically started its electronics systems diagnostics check, while she stripped herself naked, tucking her clothes into the small locker provided. There was a full-length mirror on the wall and she paused for a long, hard look at herself. She always thought she had too many bones, that somewhere along the line the sizes had gotten slightly mixed, resulting in skin a size too small for her frame or a frame a size too big. She could count her ribs and her hips were all angular hollows and sharp edges. No fat at all worth mentioning. No breasts, either—she snorted in mock dismay. Interesting, she noted to herself, how her pubic hair was so much redder than the hair on her head, which was more deep brown with red highlights. If she was really curious about it, she could always ask Chagay. And he'd give her some profound, eminently logical genetic explanation. She turned slightly, arched her back, and thrust a hip towards the mirror in a deliberately provocative pose, throwing in a smouldering look for good measure, then shook her head. Enough games. She was wasting precious time.

The status lights on her suit blinked green, which she acknowledged with the slightest of nods, and then she began a methodical manual examination. It was the first thing drummed into the heads of every astronaut trainee—your suit is your life, take it for granted and you're as good as history. And, sadly, as with almost every class, there had been the accident that proved the point. Satisfied finally that all was well, Nicole was reaching for the undersuit when she became aware of another presence in the room.

Cat held the long-legged, long-sleeved garment out to her. Nicole cursed furiously at once more being taken by surprise, and wondered if Cat was doing this deliberately, to rattle her, so that she'd screw up later. Even as the thought crossed her mind, she dismissed it, refusing to believe Cat could be so petty, especially with lives and a mission at stake.

"Ciari's done," Cat reported, "so I came over to see if you needed a hand."

"Thanks, Major."

"I've been scanning the telemetry, Nicole. DaCuhna was quite correct; this could be a real bitch."

"I know." And she thought: *Damn the woman, she was monitoring the flight deck after she left!* It was Cat's prerogative, and her responsibility, and Nicole didn't care.

"Do you?" While Nicole pulled the undersuit over her arms, flexing her shoulders to ensure a smooth, snug fit, Cat anchored her in place and closed the fastenings. Then she backed away slightly as Nicole pushed herself into the legs of the pressure suit itself; once those were on, she wriggled upward into the separate torso, while Cat snapped and sealed the waist ring shut. Again, she backed up and away, as if to view her handiwork. Nicole suddenly realized that, in free-fall, Cat always positioned herself a head above whoever she was talking to. The idea was to place her in a position of dominance, because, in gravity, her height invariably put her at a disadvantage. *Is this,* Nicole asked silently, *part of the reason we don't get along—the fact that I'm so much taller?*

"I wish I had some sage advice beyond stating the obvious," Cat continued. "Don't rush. The clock's running. Never forget that, but also never let it spook you. Take time up front to examine all your options. That way, no matter what, you'll have at least an idea of how to deal with it. The last thing you want is to get spooked. You cut corners, you get careless."

"I understand, Major."

"I hope so. Remember, a calculated risk is only as valid as the data it's based on. Garbage in, garbage out—just like with a computer.

"Trust Ciari. If he offers a suggestion, listen. If he gives a command, obey. He's been here before, which makes him an invaluable asset. Beyond that, you'll have to depend on your own judgment."

"Sooner or later, boss, it was bound to happen."

Cat allowed herself a small smile, a ghost of a grin that was more relaxed than anything Nicole had seen from her since they left the Moon, and nodded.

She didn't say another word until they were nearly done.
Nicole was thankful that she didn't have to bear the weight of
suit and backpack. The whole mess easily weighed twice what
she did. Shifting its bulky mass was misery enough and she
wasn't looking forward to clambering through *Rockhound*'s
ruined guts. They were flying the smaller of their Jeeps—the
general purpose Rovers—from Bay One and since Nicole's
locker was adjacent to Bay Four, that meant she had to cut
across the DropShaft. For convenience, she moved bare-
handed, her gloves clipped to her belt; unfortunately, the helmet had to be carried. A facemask and portable oxygen bottle
clipped to her suit, to acclimatize Nicole's system to its new
environment, added injury to insult. Cat followed her through
the extra-wide hatch, but turned upward to the flight deck
while Nicole pushed herself over to the hatch opposite. As it
cycled open, she heard Cat say, from high above: "Y'all come
back, hear?"

As *Wanderer* closed on *Rockhound,* Nicole's first thought
was, *not a prayer.* The general consensus among the crew was
that any kind of dock would be impossible, regardless of how
good a pilot Nicole was. Nearly as large as *Wanderer* herself,
the mining ship spun along like a giant cartwheel. It was rolling far faster than anticipated, the brutal torque tearing the
spacecraft apart, hurling debris off in all directions and forcing
the NASA cruiser to keep a healthy distance. Which narrowed
their already shrunken rendezvous window even further.

"That's a ship?" Nicole wondered aloud. "Christ, it looks
like a half-dozen paint cans strung together with some leftover
bits of erector set." Unlike *Wanderer*'s Command Module,
Rockhound's was spherical, and considerably smaller, since
Rockhound was never meant to carry as large a crew or the
number of ancillary craft. Chunky secondary modules were
arranged in a line behind it, with the engines bringing up the
rear. Directly aft of the CM, three fifty-meter gantries reached
away from the central core, at forty-five degree angles, each
one topped by a housing for a cargo module. The garish paint
on the open scaffolding, plus the lights and symbols, gave fair
warning that the vessel was designed to carry highly radioactive material. A horizontal ring assembly wrapped around the

base of each gantry held the communications and sensor antenna array.

"Out here," Ciari replied, "they don't have to be pretty. They just have to work."

"Looks like *Rockhound* fails in both categories. It is the ugliest thing I have ever seen." Nicole thumbed a line open to the flight deck. "Major?" she asked. *What do you think? Gimme a clue, skipper, what's my best move?* She wiped an ungloved hand across chin and cheeks slick with sweat before closing it into a half-fist and resting her chin against it as comfortably as her facemask allowed—facing command decisions in training was one thing; this was something else again. Her heart was picking up speed.

"You're in charge, Nicole," was the reply. Nicole sighed; it was the response she'd expected but she had hoped for better. Cat was giving her free rein until she fucked up.

"Paolo?"

"If we don't try, we'll never know what happened. By the time any other ship reaches her, there won't be anything left. On the other hand, my ass isn't on the line."

"What's the computer say?"

"It abstains. If you manage to touch hulls with *Rockhound* the Rover's magnaseals should hold; if they don't, you'll shoot off like a bullet. Botch the approach, and the Jeep ends up splattered against the hull or cut to pieces by those gantries. Any way you play this, the risk is substantial. And beyond the computer's safety parameters."

"Ter*ri*fic."

"It's a smart machine. Perhaps it's trying to tell us something?"

"I'm going to button up and boogey, Paolo, before I lose what's left of my nerve. I'll make my decision after we've had a close-range eyeball of the situation."

"I copy, Nicole. Cue me as soon as you and Ciari are ready, I'll void the Bay and crack Number One hatch. Be careful out there."

"Never anything but, hotshot," she said, hoping that was true.

Five minutes later, the Jeep was on its way. Nicole turned it onto a parallel course with the mining ship and closed to three thousand meters.

"There's really only one way in," she said at last, her comments as much for Paolo and the record as Ciari. "We match track and velocity, sideslip as close as we dare, and then get out and walk."

"Which way in?"

She pointed at *Rockhound*'s command module as it corkscrewed past. "We position ourselves ahead of the derelict, shoot a pair of tether lines to its nose, then rappel along the hull to the nearest hatch. If we place our grapples right, we won't have much spin to worry about, just the main rotation. And if we keep the lines fairly short, we shouldn't get thrown among the gantry arms."

"You'll have to be real close, Nicole," Paul said. "That won't leave much margin for error."

"More than we'd have trying to dock in this bucket."

"That's no error."

"What do your instincts say?" Ciari asked her.

"I need the exercise. You don't approve?"

He switched their comlink over to a private channel and said, "In Cat, I'd consider that *macha* bravado. With you, it's worth a shot."

"You're awfully hard on her, Ciari."

"No less so than you, Shea, in your own way. How come you're sticking up for her?"

"You said some lousy—hurtful—things. If they were deserved, she wouldn't be here."

He laughed ruefully, without humor. "She and Morgan were lovers, you know, a very hot item. He pulled strings to have her assigned to his command. For that stunt alone, Canfield would have had both balls and heart. But when he got his papers and Cat didn't—moreover, when she refused to quit herself and follow him—he moved out. He never forgave her for surviving and choosing her own life over his. In a sense, she hasn't forgiven herself. Everything she's done since has been a sort of penance, an attempt to prove herself. But regardless of how splendidly—even perfectly—she performs, in her own eyes she's always found wanting. Being driven by that kind of demon, Shea, is never healthy."

He reached for the comset, but her voice stopped him.

"Ben," she said, and he looked up, surprised at the use of his first name. Since the duel where he'd twisted her wrist, she'd taken to referring to him pretty much exclusively by his title, creating a deliberate distance between them.

"That mission, was it Cat's First Flight?"

He said nothing, simply nodded.

"Maybe you can judge her, Marshal, I haven't the right." She re-opened the channel to *Wanderer*. "Rover-One to Homeplate, we're ready to initiate final approach."

"We've been wondering about that, Rover," Paul replied casually. "No change in your target, I'm afraid." *I'm afraid, too, pal,* Nicole thought suddenly, absurdly. *Boy, do I wish you were here and I, there.* "Bear says your medstats are nominal, though your pulse and respiration are higher than the Marshal's."

"Unrequited passion." That provoked an amused snort both from Ciari and from someone on-line aboard *Wanderer*, she couldn't tell who.

"Confirm EVA option, Nicole?" Paul asked.

"Affirmative," she replied. "We'll close to a klick-six and use the Manned Maneuvering Units to hump the rest of the way. The Rover's systems will be slave-linked to your board so you can pull it out of trouble if any comes."

"Copy."

"Then we're gone, Paolo." While they'd been talking, Nicole had donned her gloves, flexing and stretching fingers, arms and back to push away any last-minute kinks; now, she took a deep breath, and locked her helmet securely into place. It smelled new, hardly used, and, as always, she was struck by how loudly her own breath sounded in her ears.

"Check your harness, Marshal, make sure it's snug." She did the same and, after his acknowledgment, fired the lateral thrusters.

They'd barely begun moving before Cat's voice suddenly roared in their headphones: "Breakaway, Rover—*breakaway!* Initiate negative pitch, full thrust, *now!*"

"Major, what's wrong?!" Nicole called, even as she obeyed.

"Screen," Ciari said, and tightened the focus on the Rover's camera until *Rockhound*'s midsection filled the picture. Torque had twisted one of the gantries backward and to one side, putting exceptional pressure on the joints anchoring it to the main hull; as they watched, those joints seemed to explode, the gantry buckling even more while a twenty-meter section of the antenna array tumbled away from the derelict.

"It's coming fast," he said, "we going to clear?"

"Close, it'll be close. . . ." A huge shadow passed across the canopy, blacking out the stars, and Nicole flinched, she couldn't help herself. But even as she breathed a sigh of relief, she heard the faint din of alarms aboard *Wanderer* echoing through her headset.

"Paolo?!" she called.

"The antennae, Nicole," he said, with the enforced, over-exaggerated calm that she knew meant he was truly scared, "they're heading straight for us."

She played with the thrusters, pivoting the Rover. "Can you shift position?"

"Not like that, boss. Not enough to matter. No time."

"Shit," Nicole cursed and then, in a louder voice, "Ciari, watch our back. Let me know if any more crap cuts loose!" Paul had left the communications circuit open; Nicole could hear every word said on the flight deck. Cat had taken command and was snapping rapid-fire orders.

"Everyone into gloves and helmets—pressurize your suits —we could be hit. DaCuhna, slice internal spacecraft pressure, to minimize the effect of an explosive decompression if we're breached. Seal all internal bulkheads. From now on, maintain contact via suitpack radios."

"Major, what're you doing?!" Paul cried. "Jesus Christ, Nicole, she's launched two nukes!"

Nicole saw a flash beneath the Command Module as the rockets ignited. "At this range, the blast'll fry us all!"

"That's not, I think," Ciari said from his tandem seat behind her, appreciation in his voice, "what she intends."

"Trust me," Cat echoed, speaking to Paul and Nicole both, "I know what I'm doing."

"Positive track on the missiles," Ciari reported. "Thirty seconds to contact with target."

"I didn't arm the warheads," Cat said. "It's a trick I learned from some Belt miners—using small, unarmed rockets as emergency tugs. The missiles are wire-guided, under my manual control. That, and their laser guidance system, will enable me to bring them and that mess together, as gently as possible.

Then we punch up full thrust on the motors. Which should shunt it aside."

Big bloody 'if,' Nicole thought as Paul yelled, "Impact," and the rockets erupted with eye-searing brilliance, the fire flare of their exhaust lighting one full side of the twisted mass. For a few seconds, nothing appeared to happen.

"It's moving," Paul announced. "Definite deviation from collision trajectory. And the angle's steadily increasing."

"Too late, hotshot," Nicole murmured, heartsick, "the margin's too small." She ran her hands over the console and saw her suspicions confirmed by the computer. If things didn't improve—instantly—the wreckage would tear the roof off the Command Module. Paul, with his gift for visualizing spacial relationships, must realize that too, yet his voice held no sign that he did.

Ciari tapped her shoulder and re-oriented the main camera towards *Wanderer*. It was the last thing she wanted, a close-up of the disaster as it happened, but then she spotted a faint glow along the lateral midline of the CM, between the Rover Bays and the first Carousel.

"The Auxiliary motors," she breathed, but Ciari heard her.

"Triggered, full thrust, the moment Cat fired the missiles. Wreckage shifts up, *Wanderer* pivots down. Just enough for the two to miss."

And it was.

"Still game, Shea?" Cat asked, the crisis safely past.

"We're already at our jump-off point, Major. How's our time?"

Paul answered: "Two-five-zero minutes, tops, including rendezvous and dock with *Wanderer*."

"You still intend an EVA approach?" Cat asked.

"Only way."

"I concur. But be prepared to abort at any stage."

"Yah."

"Your primary objective is to pull *Rockhound*'s flight recorder and telemetry packs," Cat reminded her, unnecessarily, "while Marshal Ciari checks for survivors or bodies."

They were moving along the same flight path as the derelict, matching its velocity so as to stay just a little ahead of it. All they had to do was make their way across roughly a mile of open space, and then board a ship that was spinning and rolling like a drunken dervish, tossing off bits of itself along the way with arbitrary, madcap abandon. No problem.

Ciari was riding back seat in the Jeep, so he went out first. Nicole switched the controls over to *Wanderer,* took a last look around, as if to reassure herself that everything was fine, even though deep down in her heart of hearts she knew she'd forgotten something, the same way she did every time she left her apartment, and gently pushed her way outside to join him. Her first impression was one of absolute emptiness; before her yawned, gaped, stretched infinite darkness, a more absolute black than she had ever conceived of. Only afterward did she become aware of stars, scattered gloriously around her. There was a moment of vertigo, when her whole world threatened to spin into oblivion, because there was no world beneath her feet. She was floating, yet her brain, evolved and born and raised at the bottom of the Terrestrial gravity well, with that welcome force to give order and shape and, more important, direction to her environment, kept insisting that was impossible. Floating was a prelude to falling and from where Nicole stood, she could fall in any direction, literally forever.

Then, she felt something—Ciari's hand—close on her arm, nudge her gently until they were face to face. Their visors were gold anodized, and for once she was glad her face was hidden from him; she figured she looked ghastly.

He touched his helmet to hers—a private exchange, just between them, not for *Wanderer*'s ears—and asked if she was all right?

She nodded, then realized he couldn't see. "Sorry," she said, "lost my bearings."

"Happens."

"Never did before."

"Earth orbit. Lunar orbit. Planetary referents can, subconsciously, be very comforting. Sort of a roof over your atavistic head. No such luck out here."

"Live and learn."

"That's the idea. The key to survival."

She pulled herself out of the shadow of the Rover and caught her breath at the sight of *Rockhound,* chasing after them but never gaining. Far off to her right, she saw *Wanderer*'s blinding navigation strobes.

"Time, Nicole," Ciari said softly.

"I'm ready," she replied, and he pulled himself away. She called *Wanderer*. "We're ready, Homeplate."

"How's the view, boss?" Paul asked and her heart skipped a beat. *He knows,* she thought.

"Got to be seen to be believed, hotshot," she told him.

"Can't wait."

"Wish there was time to enjoy it."

"Disney probably does it better."

That made her laugh, which was precisely what Paul—bless his roguish soul—intended and her medstats crawled back towards normal.

The Manned Maneuvering Units—small, self-contained rocket pods strapped onto their backpacks—took them the first leg. Nicole could feel her heart thumping harder and faster against her ribs, her breaths coming more quickly as well, and she struggled to keep herself under control. The closer they came to *Rockhound*, the more insane and impossible her plan seemed, the more she wanted simply to turn tail and flee for her life. Aboard *Wanderer*, Paul smiled as his headset picked up a throaty, absent-minded rendition of a Lila Cheney classic.

"What the hell?" Hana Murai wondered aloud.

"Nicole," he told her, on a private channel, "she does that when she's on edge; singing keeps her head in focus. The funny thing is, I doubt she's even aware of it; she'd probably deny it if you told her, even if you played her tapes."

"Her secret's safe with me," the young woman said.

"I hate to admit it," Nicole muttered to Ciari, touching helmets again, as what was left of a massive, fifty-meter scaffold swung by, "but this idea seemed a lot more sensible when we were inside the Rover."

"No argument. No alternative, either. Unless you want to abort."

"Is it feasible?"

"It's worth a try. It's also no stunt for a novice. I'll go alone, if you want."

Deep down inside, Nicole "wanted" very much, but she kept that particular fear locked up tight as she replied: "We go together." She was looking at the derelict, and missed Ciari's nod of approval.

"Me first," Ciari said. It wasn't a question, and Nicole didn't argue.

As the Command Module "fell" towards them, Ciari took aim with his grappling gun and sent a rocket powered flechette dart racing straight into the nose. The other end of the tether was clipped onto his chest harness and as the line pulled taut, he was suddenly yanked forward and down, pinwheeling in towards the main body of the derelict at what seemed to Nicole to be a terrifying speed. He was moving too fast, there was no way his maneuvering backpack could slow him; even armored as he was, his impact with the hull was sure to smash him to a pulp. She cursed her arrogance at coming up with such a dangerous lunatic scheme, unaware that she was speaking aloud, that every word was broadcast back to the *Wanderer*.

She called to Ciari, but got only harsh static in reply.

"Rover-One, Homeplate," she heard Paul's voice, calm and casual as could be, "we confirm viable medstats on both EVA personnel."

Bless you, Paolo, she thought, *for finding the niftiest, sneakiest way of telling me all is well.*

"*Wanderer,* I have no radio contact with Ciari."

"We copy, Nicole," Paolo said, "we have the same problem. His telemetry is breaking up as well, there's considerable interference."

Damn. "Anyone think it's deliberate?" She used an ALL HANDS circuit but the question was mainly directed at Cat. "Set-up maybe for a trap?"

"I doubt it," Cat replied after a moment. "According to our Lloyd's registry, *Rockhound* is specially modified to carry high-energy radioactives. She has unusually heavy shielding around the crew modules. That, added to the ship's wild motion, added to its considerable structural damage, is probably what's lousing sensors and communications. And the Marshal may also have suffered damage during his approach."

"What about my suit, have I power enough to maintain the comlink?"

Paul again: "Doubt it, boss, unless you used a tight-beam transmission aimed right at our antennae."

"Fat bloody chance, hotshot, the way that cow is wallowing."

"Precisely."

Nicole thought fast, and unconsciously started humming, more vintage rock and roll.

"Boss," Paul called, "we got nothing now from the Marshal. He's either in a completely blocked location . . ."

". . . or he's stopped transmitting," she finished. "Okay, my turn. The belly's just swung by, I'm going to catch my ride on this rotation."

And she did.

The harness took the brunt of the shock. Actually, it felt no worse than lifting off aboard the Shuttle from Earth, but she had no time, less chance, to enjoy the ride. The major risk of this approach was that a piece of wreckage might shear off while she was spinning in; she couldn't manuever and the slightest contact, to her or her line, meant disaster. This was the risk; the calculation was that it wouldn't happen during the few seconds she was vulnerable.

She saw the hull rushing up below her and slapped the MMU controls on her left forearm. A flash on her helmet head-up display told her the thrusters had fired, confirmed physically by an annoying vibration down her back. That same display showed her fuel consumption; she watched it with one eye while the other—and most of her mind—concentrated on landing. She decided to err on the side of caution and cut power short of the mark she and Ciari had agreed upon. Then, her feet made contact—too hard on the steeply sloped, surprisingly slick surface. She'd hit too fast, she lost control. The magnaseals on her boots couldn't hold and she went sprawling, inertia stretching her line taut while the ship's spin rolled her across the hull. She flailed desperately for a handhold, terrified that she might tear her suit or damage her backpack, or that her anchor might pull loose and send her flying into the ruined gantries below. Finally, she latched onto a stanchion to lie flat on her face, panting like a marathoner, unwilling to let herself believe that she'd survived.

"Woman," a welcome voice said, the words painfully shot through with static, "you do not deserve such luck."

Ciari stood on the hull, anchored by boots and a safety line clipped outside an access hatch. With careful steps, he made his way to Nicole and locked another line to her harness; then, a final piece of insurance, he hooked the two of them together.

"You computed the safety margins," he continued, speaking while working. "Don't you trust your own numbers?"

"I figured a little extra couldn't hurt."

"Now you know differently. What's your suit status?"

"Whole. Fully . . . functional. I'm in worse shape."

"You deserve to be. Can you stand?"

He gave her a hand up and, as soon as her boot seals made solid contact with the hull, led her to the hatch, where he unclipped the tether from her chest harness and fastened it to his own. The double spin gave *Rockhound* a semblance of gravity, piling every loose object in a corner formed by the junction of what appeared to be walls and floor; they found themselves walking on the one and forced to climb the other, usually on hands and knees, using portable magnaseals slipped over the palms of their gloves. More often than not, they had to haul debris clear of interior hatchways, to clear space enough for their bulky backpacks to pass. Nicole was soon drenched in sweat, fire twisting along shoulders, back and legs as she endured the full weight of her suit and more.

"This is taking too long," she gasped, eyes widening a little as Ciari's voice came back as hoarse with fatigue as her own.

"Can't be helped. Come this far . . . hate to pull out empty."

"Where . . . are we?"

"Mid level . . . Command Module—flight deck's through that hatch."

"Ciari—you see . . . something wedged in the opening?"

Now the power armor proved its worth, as he braced himself in place and shoved the hatch all the way open. Immediately, the object popped loose, bouncing off the ceiling and ricochetting down towards Nicole, who was standing on the bulkhead at the "bottom" end of the passage. She caught it easily.

"It's a helmet," she said.

"Any name or number?"

"'Wolfe.' That's it. What about the rest of this bucket? Do we search . . . ?"

"For survivors?" he finished, and he handsigned the negative vehemently. "Can't separate—too dangerous—take way too long—have to trust . . . *Wanderer* external scan."

Without warning, a frightful sound exploded from Nicole's

headset and she screamed, hands flying to her helmet. Ciari dropped towards her and held them tight until the panic spasm ran its course.

"Thanks," she sobbed, trying to regain her equilibrium. "I . . . lost my head. The noise. Couldn't think. Just wanted to make it go away. If you hadn't stopped me, I was ready, I really believe I'd have torn my helmet off."

"I know."

"What the hell *was* that?" Even as she spoke, she stiffened, eyes closing to slits with pain. It wasn't as bad, this time, and she could make out words.

"Wanderer to Rover-One, do you copy? Boss, this is Paolo . . ."

"I hear you," she cried, *"I hear you!"*

The quality of reception was wretched. Paul's voice was intermixed with a dreadful amount of static and he kept wavering in and out, loud one moment, whisper faint the next, according to the motion of the derelict. But at least contact had been restored.

"Christ," Nicole told him, when all was sorted out, "you boomed in here like the Wrath of God."

"Sorry about that," he replied. "We were worried."

"What—?!"

"You mean this? Simple, really. Hana's idea." *I'll kill her,* Nicole thought. "Extrapolating off of something you said. She took the main antenna off EarthLine and centered it on *Rockhound*'s Command Module." Nicole was astonished. *"Wanderer* generates enough power to punch a signal through that dish all the way, unaided, from Pluto to Houston. With it locked on *Rockhound,* and from this range, she figured all the shielding in the System wouldn't be able to block us out."

"Clever girl. Someday, I'll return the favor."

"Nicole," Ciari touched her arm, and she started; she hadn't realized he'd left her. His approach to *Rockhound* had been more eventful than hers; he'd caromed off a spar, losing a brace of antennae in the process, which is why he'd been spared her agony. She patched him through to *Wanderer.* "I found a crewman," he told them with a crisp, efficient lack of emotion, a part of his job he'd done often before. "Dead. Male, dark-skinned, caucasian features, age indeterminate.

Suit tags and registry tapes ident him as Phillip Wolfe. I also have the primary datapack."

Nicole held up the helmet and Ciari handsigned. "Yes."

"Phil?" Cat asked.

"You knew him, Major?" Nicole asked.

"Him and his entire Clan. *Rockhound* is theirs. I planned to visit Wolfe Station on our Inbound leg. Ben, how did he die?"

"Quickly. Explosive decompression."

"Is that it?" Nicole asked.

Before Ciari could answer, Hana came on-line. *"Fracture!"* she yelled, and the Command Module tipped over with a great, shuddering vibration as something huge gave way aft. Nicole's eyes went wide as the stout bulkheads twisted like paper and part of the corridor compressed, as if some giant had taken his toy and crumpled it in opposite directions.

"Status," she demanded, voice taut with strain.

"Half my telltales went off the board," Paul told her. *"Rockhound's* hull has buckled—number two gantry has given way—"

"Any danger to *Wanderer?!"*

"Negative. It blew the other way. But the core hull has a definite bow to it. Motion's going all to hell. We're unable to predict the effect this new torque stress will have on the frame. If you've got the datapacks . . ."

"Forget them," Cat broke in. "This is a direct order, both of you—abort the mission. Pull out, as fast as you can, any way you can."

"Where?" Nicole asked Ciari.

Retracing their steps was easier, they were descending the gravity well, but the spin/roll was no longer consistent and the condition of the ship itself was deteriorating markedly. A hatchway bent sideways as Nicole struggled through, pinning her so tightly she couldn't catch a breath. Ominous flashes appeared on her head-up display, indicating damage to her backpack. But Ciari was there, with his enhanced muscles, to lever her free. The pain faded quickly, but not the alarms on her faceplate.

"I may have a problem," she said simply.

"Housing's cracked," he reported, after a quick check. "Can't tell if anything's busted inside. No vapor, though; you're not losing atmosphere."

"Things are stable so far, but I don't think I can take another shock like that. Or push too hard."

"Almost there."

By the time they reached the outer hull, *Rockhound* had bent almost double, into an L-shape that made the engineering assembly a looming, towering cliff above their heads, the remaining gantries flaring off to each side like skeletal wings.

"We can't jump off from here, the way we planned," Ciari said. "We'll just splatter against that."

"Look," Nicole told him, pointing at the gantries. "The one on our right is pretty much clear. Can we fire a grapple right out to the end, the cargo housing, with us on a tether, and let it pivot us away?"

"It's possible."

"If we stay together, use our MMUs in sync, we should be able to brake once we're clear. Then, *Wanderer* can vector the Rover to pick us up and we can ride it home. Paolo," she called, "you copy?" Silence. "Paolo?" She spoke louder, as if that made any difference with her gain pushed wide open.

"Are we deaf, Ciari? Or is it worse?"

"Doesn't matter. We have no option. All we can do is flash the Mayday beacons and hope."

"How do we play this?"

"We stand facing each other. You shoot, I'll hold us together."

"How romantic. Just don't squeeze too hard, okay; my ribs are sore enough."

They fastened their chest harnesses and Ciari took Nicole in his arms. The tether line itself was their weak link; it had to be clipped onto a quick-release latch, so they could cut completely loose from the derclict once they were clear. Otherwise, they'd simply be dragged along behind it until the rope fouled some other piece of wreckage and spun them back into the main hull. Of course, by then, chances were they'd be long dead of suffocation. That might be their fate, regardless, if *Wanderer* missed their transmission, if the crew wasn't on the ball. A pop of color caught Nicole's eye—one of her internal status telltales shifting from orange to red, backpack malfunction. Nothing critical but a harbinger of worse to come.

She couldn't fit both arms around Ciari's helmet and had to

aim the bulky pistol one-handed. Naturally, that hand shook. To her, it seemed to jump all over the place. They only had this one shot; it had to be perfect. But, she remembered, that was true for everything in space. Perfection was the rule, death the reward for cheating. *Hold your breath*—in her mind's eye, she returned to the Colorado mountains, her goonie summer at the Academy, when civilians were processed quickly, efficiently, ruthlessly into fledgling officers; she lay on her belly, squinting at a target, listening to her instructor, squeezing off round after careful round. *Let it out slow.* She'd surprised herself with a respectable score. Paul Da-Cuhna went to the Olympics on the rifle team. She didn't mind. In the air, dogfighting, she invariably blew him to kingdom come. *Squeeze the trigger.*

She felt a slight pressure up her arm as the dart's solid-fuel package ignited and the minature rocket sped away; seconds later, a flash from the top of the gantry told her she'd scored a bull's-eye. An hour ago, she would have cheered. Instead she told Ciari to let go.

He de-powered his boot magnaseals and pushed away from the CM hull. Next, he fired his thrusters, which pulled the line taut and sent them shooting outward from *Rockhound* in a great, sweeping curve. They had passed the apex and were beginning to swing back in towards the derelict before he gave Nicole the signal to release the tether. It separated without a glitch, leaving *Rockhound* going one way, while they tumbled the other. Nicole brought her right arm down and he pressed the EMERGENCY switch on her signals panel; then, she did the same on the opposite side for him. Only when they were both broadcasting at full power did they apply the thrust needed to stabilize their flight; and only after that did they get around to unloosing their harnesses.

Nicole thought of asking where they were, then decided there was no point. Another telltale had shifted red—a steady and degrading pattern—which meant that her brilliant escape, at least insofar as she was concerned, looked to be an utterly wasted effort. She thought she would mind more than she did. All she felt, though, was sleepy. Adrenaline crash? More likely, lack of oxygen or carbon monoxide poisoning as her LifeSystems collapsed. She was even starting to see things—like stars suddenly rear up all big and bright and funny-colored right in front of her, when they should be a cool and unreachable part of the celestial background.

"You planning on staying out there?" Ciari asked from the step of the Rover hatch. A hand reached out to her. "Or would you rather follow me inside, where there's air to breathe?"

"I'll follow you anywhere, chum." But she missed with her first try and spun herself into a lazy circle, muttering: "Worse than grabbing the fucking brass ring on the fucking carousel," as she tried again. This time, he left nothing to chance but caught her harness and pulled her through the hatch. He used the EMERGENCY FLOOD as soon as the Rover was secure, the quickest way of establishing an atmosphere, and the moment he had adequate pressure, snapped the locking levers on Nicole's helmet and and yanked it off her head. They'd both been floating in near absolute zero space and even though the Rover's internal heaters were full on, the air was bitterly cold, worse than the arctic in mid-winter. But it could be breathed and Nicole thought it wonderful. She hadn't realized how bad off she'd been; five minutes more, max, would have been too late.

It was the better part of a day before Cat gathered the crew in the C-1 wardroom for a conference. Nicole was half stretched out on one of the bulkhead benches, head back, eyes closed, a steaming cup of chicken soup cradled on her breast. Even with the shots Chagay had given her, she still ached from top to toe and she doubted she'd ever again be warm. There was a hollowness deep in her chest as well, made worse by ever-more-frequent fits of coughing, which reminded her of how she'd felt after smoking, on a dare, a twenty-dollar Havana cigar.

Noise from above prompted her to crease open one eye. When Nicole saw Paul and Hana clambering down the accessway from the DropShaft, she let the eye close. They'd been closeted with the *Rockhound* data packs ever since she and Ciari had returned, trying to decipher them. Judging by their expressions, they hadn't had much success.

Once everyone was present, the Marshal led off the briefing.

"I found Citizen Wolfe wearing a full pressure suit." he began, "except for gloves and helmet. I found one glove among a pile of debris at the base of the passage leading to the flight deck, and Lt. Shea found the helmet, wedged tight in a warped, partially closed interior hatch. Presumably, *Rockhound* suffered a massive explosive decompression and Wolfe was unable to seal his suit before his atmosphere blew away. Under the circumstances, death was probably instantaneous."

"Any reason to doubt it was an accident?" Cat asked, taking longhand notes as a supplement to the automatic audio-video record the ship's computer was making for the log.

"You could achieve the same results by tossing the body out an airlock without a helmet and then placing the corpse in *Rockhound*'s Command Module. Or strapping him in his chair and blowing a hatch. There are, as you know, near-infinite possibilities. Unfortunately, all the things we might check to prove or disprove any such suppositions are either missing or heavily damaged. That in itself might indicate foul play, but thus far it would be no more than a circumstantial judgment. And a pretty thin one," he added.

"Why would anyone go to such trouble?" Chagay asked. "Why would pirates leave a derelict, or even a corpse, when complete destruction would be so much easier, and safer for them? Most illogical."

"No signs of violence on Phil's body?" Cat asked.

Ciari shook his head. "I could only make a superficial examination, Cat. From what I saw, what I recorded for Chagay, no."

She looked across the floor, up the curve, and Chagay replied: "Injuries appeared consistent with the extant situation."

"What about the flight recorders?" she asked Paul.

He snorted. "Junk," putting into that one word all a technologist's innate contempt for shoddy workmanship and second-rate material. "Firstly, they're cheap-shop units that barely make minimum NASA standards for a deep space vessel. In addition, there was substantial damage. Evidently, when *Rockhound* decompressed, some main panels short circuited. Tapes are either burned out or, where they're intact, the magnetic bubble memory fields are so scrambled that data retrieval is impossible."

Nicole shoved herself up, wincing as phantom shards tore up her side, and tapped a command into the library console. She frowned. "You say the equipment was bad, Paolo?"

"The pits."

"Not unusual for a free-lance spacer," Ciari said. "Everything out this far is so expensive, and so scarce, that people buy as cheap as they can, as rarely as they can, and then jury-rig improvements."

"I know that, Marshal, but it doesn't square with this purchase order."

"What order, Nicole?" Cat asked.

"While I was in sickbay, I had Paul query Ceres Base for all the data they had on Mr. Wolfe. According to their file, when *Rockhound* docked at Ceres this last trip, Wolfe put her through a complete electronics refit; he had all his existing equipment removed and replaced."

"Obviously with crap."

"Not so, Paolo. At most, five years old, purchased from Air Force and NASA. Used, but top line all the way."

That brought Paul over to her bench. He peered intently at her screen, then called for his compad. Hana passed it over.

"Curiouser and curiouser," he muttered when he'd finished comparing notes. "The serial numbers aren't even close. There's been a switch."

"NASA seconds are cheap compared to brand-new, mint condition hardware," Nicole said, "but we're still talking bucks."

"A strike," Ciari said softly. "That's the only answer. A Belter upgrades his equipment when he has no choice, or when he's loaded."

"The stuff Wolfe dumped was comparatively old and worn, nowhere near state of the art," Nicole told them, "but still functional. The refit was a matter of choice, not necessity." She pointed to her scanscreen. "According to Ceres, his bank balance was almost nil, so the purchase price had to be taken out of whatever Wolfe received for his cargo."

"Which was?" Ciari asked.

"One megagram cannister—shielded—*damn!* Catch this: 'Contents bonded and secured.' Farallon Associates, licensed shippers. He also stocked up on fresh food."

"That's the clincher." Ciari leaned over Nicole and tapped the screen. "He splurged, the bleeding asshole. Goddammit, after all these years, with a family at stake, you'd think the fool would know better."

"So what are we talking about?" Paul wondered aloud.

"Wolfe hit, what, a Mother Lode and got ambushed for his good fortune? Claim-jumped?"

"Archaic terms, DaCuhna," Cat said, voice tinged with sadness and a suddenly pronounced West Texas twang, an indication of how deeply she was affected, "but appropriate. Hardly funny." Paul's grin faded and he muttered an apology. Nicole punched him softly in the shoulder. "The Belt," Cat went on, "is simply too by-God big, our forces stretched too thin. If we had a thousand times as many ships, plus the crews to fly them, it still wouldn't be enough. The profits to be made out here are too high, the risks to a hijack operation virtually non-existent. These raider outfits — pirates, bandits, buccaneers, wolfpacks, call 'em what you will — keep tabs on the small independent miners, like Phil Wolfe and his Clan, and whenever someone hits it big, they move in, wipe everybody out, and loot the claim. We've tried to stop them. Might as well try to stop the turning of the Earth."

"How far to Wolfe's asteroid?" Nicole asked Paul, who scribbled some quick equations before replying, preferring to figure the answer himself rather than ask the computer. He was showing off. Nicole let him.

"Figure a week," he said, "if we light the torch full. Gonna play merry hell with our mission profile, though. We'll probably have to call for a refueling rendezvous at Cocytus."

"One step at a time, Paolo. Alert goes out first — to them and Ceres both, copy to DaVinci." Nicole had already made up her own mind but this decision was properly Cat's. "Major?" she asked.

Cat thumbed through her own notes, then looked at Ciari, who nodded fractionally, then back at Nicole.

"Do it."

six

THE ROCK WASN'T much to look at—a jagged, lopsided spheroid, roughly four kilometers in diameter. Nicole kept a twenty kilo-klick separation between *Wanderer* and the asteroid as they turned parallel to its orbital track; that way, they'd have time to react to any attack from the rock itself, and room to maneuver. They'd been trying to raise Wolfe Station for the previous two days and, from the moment they'd come within range, they'd begun scanning the asteroid with the cruiser's most powerful and sophisticated external sensors.

Thus far, they'd determined that the station's habitat domes were intact, its powersystems operational, and that this was indeed one of the fabled "Mother Lode" strikes that all Belt miners dream of. But they'd found no sign of life—on a station supposedly inhabited by six men, seven women, four children, two cats and a parakeet.

"Next move?" Nicole asked, slumped in her chair on *Wanderer*'s flight deck. She was wearing the heaviest clothes she had, plus her leather flight jacket, yet she still felt cold, and only over the last day had her cough and sniffles finally begun to subside. The blast of icy air in the Rover may have saved her life, but the price was fifty hours flat on her back with a fever. Even now, well on the way to recovery, shot full of antibiotics, she felt utterly miserable.

"There's no way we're going to learn any more sitting on

our butts up here," Cat replied between bites as she finished her sandwich. Nicole kept her eyes on her own console; even the thought of food was more than she could bear. "We've got to go dirtside and eyeball the scene for ourselves."

"That could be what they want."

"True. But who are 'they?'"

"Who flies this one?"

"You volunteering?" Cat asked with a grin that prompted a smile back from Nicole.

"You'd let me if I did?"

"Not a chance. You're lucky I let you on this deck."

"The Bear pronounced me fit for duty, Cat."

"He has his standards, I have mine. Anyway, I'll run this jump."

"You're Mission Commander."

"Meaning I should stay behind and let others do the dirty work? Not my style, youngster. I'll take DaCuhna as pilot and Dr. Shomron, in case there are any casualties."

Nicole tried one more time: "Couldn't Marshal Ciari . . . ?"

"Of course. It's right up his proverbial alley. Except that, if there has been trouble, the Wolfes will blast a stranger on sight, regardless of his eye-dee. They know me, though; they'll talk before they shoot."

"Fair enough." Nicole flipped an intercom switch. "Paolo, action stations. Prep Rover-Two for launch, combat mode; Major Garcia will be in command, with you flying right seat. Break out battle armor as well, three suits."

"Copy, boss," Paul acknowledged.

Nicole changed channels. "Bear, would you please meet Major Garcia in Shuttle Bay Two in ten minutes—full medi-kit."

"On my way, Lieutenant."

"I'll give a hand," Hana called from the level below, but Nicole cut her off, calling her back to her console.

"If the hotshot needs help," she told her, "he can use Andrei or Cat. I want you on the scanners."

Cat looked at Nicole quizzically as Hana obeyed, muttering darkly in Japanese under her breath.

"Something?" she asked.

Nicole shrugged, and sneezed violently. "An itch, that for all I know could be due to this bloody cold." She sighed, wiping a nose that felt raw and tender and big as Jupiter. "A . . . sense I'd rather be somewhere else."

"I know what you mean. Keep your eyes open. If you spot anything, no matter how trivial . . ."

"You'll be the first to know. Good luck, skipper."

"Be seeing you, Shea."

As Cat started down the DropShaft, Nicole called out: "Y'all come back safe, hear?"

Cat smiled and waved, and was gone. Nicole sat in silence for a minute, gazing at nothing through the canopy, then buzzed Hanako. "Punch up the positions of those remote scanners we dumped during our approach. I want to see our 'eyes.'"

"Flat screen or holo?"

"In the tank. And don't worry, Hana, I'll give you a chance to say good-bye to Paul before he leaves."

Nicole heard a wry sigh. "It means a lot to him."

"What about you?"

"Like I said, I like him. Here's your picture."

Inside the hologram tank was a three-dimensional representation of their local space. *Wanderer* was a bright dot floating in the center of the transparent polycrystal sphere, with Wolfe's asteroid outlined nearby. There were other rocks in the immediate vicinity, each labeled by the computer. They'd noted during their approach that this was an unusually crowded asteroid cluster; indeed, Wolfe had laid claim to the entire group. Tiny dots of color indicated the sensor packages scattered to augment the instruments aboard *Wanderer* herself.

"What's our effective scanning range?" Nicole wondered aloud.

"Depends," replied Hana. "You could say that our optical and radio research telescopes have an almost infinite range, especially with computer enhancement of their images."

"Yes, but then I'm not a smart ass."

A smile slipped into Hana's voice as she continued without pause: "In a more practical sense, figure a sphere roughly a half-million kilometers in radius around *Wanderer*."

"Seems like a lot of room."

"It isn't," Ben Ciari said, as he slid into the right-hand command chair, next to Nicole's. "A laser or particle beam can cross that distance in seconds."

"Except that no one's built combat lasers or particle beams with that kind of power," Hana countered.

"First time for everything. Also, a high-acceleration nuclear missile, pulling, say, a hundred-plus Gs, will be here almost as quickly."

"Terrific. So it isn't such a great cushion," Nicole conceded with a shrug, "but it's the best we've got." She opened a line and picture to the shuttle bay. "Paolo, status?"

"Nearly finished, Nicole. The Major and the Bear are already aboard, I'll be following shortly. So far, the gunship's preflight is nominal."

"Nicole," came a whisper over her headset.

"Andrei," she called, and when he acknowledged, "watch Hana's board, please. I want to hear about any bogies." Then, to Hana, "On your way back, swing by the galley and work up an order of munchies and drinks."

"I thought you'd sworn off food."

"Please, don't remind me. But we're likely to be on watch for quite a while and I'd rather we eat while things are still quiet rather than on the run."

"No problem. Punch your orders into the computer so they'll be ready and waiting when I arrive. I shouldn't be long. Thanks, Nicole."

"The team supreme sticks together. For my co-pilot, I do anything."

"I'll remember that," Ciari said from Paul's place.

"Don't push your luck, chum," she growled back, and partly meant it.

Nicole tapped her panel and a couple of scanscreens flickered to life—one showing a panoramic view of Bay Two; the other, telemetry relevant to the Rover. Nicole zoomed the camera in on the wedge-shaped gunship; through its clear canopy, she could see Cat and Dr. Shomron in the cockpit, stowing their equipment and finishing a pre-flight checklist. Cat looked up, saw the camera and waved. Nicole backed the image and swung the lens to find Paul. He was just beyond the interior airlock, with Hana trying her best to embrace him—not the easiest thing to do with him wearing full armor. Finally, since the Bay was zero-gravity, she pushed herself off the deck and wrapped herself around him. Nicole flushed slightly, uncomfortable at having caught her friends at such an intimate moment. Yet, she'd been perfectly aware of the possibility when she activated the camera, had she wanted to play voyeur? She refocused on the gunship. Seconds later, Paul came into view, tossing a jaunty wave towards the airlock before clambering aboard.

"Mr. DaCuhna and Dr. Murai seem quite . . . involved with each other," Ciari said blandly. He might as well have been describing the weather.

"So it would appear." Nicole matched his tone. "I want everyone in suits," she said, deliberately changing the subject. "Marshal, you first. Andrei, you go as soon as Hana returns. Then me." She buzzed Hana on remote and told her to don her own pressure suit before leaving the Bay.

"Something on your mind, Lieutenant?" Ciari asked.

"Quite a bit."

"Don't be coy, it doesn't suit you."

"This isn't the time, or the place . . ." She stopped, thinking, *Maybe it is?* And, *Do I really need this shit?* And, *Why in hell can't anything ever be simple?!*

"Are we 'involved,' Ben?" she finally asked.

"I think we could be. Is that what you wanted to hear?"

"To be honest, I'm not sure what I want. You don't sound terribly enthusiastic, or committal."

"I know the risks, and the realities."

"Suppose I'm willing to take a chance?"

"The daring of ignorance."

"You're laughing at me, you fuck!"

"Nicole, I'm a Federal Marshal, near the top of the seniority list; you're Air Force, on your novice run. As far as our careers are concerned, we couldn't be farther apart if we tried. Once this mission's complete, you'll probably be given another year or two of local / long-haul duty, around the Earth or perhaps additional *Wanderer* flights, before you get any Belt or OutSystem assignments. You'll have no discretion over where you're sent, not for years. I can name my station. But I hate the Earth, and I can barely stand Luna. I'm a loner. I do my work in singleships. You want a relationship? Fine. I guarantee it for the length of this trip. Not because I don't care for you, and not because I can't hack permanence, but because the practical obstacles are so bloody huge I don't think our feelings for each other, whatever the hell they are, would survive very long."

There was a long silence, broken by Nicole.

"Makes sense," she said simply.

"I'm sorry. I didn't mean to come on quite so strongly."

"I'll survive." She hit the intercom board, deliberately ending the conversation. "Hanako, what's keeping dinner?"

"Your waitress had to go to the bathroom," came the reply over the CM speakers, "while she changed, d'you mind?"

"Merely curious. And hungry."

"That's a switch. Be patient, Nicole. Suffering, they say, is good for the soul."

"My lucky day, then. Paolo, status?" she requested.

"Ready to roll, boss."

She held the Rover on its cradle until Ciari and Andrei returned to their stations in pressure suits and then watched silently as the gunship rose slowly past the bow view ports. When it was clear of the Command Module, it turned towards Wolfe's Asteroid, lights flashing on Nicole's panel, confirming ignition, as its main engine fired.

"What's their ETA?" Nicole asked, squinting slightly as she tried to find the Rover's identification strobes against the starscape, muttering in annoyance when she failed. Ciari handed her a pair of electronic binoculars, but she shook her head, waving them away.

"Sixty-three minutes," Hana told her. "Cat and Paolo are taking their time." She floated up to Nicole's level, foodbox in her arms. "This is for you two; Andrei and I already took ours."

"Thanks. Soon as you're done, I want you to plot the tightest vector possible past that rock."

"In case we have to run?" Nicole nodded. "No problem."

"Andrei," Nicole called, and when he answered, calling up from the deck below rather than using the intercom, she told him, "prime the mains. I want us ready to establish full thrust at the flick of a switch."

Then, as she sipped some welcome chicken soup, Ciari unzipped a thigh pocket and pulled out a large, gleaming key. Nicole's face paled the moment she saw it—though, in truth, she was far from surprised. Without a word, she resealed her soup, replaced it in the box, and reached under her sweatshirt for an identical key, on a lanyard around her neck.

"Weapons system checklist, Nicole," Ciari told her. Without being asked, Hana moved the foodbox out of the way as Nicole activated the appropriate sequence on the computer and opened the hard-copy manual as well.

"All warsystems to primary operational mode," she began, marking each item in her book, while Ciari did the same on his scanscreen. He repeated her words, her actions, the pair of them pulling switches and pressing buttons. "On my mark," Nicole said finally, "insert command keys and execute a 180-degree clockwise turn: five . . . four . . . three . . . two . . . one— *mark!*"

For a moment, neither of them said anything. Nicole looked at Ciari, at the console, at Ciari once more. Somehow, turning those keys made everything different. In all her years of training and drills, it was the one thing she'd never done, in a real spacecraft, in a real, potentially shooting, situation. Now, *Wanderer*'s nuclear missiles were armed. All she had to do was lock on to a target, press a button and people would die. With nukes, there were no warning shots. *Pressing* that button bespoke a willingness to kill.

"Moment of truth?" she wondered, her voice barely a whisper.

"Let's hope not," Ciari reassured her. Then, to change the mood, he gave an exaggerated groan and stretched his arms as high overhead as his suit would let him.

"Now, Shea," he announced, "we wait."

"Hold the fort," she told him, snapping herself free of her harness and twisting up and out of the chair, "while I change."

Before leaving the flight deck, she typed up a display of the Rover's status; thus far, Paul was flying a nominal approach. There wasn't a hint of trouble. *Too good,* she thought, *to be true.* And then mentally kicked herself for being melodramatic. She made a quick stop by Andrei and Hana's consoles, nodding in approval at the escape course Hana had set up. Both women hoped it would never be needed. The engines were ready as well.

She'd just reached the Changing Room when the alarm sounded. She was back in her chair in seconds.

The blip was right at the edge of the holo tank, its brightness indicating a large, powerful contact, and it was closing on them fast.

"Sensors have anything?" Nicole asked Hana, who frowned and shook her head.

"Still too distant for a decent reading. But if it maintains its current heading, it'll pass two of our remotes; we can query them for data."

Now it was Nicole's turn to shake her head. "Leave 'em be. Even if we use a tight-beam, pulsed transmission, there's too great a risk of that ship spotting them. The remotes are our ace in the hole; I don't want to throw them away."

"Good, Nicole." Ciari nodded approvingly. "That bogie is very large—twice our size, at least—and its straight-in approach is creating a corridor behind it that our on-board sensors can't scan. Anything could be hidden in that blind spot and, without the remotes, we wouldn't know it till it was too late."

"Nicole," Hana said, "your panel. That ship's transmitting."

Nicole plugged in her headset, switching the incoming call onto the flight deck speakers as well, so everyone could hear.

". . . to unknown spacecraft, please acknowledge our transmission. I repeat, this is the *USS von Braun,* on Belt patrol, calling unknown spacecraft near Wolfe's asteroid. If you do not acknowledge, we must assume you to be hostile, and you will be fired upon. . . ."

"Feisty bastard," Hana growled. "Contact still closing; no deviation from previous course."

"Answer him, Marshal. Tell him who we are and flash our recognition code. I'm calling the Major.

"Deuce," she said, while Ciari responded to the challenge, "Deuce, this is Homeplate—trouble call—acknowledge, please."

Cat didn't reply, forcing Nicole to repeat her broadcast twice; when she finally did answer, her voice was broken by heavy static.

"What's up?" she asked. Nicole stroked the radio controls, wishing she had Paul's instinctive, delicate touch, and managed to smooth out a fair chunk of the interference.

"Contact—verbal eye-dee, *USS von Braun.* Intercept." Ciari caught her attention. "Hang on."

"Recognition signals transmitted and answered," he told her. "Everything checks out."

Nicole repeated that report to Cat. "Sounds right," she was told. "This is *von Braun*'s sector. Tell Scotty howdy for me, and remind him of our last poker game at Copernicus."

Nicole relayed the message and heard a man laugh at the other end.

"Tell Cat that was a nice try, *Wanderer*, but as I recall, we were at Oberon's on Pico Station last time we played for money. Which reminds me. Babe, you still owe me a couple of *C*s."

"Two hundred sixty-three, to be exact," Cat said. From her tone of voice, Nicole thought it must have been a marvellous game. "Certainly sounds like Scotty. Except for this by-god static, I'd rate everything green board. I'm continuing my approach to Wolfe Station, Nicole. You might ask Scotty if he'll provide back-up; he can front a landing party more easily than *Wanderer* if I hit trouble dirtside. Otherwise, keep me posted."

"We'll be in touch, Major."

Ciari was speaking, but she wasn't paying attention and missed most of it. "Do we stand down the warsystems?" he repeated. Nicole shook her head. "What about passing along Cat's request for back-up?" Another shake. "Reason?" A shrug. "Shea, you're turning paranoid."

"And you're not?"

"I was born paranoid. That's why I'm such a good cop, and still alive."

"Which is why I'm learning to follow your example. Expect nothing, trust no one, correct?"

"Range to *von Braun*, three hundred thousand kilometers and closing," Hana reported as Cat began her final descent to the asteroid, "course unchanged. If he doesn't initiate retrofire, or modify his track, things could get a bit dicey. On the other hand, if he maintains present velocity, *Wanderer*'s main sensors should be able to get a pretty detailed scan of him fairly soon."

"Anything behind him?" she asked, while thinking, a little absurdly, *Jesus, Dr. Elias and his proficiency board are just going to love this; a potentially hostile situation and here I am, wearing sneaks and sweats.*

"Nothing I can see. The remotes are programmed to scream if they spot anything out of the ordinary..."

Right on cue, another alarm *branged* and the image on the main screen dissolved, to be replaced by a computer-generated schematic of local space from the point of view of their outermost remote scanner. Just moving into view, following precisely along the trajectory established by *von Braun,* was another vessel. At first, it appeared as no more than an unusually bright blip, but as the remote acquired more data and transmitted it to *Wanderer,* the screen dissolved once again and the computer painted a silhouette diagram of the new contact.

All this occurred in five seconds; then, in the holo tank—its image still centered on *Wanderer,* showing the complete layout of the remotes—a brilliant flash suddenly enveloped the unit that had tagged the second ship. When the glow faded, all trace of the remote was gone. More lights burst in the tank and, again in a matter of seconds, every scanner had been destroyed.

While this was occurring, *Wanderer*'s crew was reacting. Ciari started things off, as soon as the silhouette appeared, with a cry of recognition: "A refinery!"

"Andrei," Nicole snapped, "hit that switch—main engines, emergency ignition—*now!* Full thrust, maximum acceleration, along Hana's vector!"

"Laser tracks," Ciari reported, voice calm, unnervingly unconcerned. Everyone looked at the holo tank. Arrowing towards them from the other spacecraft were two streaks of color, moving almost faster than the eye could follow.

"Shields?"

"Already up."

A second later, another screen, revealing the view aft from the Command Module along *Wanderer*'s upper spine, showed a magnificent auroral display as the twin bolts were deflected. But the protection, Nicole knew, was as temporary as it was illusory. The lasers were a probe; the real attack would come afterwards, with conventional missiles or nukes. The shields would be useless against those.

"Deuce, Deuce," she called, "abort your landing. We got big trouble!"

She thought she heard Cat reply, but a sudden sleetstorm of

static made her tear off the headset, breath hissing through teeth clenched tight against the pain. Try as she might, she couldn't clear a two-way channel through to the gunship. Rover-Two might be able to hear her transmissions, but she couldn't receive them. And because it was below *Wanderer*'s line of flight, she couldn't use the main antennae, the way Paolo did to contact her aboard *Rockhound*. Fortunately, that worked in their favor as well, since *Wanderer*'s bulk also blocked the tight-beam transmissions from being intercepted by their attacker.

Instead, she bumped the gain to the red line and prayed that would do the trick. "We've been ambushed, Major," she said. "Our contact isn't *von Braun*, unless it's been hijacked or gone rogue. They've too big an edge in size and firepower for us to risk a standing fight, so we're going to pick you up and rabbit the hell out of here, using Wolfe's rock for cover."

Even as she spoke, she knew whoever was commanding their attacker had to be thinking along the same lines. *Wanderer* simply had no other viable option. She wondered how he planned to stop them. The Command Module was beginning to vibrate as the giant primary engines slowly—*too slowly,* thought Nicole, *not that we can do anything about it*—built up thrust.

She reached out to seal the internal bulkheads and trim life support everywhere but on the flight deck, only to discover it had already been done. When she spoke, her voice was tight, too controlled, and although her hands were steady, the palms were sheened with sweat. She was reacting as she'd been trained, her mind cool, surprisingly calm, yet the fear existed, manifesting itself in shades of speech, or tiny movements of the face and hands. The "moment of truth," Ciari had said.

Now she'd learn.

"Missile signatures," he announced.

"How many?"

"Four, coming fast."

"Let the computer have 'em. Electronics Counter-Measure systems to divert the missiles away from us and then our shipboard lasers and ABMs to ace 'em. I don't want them within ten thousand kilometers of us; we can't risk the ElectroMagnetic Pulse of a nuclear blast screwing up our instrumentation."

"Understood."

The computer did its job to perfection, obliterating its targets with ease. The explosions confirmed their worst suspicions, however; the raider was using nukes, with megaton yields. One direct hit—even a respectable near miss—would finish them. And as salvo followed salvo, with heat flashes and radiation filling the gap between the two spacecraft, it became increasingly hard for *Wanderer*'s defenses to cope. At which point, the raider began throwing smaller, conventional, multiple-warhead missiles at them; while still out of range of *Wanderer*'s anti-missile beams, the primary vehicle separated into a dozen smaller units, each pursuing its own wildly corkscrewing track. Without warning, they had a hundred targets coming their way. Since the cruiser's supply of anti-missile missiles was limited, the lasers had to bear the brunt of this new attack. That limited their effectiveness against the nukes, which allowed that barrage to come significantly closer. *Wanderer* shook slightly and red lights flashed on Nicole's board. They'd been hit. A hundred-kilogram blast along the main frame that cracked one spar and bent three others nearby; *could be worse*, Nicole thought, *and probably will be*. The biggest danger was one of the little buggers connecting with the Command Module; a direct hit on the windows would effectively end the duel.

"How will we dock the gunship, Nicole?" Andrei asked, as the asteroid grew in their screens and view ports.

"On the run. We cut power immediately prior to rendezvous; Cat matches velocity with us. We slide out the cradle, she drops on, we reel her in, close the hatch and crank up the motors. Start to finish, the whole maneuver shouldn't take more than two hundred seconds."

"And should something go wrong?"

Suddenly, Nicole felt very old, and weary far beyond her time. Whatever happened, she knew that, in certain, precious ways, she'd never again be as young, as carefree, as... innocent.

"We leave them, Andrei."

"Welcome to the club," Ciari said, in a voice meant for her ears alone. She didn't look around, for fear he'd see the hate burning within her eyes.

"Coming up on Wolfe Station range, Nicole," Hana said,

"but the Deuce isn't climbing to meet us. D'you think Cat didn't receive your message!"

"Andrei, cut the mains," Nicole snapped. "Hana, can they still achieve rendezvous?"

"Not on this side of the rock. She's too far away and even with us just coasting, she'll need too much Delta-Vee. If she loops the rock and meets us on farside, though, she has a chance. But that window's minuscule; she's got no time to waste."

"Punch me a hole through that static, Hana. Divert power from all nonessential systems to do it. I have to be able to talk to Cat, tell her what to do."

"Goddammit."

"Ciari, what's wrong?"

"Missile signatures. Not from the raider, Shea, from the fucking *rock.*"

She looked at the screens, too stunned to speak as fire scarred the dark surface of the asteroid. Three missiles. Probably part of Wolfe Clan's own inventory. A perfect trap, and Nicole had rushed right into it.

"Can we block them?" she asked because she had to, though she already knew the answer.

"No," Ciari replied in a flat, passionless voice. "Our defensive systems are callibrated aft, towards the raider."

The speakers crackled, and they all jumped at the sound of Cat's voice. Reception was far from ideal, but she could be understood.

"Wanderer from Rover-Two, do you copy? *Wanderer . . ."*

"There's your channel, Nicole," Hana announced with grim determination, "but talk fast; I can't guarantee how long I can keep it clear."

"We can see your situation, *Wanderer,"* Cat continued after Nicole had acknowledged her call. "I count three missiles, is that correct?'

"Affirmative, Major. I'm sorry I fouled up."

"Later. Maintain your present vector and re-establish full thrust on the primaries. We'll run blocker for you against these bogies."

"Major, you can't!"

"Child, I have no intention of committing suicide, believe

me. We'll zap the missiles, then their silos, and meet you round back. Copy?"

"Copy. Good luck."

"*Gracias*. Now pay attention, novice, you might learn something."

"Show off," Ciari muttered.

"She'll be cutting things real damn close, Nicole," Hana said.

"Cat knows what she's doing, Hanako."

"Perhaps," Ciari said.

"You have a better way, Marshal?" Nicole snapped.

"They knew we EVA'd a gunship, they know what it can do. This can't be a surprise to them, which means there's something else in the works, has to be. Once they started shooting, they couldn't let us out alive. They'd be the target, then, no match for the starship that'd be scrambled once we got a signal through to base."

They had mere seconds to register the trio of fat, overpowered missiles leaping towards *Wanderer* from the asteroid before the gunship, too tiny to be seen with the naked eye, cut across their path. There were three laser flashes.

Nicole couldn't help crying out as the flight deck filled with light so quickly that the automatic polarizers built into the camera lenses couldn't compensate in time. As she looked away, blinking the spots from her vision, she couldn't help thinking, absurdly, that so monumental an explosion didn't seem quite right without any sound to accompany it.

"Hana," she called, her voice unnaturally loud, "status on the Deuce. Are they all right?"

"Can't tell. The blast established an ionization field that's blocking my probes."

"Shit!"

"More contacts approaching from aft," Ciari reported. "Also laser tracks. That bastard must have the firepower of a battle cruiser; he's pushing our defensive systems close to their saturation levels. Another hit—conventional, way aft—minimal effect, it splattered against the heavy structural shielding around the engines."

"Once we reach farside, we'll have some breathing space."

"That's what worries me."

Nicole wanted to snarl at him, but in truth it worried her, too. His words made too much sense to be ignored.

"Explosions on the surface," Hana cried, and almost simultaneously they heard Paul DaCuhna's jubilant voice.

"Nailed the sods! *Wanderer!* Hana, Nicole, you guys see that?! I hit 'em square! Some Class-A shooting—*wow!*"

"Lovely piece of work, hotshot," Hana agreed.

"Major," Nicole said, as a horrible thought struck her, "what if those weren't raiders down there? Suppose they were Wolfe Clan, thinking *we* were raiders?"

"I used a private challenge, Nicole, worked out between Phil, his senior partner and myself to cover just such an eventuality. Also, I know—I . . . knew—everyone on that rock. They botched the reply and I didn't recognize the voice. Whoever was down there wasn't Wolfe Clan. And raiders don't take prisoners."

Nicole looked at Ciari. "They've been here awhile."

"Advance party. To do the dirty work and prep the rock for the refinery."

"But why let us come in? Why the silence? Why not try to warn us off days ago, when we first started calling? They put themselves in this box."

"Or us."

"We're masked," Hana broke in. "Wolfe's asteroid now shields us from the raider's sensors."

"Hurry up, Cat," Nicole said urgently, "before they start shooting at you."

"That's odd," Cat said, her tone slightly bewildered. "My scanners indicate that both the raider and the refinery have modified their approach. Hell and damnation! With all the by-God electromagnetic 'clutter' created by these multiple nuke detonations, it's impossible to get a solid fix. I can't be sure."

"Hana—!"

"Waste of effort, Nicole. The rock hides them from us as effectively as it does us from them. Major, you have a two-hundred-second window; if you don't initiate the rendezvous maneuver within that time frame, you'll never catch us."

"Plenty of time, Doctor. Something about this pattern rubs me the wrong way. It's . . . familiar, but I can't quite place it. Do *Wanderer* sensors read anything ahead of you?"

"Negative. Clear space . . ." Nicole fell silent as she caught part of a background line from Paul to Cat.

"A single missile?" Cat asked, doubt unmistakable. "Vectoring for the asteroid?"

"They must know we've slipped past," Andrei muttered.

"Or they don't care," Ciari said with a look to Nicole.

"Cat," she called, "a hundred seventy seconds. Your clock is running, you guys, quit farting around."

"Oh my God," Cat whispered.

"Say again, Deuce," Nicole demanded.

"Get out of here, *Wanderer*," Cat told them, trying to keep her voice crisp and businesslike and failing. "Run as hard and fast as you can. Push the engines for all they're worth."

"Major, what's happening?"

"I haven't time to explain. We have to run blocker against this bogie; we have to . . . detonate it before it strikes the asteroid. It's your only hope—and a slim one at that."

"Cat!"

"It's an anti-matter warhead, Nicole, has to be. A friend of mine—Morgan, the one you met at DaVinci—pulled this stunt against a raider outfit in the colonies. The missile feeds on the mass of its target; if it strikes the rock, it'll convert the entire asteroid into a pint-sized supernova. But if I can detonate the warhead prematurely—if all it has to feed on is open space, or . . . the mass of this Rover, not only will the primary explosion be that much weaker, the asteroid itself will act as a buffer, protecting you for a few seconds before the anti-matter fireball consumes it. Not much, but it might prove the difference necessary for your survival."

"What about you guys?" Nicole asked softly.

All they heard was a small sigh.

"Paul," Hana cried, *"no!"*

"It's done, babe. We're committed." He tried a laugh. "Y'know, Nicole, I dreamed of going out in a blaze of glory, but this is ridiculous." A pause. "Oh well, when you can't even manage a decent laugh for your own jokes it's a definite cue for the final exit. Famous last words, Major and Bear, if you have any; we're approaching firing point."

"Ms. Shea," Dr. Shomron said, in his grave, slow voice, "among my effects . . . a letter for my wife . . ."

"She'll get it, Bear. You have my word."

"*Wanderer,*" Cat said, "Nicole, you're good people, some of the best I've known. It's been a privilege."

"Good-bye, Cat," Nicole whispered. "*A . . . a dio, Paolo.*"

For once, Paul had no words and Nicole was thankful he couldn't see her face as she bent over the console, fists clenching so tight the nails drew blood.

Over the constant susurrus of static, they could hear the interplay between Cat and Paul as they closed on their target. *Wanderer* was developing a five-gravity acceleration, well beyond its design maximums, the pressure forcing Nicole up and back into her seat, alarm lights flashing all across her board as systems protested and threatened to fail. In the main screen, Wolfe's asteroid grew perceptibly smaller as they shot away from it.

"Ready," Cat said, Paul echoing her commands. "Systems set and locked. Fire."

"Got it!" Paul had time to yell, before his voice—and Cat's and Bear's as well—spiraled upward into a primal, falsetto shriek of atavistic terror. Then, the voices disintegrated, replaced by an agonizingly high-pitched electronic squeal—the gunship's own scream as it was instantly vaporized. The noise ended almost as soon as it began; after that, nothing was heard but background static.

"If anyone's interested," Hana noted, "I'm monitoring a huge spike in infrared emissions on the opposite side of the rock."

Nicole saw the asteroid outlined in a corona of whiter-than-white fire and, even as she watched, its rim seemed to melt and crumple in on itelf. The fire cascaded along the surface, seared through the rock's heart, and a star was born before their eyes.

The asteroid had looked so small, so far away, a moment ago, yet the awful, unendurable fire reached out to catch them with terrifying ease. *Wanderer* twisted and groaned around her. In the distance, aft, there was a hollow thump that had to be an explosion. Every telltale turned red at once and boards shorted, sparks and small flames popping alive and into the air. Nicole didn't care. Instinctively, she covered her eyes, but it didn't help as light enveloped them, growing brighter and brighter until it filled her mind, became all she could conceive of.

Her last thought was that this must have been what the Universe looked like on the day of Creation. Beautiful and terrible, at the same time.

seven

WHEN AT LAST Nicole opened her eyes, she thought she'd gone blind. All around her was darkness, more complete and absolute than any she'd ever experienced. She blinked once, twice. There was no change. She didn't react at first, amazed enough to find herself alive. It was as if body and mind were disconnected, one functioning, the other not. She was capable of movement, action; she was aware of what was happening; and yet, those events seemed to have no real meaning.

She could hear, though; a loud, variable *whoosh* echoed in her ears. She didn't understand what it was until she started groping around with her hands; that was when she discovered they were gloved, that she was wearing a pressure suit, helmet included. The noise she heard was the sound of her own breathing.

With that realization, she couldn't help laughing. But the laughter quickly leapt into falsetto, threatening to slip irrevocably out of control. She was awake now; she couldn't duck reality any longer, the reality that she was blind. She remembered the awful radiance of the anti-matter explosion, her eyes suddenly burning with tears as Paul's death shriek echoed in her thoughts, and assumed that the fireball had somehow burned out her optic nerves.

She tried to move, only to discover she couldn't. She nearly panicked, until her hands found the buckles of a safety harness drawn tight across her torso. *Makes sense,* she thought, *the last thing anyone needs is a crip blundering about, making a nuisance of herself.* She kept exploring and soon came across air hoses connecting her suit to a backpack. That gave her pause. Usually, suits were hooked into the ship's cycler system through plugs built into the base of every Command Module chair. A backpack meant the primary Life-Systems couldn't be trusted.

She tried to say something, but only a ragged croak emerged. She was so dry she couldn't even sneeze. It seemed to take forever to moisten her lips enough to talk; as she started to speak, she wondered how she'd keep from screaming if no one answered. Hell, she had no idea if her suit radio even *worked.*

"Shea . . . Shea here—anybody there?" was what she meant to say, thought she said. Hard to tell. Her head had begun to ache—a merciless pounding against the back of her skull—and her mouth tasted fuzzy and metallic. Legacy of a concussion, most likely, combined with bad air. She wondered how long she'd been on this pack, and what to do if it ran out, which was suddenly becoming a distinct possibility. The fact she was in a suit meant *Wanderer* had most likely been holed, its internal atmosphere voided into space. Unfortunately, the only way Nicole could be certain would be to open her helmet and take a breath, a definite mistake if she was sitting in a hard vacuum.

Hobson's choice, as per bloody usual, she sighed to herself, *damned if I do, damned if I bloody don't. Terrific.*

She felt something touch her right arm and jumped, yelping as well in shock and surprise, before sagging in relief when she realized it was only another hand.

"Nicole," she heard Andrei call over the radio, "can you hear me? Respond, please?"

Nicole nodded, grunted aloud, and he asked, "Are you all right?"

"Yeh—yes, I . . . I think so," she stammered, while her brain screamed, *liar!* "Andrei, I can't see. I'm blind."

"Zdorovo," he cursed, then paused. "Wait a moment. Why do you think so?"

"Because my eyes are open, chum, and I can't see a fucking thing!"

"One simple way to be certain." Andrei flicked on a torch and Nicole brought her hands up to protect her eyes.

"I—that light! I can see!" she yelled. "I can *see!*"

When she'd calmed down, removing helmet and safety harness, she pulled herself up to the top of the flight deck and stared out the big view ports at the stars. She'd never seen anything more beautiful. It was only after her initial euphoria had passed that she realized the air she was breathing now was, if anything, worse than in her suit and that, with each breath, a cloud of frost appeared before her face.

She looked at Andrei. There was sufficient starlight on this level to show her that the Russian was also in a full suit, wearing an airpack, lacking only his helmet. He was nodding, his thoughts paralleling hers.

"Correct, Nicole; we have no power. And without power, we have no atmosphere recyclers, which means no fresh air. We've been bleeding pure oxygen from the undamaged reservoirs into the CM but without the cyclers we can't do a thing about carbon dioxide build-up. Already, we're skirting the danger levels; in a few hours, we'll be past them. We have perhaps a day, no more."

"No power means no heat, either," Nicole noted quietly.

Andrei nodded. "True. *Wanderer* is marvelously well insulated, but we're still losing heat along a steady curve. After all, it is near absolute zero outside. But we'll suffocate before we freeze."

"Ter*rif*ic. Crew status?"

"Hanako is working on the powersystems, trying to jury-rig a feed from the fuel cells. Marshal Ciari is EVA, on a reconnaissance, to see how badly we're damaged."

"Isn't engineering your specialty?"

Andrei smiled wanly and shone his torch down his right side. The arm was empty and Nicole could see the angular outlines of splints against the bulky fabric of the suit torso. "Most uncomfortable," he said.

"Bad?"

"Two places, compound fracture. It was a very rough ride."

"I can guess. I think I banged my head."

"You'll have a very rakish scar above your left eyebrow. Quite a mess. Possibly concussed, but since we had no means, and no decent opportunity to give more than first aid, we decided to let you be."

And if I happened to die, she realized, *probably my good fortune.* She shook her head in a vain attempt to dislodge the cobwebs still crowding her brain. "How long have I been out," she asked.

"A day, more or less."

"You should have waked me."

"To what purpose? You would have been of less help than I and"—he paused—"we felt it would be kinder, should worst come to worst, to let you die in your sleep."

She drew him into a gentle, sisterly embrace. "I appreciate the thought. But if I have to die, I'd rather do so with friends than by myself. I'd like to have *my* chance . . . to say goodbye."

At that point, the lights came on.

Nicole reacted first, sprawling across her console and slapping the intercom. "Hana," she called, "Hanako, you did it! Way to go, girl, we have power on the flight deck."

"Power in Command and Service Modules, thank you very much. But how long it'll last is anyone's guess. Hey—Nicole, is that you?"

"The one and only, aching but alive."

"Will wonders never cease. I've some work to finish. Better to lock as much of this mess down as I can while I'm here. So I'll see you two in a bit, okay?"

"I copy. Hana, you want some help?"

"I can handle it. Thanks, though. Maybe later."

A new voice came on-line: "Glad to hear you're up and about, Shea. Now that the hard work's all but done."

"Gimme a break, Ciari. You InShip? The EVA complete? How do we look?"

His voice was bleak as he replied, "It's something we should all hear together. I suggest we meet in C-1, as soon as possible."

They parked themselves wherever they pleased. The Carousel wasn't spinning anymore. That took more power than the fuel cells could provide. The great wheel was far darker than they'd ever seen it, more raw illumination coming from the few functional status telltales than the lighting panels that framed the hub above their heads. They were still in suits, because it was still bitter cold inside the spacecraft and would be for some time, as the heaters slowly and gradually took effect. They were taking things as easy as possible for the moment, trying to put an absolute minimum of strain on their improvised power system. It was their lifeline; if it failed, they died. The equation was as basic — as final — as that.

Nicole sipped some soup, cursing under her breath as it burned her tongue, while Ciari floated forward to face them all.

"In a nutshell, folks," he said, "if we were any worse off, we'd be dead." Nobody reacted, they were all too tired, too empty. She held the heatercup under her jaw, luxuriating in its warmth.

"We took some hits during the fight," he continued, "but it was the anti-matter blast that pretty much did us in. When Wolfe's asteroid shattered, some fair-sized chunks of rock must have slammed into the main engines. It's a miracle nothing blew. *Wanderer*'s tail looks like an inspired piece of free-form sculpture, even more impressive than our last sight of *Rockhound*. Everything aft of the C-1 ring of the Service Module is open to space. Hana and I had to improvise an airlock in the DropShaft so she could get downship to work on the fuel cells."

"That's our second miracle," Hana broke in. "We're getting nominal function out of the undamaged cells. And I'm fairly sure a number of the others can be salvaged. For the moment at least, power isn't a major problem.

"Unfortunately, that's about all the good news there is. The heat-flare of the blast, plus impact with the debris, stripped us clean of our external antennae and sensor modules. For all intents and purposes, *Wanderer* is blind, deaf, dumb and retarded. The ElectroMagnetic Pulse that hit us was so intense it even scrambled the circuitry of our hand calculators. The across-the-board outage suffered when we lost the main engines was the *coup de grace.* Now, I've managed to restore the idiot systems — air cyclers, environmental units, basic life support — but beyond that, *nada.*"

"The Auxiliary Propulsion System appears fully operational," Ciari said, picking up the briefing again. "Fuel levels are at 93% capacity. Mind you, we'll have to improvise firing circuits, and do any astrogational calculations by hand, but if we ever want to move, the APS will do the job. The glitch in that program, however, is that it hasn't the power to move the entire spacecraft; we'd expend all our fuel simply trying to turn *Wanderer* around. So, to utilize the APS, we'll have to separate the Command Module, which will cost us the benefit of the fuel cells. CM batteries will sustain us about a day at normal operational levels; at bare minimums, a week. After that, lights out."

"Anyone have any idea precisely where we are?" Nicole asked.

"A long, long way from home," Andrei cracked, but no one even smiled.

"As soon as I'm rested," Ciari replied, "I'll go EVA and shoot some starsights."

"How long before anyone comes looking for us?" Hana wondered.

"Depends," said Nicole thoughtfully. "If there was a starship handy, a week tops. Sublight, figure a month minimum. But that assumes they know we're in trouble."

"C'mon, Nicole, they'll start worrying the minute we go off the air."

"I wouldn't count on that."

"Why not? They could hardly have missed that explosion."

"The raider had our communications protocols down pat, official and unofficial. They even had the right reply to Cat's personal challenge. Stands to reason they'll be just as efficient and effective at covering our tracks. They could fake our traffic, or give DaVinci a plausible explanation for our silence. For all Mission Control might know, that blast might have been us. Wolfe's people got a little overedgy, they shot first, ignited our fuel and armaments. Rest in Peace, *Wanderer*."

"A disaster beacon would tell 'em different."

Nicole shook her head, "That's right. And who d'you think would be most likely to hear the Mayday? Those raiders may assume they nailed us—maybe we got lucky and the explosion played as much havoc with their scanning systems as ours—but they won't take it for granted. Not their style at all."

"Shit!" Hana cried, and then shifted into passionately furious Japanese.

"What?"

"I'm an idiot. A senile fool! We may not have lost every computer."

"What!"

"Nicole, the Rovers! Outside of engineering, the shuttle bay is the most heavily shielded area aboard *Wanderer*, because it's designed to open to space. And when you add to that the shielding on the Rovers themselves—!" She kicked herself up and away from her perch, angling towards the DropShaft access, but Nicole stopped her.

"Check it out tomorrow. Same goes for you, Marshal, and your starsight EVA."

"Tomorrow!" Hana protested.

"Tomorrow," Nicole said, with flat finality. "Right now, everyone relax, take it easy, eat some food, get some rest. We need it, more than any of us are willing to admit. Twenty-four hours won't make that much difference to our eventual survival, but rushing off half-cocked and half-zonked could ace us all."

Despite her own orders, Nicole couldn't sleep. She prowled what was left of her first command, swimming through the air from compartment to compartment, inspecting the Command and Service Modules from the sealed DropShaft forward to the flight deck. The temperature had risen perceptibly, though it was still chilly, and she soon shucked her pressure suit in favor of sneaks and two layers of sweats and her Edwards jacket. Floating in the shaft, she admired Hana's and Ciari's jury-rigged hatch, and thought about Chagay's experiments—all his effort, his meticulous work—lost in the Lab ring beyond. They didn't even have his notes; the electronic records were lost with the computer and the hard copies denied them by the radiation levels on C-2.

Finally, her roaming mood took her back to C-1. The great wheel was empty. Everyone had decided to crash on the Flight Deck. The darkness was broken by the dull red glow of the emergency lights. She moved without conscious thought, hardly aware of what she was doing until she found herself pulling her guitar off its bulkhead clamps.

She floated there a moment, idly running her hands across the smooth, curved wood. It was an acoustic model, handmade, and far older than she was. It had been her father's and when Conal Shea had seen his very young daughter eyeing it, even sneaking a touch whenever the girl thought no one was looking, he'd given it to Nicole. It was one of the few possessions she'd brought with her from Earth, despite the outrageous cost.

Nicole strummed a single chord, and winced.

"Baby, you are out of tune," she muttered, thinking: *no wonder! I haven't touched it in over a fortnight. Poor dear's probably furious with me.* She pulled her tuner out of the bedside tabouret and got to work.

Awhile later, finally satisfied, she ran through some fast finger exercises as a warm-up. Her hands were stiff. It felt like she was playing with a set of HardSuit gloves on. But even clumsy as she thought she was, she felt better.

She pulled her legs into a lotus cross, smiling as she noticed she was hovering a meter or so above the deck, and wondered what to play. Her hands began her favorite Lila piece but as soon as she recognized the song, she stopped herself, remembering how pleased Paul had looked when he'd given her the bootleg tapes. There were more tears and her body hunched in on itself with pain. Then, she plucked at the strings, a Bach *Chaconne* that was the first thing her father had taught her to play.

"Very nice," a voice said beyond her when she finished. It was Ciari.

"Not really," she replied, though she was glad he liked it. "I'm dreadfully out of practice." She strummed some random chords, adjusted the tuning.

"Would you rather be alone, Nicole? I didn't mean to disturb you."

"That's okay, Ben. I could use the company."

"We all could, I think."

He slipped into the cubicle beside her and slid a flute out of its traveling case. "What'll we play?" he asked.

After a couple of rough starts, they settled on folk songs. The ones that both knew were no problem; when they ran into a song that only one was familiar with, the other improvised a harmony, or followed along the melody. Nicole had acquired an awesome knowledge of traditional songs from an Irish uncle who was a professional balladeer; that night, in her corner of the darkened Carousel, she ran through the entire repertoire.

They were midway through a spirited reel when the wail of a harmonica suddenly joined them. They stopped, surprised. It was Andrei, grinning sheepishly as they looked in his direction.

"We heard you playing," he said. "It sounded like fun."

"The more the merrier," Nicole smiled, "but it looks to me as though we're a body short. Where's Hana?"

"Scrounging," she called from the DropShaft as she heaved something into the Carousel. In the dim, broken light, as they emerged from Nicole's cubicle for a look, no one could make out what it was. Hana palmed a control plate, and the lights came on.

"You sure the system can cope, Hana?" Nicole asked, her voice and manner serious

"If it can't, boss, we might as well learn now. Don't fret, Nicole; it's only an extra couple of centawatts. Nothing'll go wrong, you have my guarantee. Hell," she went on as she twisted over to open the sealed case she'd been hauling, "I'd stack that wiring rig of mine against most dockyard jobs any day."

"We'll take your word for it," Nicole said, angry inside at the way reality had intruded into the gentle, almost fairy-tale mood their music had created. "What have you got there, anyway?"

"See for yourself." Hana backed off slightly as the others all crowded over; inside were seven bottles.

"OJ," she said. "Fresh-squeezed, flash-frozen, perfectly preserved—I've been thawing it. Major Garcia had me pick it up at DaVinci just before we left, something special to celebrate the successful completion of our mission to Pluto. Since it appears unlikely that we'll even reach Pluto this trip, I figured it wouldn't do any harm to drink the stuff now."

"A New Wave, nonalcoholic Irish wake," Nicole said softly, pulling a bottle from the case. "Pity we can't get drunk."

"It's the thought that counts, boss," Hana said.

Nicole held the bottle up in a toast, then tapped Hana with it. "Since you've come this far, hon, you might as well go for broke and pull some of the emergency foodpaks. We'll use 'em for munchies."

The taste was tarter than Nicole liked but she wasn't really bothered as she took a hefty swallow and passed it to Ciari. As he drank, she began another song, Andrei doing his best to follow along with his harmonica; but his broken arm caused too much trouble and he and Hana ended up providing enthusiastic, albeit increasingly off-key, vocals instead. Ciari introduced them to Belter and OutSystem songs, and Andrei countered with Russian ones, mixed up with some classic Mississippi Delta blues riffs he'd learned in childhood from records brought back from American tours by parental friends in the Soviet State Opera. Ciari's voice was lower, naturally rich, while Andrei filled the Ring with a pure, resonant tenor. They played and sang and talked and ate and drank until the bottles were empty, the munchies gone, their songs finished, their throats sore and voices hoarse. No one had any idea how much time had passed; no one really cared.

Hana was the first to cry. Nicole was singing an old ballad, passed down from generation to generation in her family for so long that no one knew when it had first been written, or who had done so. She sang alone; the others just sat and listened. And when she was done there was no applause, though they'd cheered riotously and whooped it up in a fine old fashion after every other tune, merely an awkward, awful, empty silence. Nicole saw Hana cover her eyes and turn a little away. Before she could make a move of her own—she wanted to cross to Hana, embrace her, comfort her for the loss they all felt—Nicole felt Ciari's hand on hers, a touch so gentle she barely felt it, yet strong enough to hold her back.

He moved her guitar out of the way as she flowed into his arms; she shook with the force of sudden sobs. He cradled her against his body as best he could, gently stroking the back of her neck. She made no sound as she wept, her very silence making the impact of her emotions that much more intense. There was an ache deep within her chest, a hollowed-out sensation that grew with every breath until it consumed her. She felt Ciari cup her head, heard his voice—understanding the tone, if not the words—knew he was trying to comfort her as all the emotions she'd held bottled up inside cut loose at once. She remembered the first time she met Paul—in the Academy's sprawling central plaza, surrounded by a thousand other terrified, terrorized cadets, ears verbally assaulted by shrieking, berserker upperclassmen, senses overwhelmed by so many things they'd had no chance to learn but were expected to know—and the good times, bad times that followed. A summer bivouac in the Rockies, where she'd stunned her classmates with her knowledge of ribald ballads, while Paul kept them all in hysterics by creating scores of inspired, hilariously funny limericks. A trip to Denver, to the ballet, with Paul looking handsome as could be in dress uniform, the young ladies falling over themselves to be near him, the young men ignoring her completely.

Now, he was gone. And Cat. And the Bear.

Why couldn't someone cut out her heart, so it wouldn't hurt so much?

She sniffed noisily and looked blearily around to ask if there was anything left to drink?

Hana shook various bottles, found one that wasn't quite empty. Nicole took it, held it high in a toast, and said, "Here's to you, Paolo. Wherever you are, partner, may you fly in peace and happiness, forever!" She took a fast, deep slug of juice and passed the bottle to Ciari. His toast was to Cat, and Andrei's to Chagay. Hana, though, paused before she spoke, and looked at them all in turn, lastly, for the longest time, at Nicole.

"To us," she said, "because we yet live."

Then, the bottle was dry.

She reached out and Nicole was the first to respond to her mute appeal, moving in close, arms going around each other in a tender, loving embrace. Nicole felt Ciari by one side, Andrei by the other, and they held each other tighter. There were more tears, but these were as much of joy and love as grief. As she looked from face to face, Nicole felt closer to these three people than to anyone else she'd ever known.

One by one, they fell asleep. But her mind refused to take the hint. She closed her eyes, slowed her breathing, thought of nothing—even turned to her private ever-reliable *mantra,* but it failed her.

With a sigh of betrayal, she opened her eyes. Bodies had shifted in sleep, shunting her to the outside of the group, and only the slightest of twists was necessary to float herself free. A flick of the wrist sent her upward, to the DropShaft access. A good pull with both arms rocketed her onto the flight deck. Some basic status lights had reactivated when power was restored but for the most part, the consoles were dark. Nothing worked. Nicole hovered by Cat's chair, absently stroking a palm across its back, before climbing into her own, bracing herself in place with her feet on the panel. The stars hung in place beyond the window, like a backdrop on a stage set, hardly moving — though, by its own standards, *Wanderer* was hurtling through the sky.

"It's no sin to survive," Ciari said suddenly beside her. "D'you know why?" He asked in the same surprisingly gentle voice, when she didn't respond. "Because, sooner or later, you won't. Nobody does."

"I hate it."

"Death?"

"We're surrounded by so much ... majesty. Wonder. Beauty. Things that can't — maybe shouldn't — be explained. Miracle upon miracles. Why do we lost sight of that? Why do we deliberately close our eyes?"

"If I had the answer...?"

"I thought you were a philosopher, Ciari."

He kissed her, a quick, tender touch of the lips. Then, he moved back a little to look at her. As he did, Nicole made a sound deep in her throat that was halfway between a growl and a moan, clutching at his jumpsuit, catching her breath sharply as his hand slipped between her legs. She looked back and forth between his eyes, but their expression was hidden by shadow and their own dark color. She wondered what was in hers. It was strange, and frightening — she wasn't sure she liked him, would ever like him, yet she hungered for him, to be a part of him, make him part of her. It was unlike anything she'd ever felt, reminding her of the horror stories she devoured as a kid, wherein heroes and heroines found themselves entranced by some demon or vampire's fatal glamour.

The second kiss was as tender, her tongue touching his lips, answered in kind. A hand went behind his head to hold him as close as she could. She wanted him to feel her strength, to understand she was an equal partner, not a conquest. She felt him stroke across her hips, up her sides, over her breasts. His hair was so much longer than hers and finer; she pulled off the clip that held it in place and laughed to see it fan out from his head

like a halo. There was no excess to his body, the skin was
stretched taut over muscle and bone. The curves were sharp
and marred by ridges of scar tissue. He'd seen hard times,
and hadn't emerged unscathed. And she wondered if that went
deeper than the skin. *Who has he known,* she asked herself,
as he kissed the hollow of her throat and she his brow and
eyes, and his hands moved beneath her shirt, *who has he hurt?
And who's hurt him? Will I be one? Probably — but which?*
And as she thought the question, she realized she didn't care.
The moment mattered — the need, the gamble for joy, the trust
that this was an act of friendship — whatever came tomorrow,
she'd survive.

She didn't remember losing her clothes until the chill air
raised goosebumps over her entire body. Or was it his hands
and mouth on her breasts? There was ice inside, a delicious
agony, and then he was inside her as well and all she could
manage that initial moment was a long, shuddering moan. He
flexed, nearly slipping free, and she locked her ankles together behind his back to hold him. Belatedly, she realized he
had fastened her harness. Otherwise, their wild movements
would have sent them tumbling about the cabin. She laughed,
which broke his rhythm. He was flushed — she could feel his
heat when she kissed him — and panting as he asked what was
so funny. And then he laughed, when she told him. He thrust
in long, slow strokes and she responded with her own inner
muscles, flashing her teeth in delight to hear him groan. He
moved faster and deeper, and she helped him. Time and again,
she thought him ready to climax, and told him it was all right,
but nothing happened except that his hands moved to new
locations, stroked new sensations from her, making her move
with more urgency, stretching long and tight in the chair,
against the man and the bonds that imprisoned her, fighting
as much to be free as to be held. A great and terrible wave
was building within her, more intense than she had ever experienced, ever imagined. She wasn't sure she wanted it, she
was losing control, but he held her as the wave crested and
her head arched back, every tendon taut, unable to give voice
to this burst of ecstasy, as blinding and ravaging in its own
way as the explosion that had wrecked *Wanderer.*

She found herself crying as she relaxed. There was no

strength in her body and she was pleased to see he was exhausted as well, gleaming with sweat. She draped her arms
around his neck and gave him a slow, passionate kiss. She
began to laugh, with wicked, irrepressible joy. He snapped the
buckle on her harness and they rolled up and away from her
chair, holding themselves together.

"Review Board would definitely have my ass for this,"
Nicole said with a grin.

"They'll have to stand in line." Ciari grinned back, and she
swatted him on his own, gasping with surprise and delight as
that made him shift position; spent though he was, he still felt
hard within her.

"Tell me, Red," he asked, "was it worth the anticipation?"

"Men," she muttered in mock disgust. "Is that what's important, how well you scored?"

"Of course. To enter in my log."

"Bastard."

"Takes one to know one."

"God," Nicole shook her head, "what Hana and Andrei
must think."

"They're asleep in the Carousel, unless you want to wake
them and announce the fact."

"Don't play with me, Ben. And don't mock me."

"Don't ask for it."

He shifted in her arms, as if to move away, but she
wouldn't let him, tightening her grasp. For a few seconds, he
looked anywhere but at her and even in the dim light of the
status telltales, she could see small bursts of tension around
his jaw.

"Surprised yourself, did you?" she asked him. "Now who's
thrown caution to the wind?"

He sighed, glanced sideways at her, and she let him go,
shivering with pleasure at the purely physical sensations of his
withdrawal.

"There are enough complications in a solo spacer's life,
Nicole, without adding a relationship to them."

"So you told me. But every life ends, is that it? Nothing to
look forward to, nothing now to risk."

"We have a chance."

"The difference between us, Ciari, is that I believe it." She took him in her arms and they held each other close, desire vying with fatigue in both of them and winning without a contest. She laid her head on his shoulder and said, "We'll survive, Ben," so softly she was certain he wouldn't hear, but he did. "I don't know how, but we will. *We will!*"

─────── **eight** ───────

FOR THE NEXT week, much of their work was basic house-keeping and spacecraft maintenance, as they fleshed out the rough, preliminary survey carried out in those first, desperate hours. Most of their primary organic stores had been lost when debris had ruptured the hull, either destroyed outright or contaminated by radiation, but they had sufficient emergency rations to last them for the foreseeable future. Hana's improvised wiring set-up proved to be as good as she said it was and, over the days that followed, more and more systems were brought back on-line.

As soon as the shuttle bay was fully operational, Ciari went EVA with one of their two Science Modules for a starscan. The results didn't cheer anyone.

"We've come a pretty fair piece from Wolfe's Asteroid," he told them. "We were developing full emergency thrust on the mains when that rock blew, remember, and when the fuel elements in the engines themselves detonated, they added considerably to our Delta-Vee. At the moment, we seem to be in a 'Kirkwood Gap,' a sector of the Belt where there are no asteroids. We're also moving through the outer fringes of the Belt, about three astronomical units from Earth's orbit. Since Earth herself is on the far side of the sun, the distance home is a lot farther. I doubt we could be more remote if we tried."

"What about our own orbit?" Nicole asked.

Ciari shrugged. "Too soon to tell, but I wouldn't hope for much. We're moving up from the plane of the ecliptic, and away from the System. None of the Outer Planets are near enough to do any good, which leaves only one significant gravity source which can affect our trajectory—the Sun itself, six hundred million kilometers, thataway." He pointed across the Carousel.

"We're very small," he continued, "and in relation to our mass, moving very fast. If we're in a Solar orbit, it's bound to be shallow; I'd lay fair odds we won't be back in this neighborhood for quite a while."

"If ever," Nicole finished. Ciari nodded.

"Well," she said, "not the end, by any means. Not even close. We play for time, drift as far from where we were ambushed as possible—as far OutSystem—and then we start yelling. True, the raiders may hear us. True, they may arrive before sublight rescue. But a starship . . ."

"A triangle run," Ciari asked, "out half a light from DaVinci, and then back to us? If there's minimal risk of any collision, that's . . . feasible."

"Assuming anyone hears us," Hana countered. "It'll take our signal better than two hours to reach Earth; even pushing it with every spare erg of power, it'll be barely a whisper when it arrives. The disaster beacon's omni-directional, as well; there's no way to focus its transmission. So who's to say it'll be noticed?"

"No guarantees, but we've nothing else. All it requires is that we keep ourselves and this bucket functional for a couple or three months. Is *that* feasible?"

"Maybe," Hana said slowly. "The longer we wait, the greater the risk."

"We know the obvious, Hana," Nicole told her and the other woman's eyes flashed. But then, Hana gave a shallow nod; she was willing to concede at least the possibility. Andrei agreed. Nicole felt indecently pleased with herself. They'd appeared utterly without hope, yet she'd found some. A little victory to balance the grand disaster, a vindication to eat away at her sense of loss, and failure.

But as the first month crawled by, the crew found themselves confronted by a problem she hadn't anticipated: boredom. Ciari rigged a zero-gee exercise set-up and committed everyone to a rigorous schedule, at least an hour a day, and he doubled it if a session was skipped. He forced Nicole to continue her unarmed combat lessons and drove her harder than he had before. Unfortunately, that did nothing to fill the rest of their time. With access to his lab denied by the lethal radiation levels, Andrei could do little work on his experimental program. All the entertainment modules had crashed with the main computer system. Games, books, movies, records—everything stored in its memory was gone. Their musical instruments helped some but only so many concert singalongs could be staged, so many pieces taught. Andrei had a chess set, but he and Ciari were Grand Masters and even at their most inspired, the women couldn't even come close to making it a decent contest, let alone win. Cards were tried, and there Nicole got some revenge, winning at poker, losing at gin, hating bridge. The four of them began to get on each other's nerves.

After their night together on the flight deck, Nicole and Ciari stayed apart by mutual choice. The ship had become too small, there was no real privacy, and each felt it wouldn't be fair to the others. And yet, it was equally hard to hide what had happened, the changes it had made between them. Nicole would look up to discover Ciari watching her, or at other times, she would watch him, fixing face and body indelibly in her memory, as if both sensed it wouldn't, couldn't, last. Nicole remembered her conversation with Hana, and thought she understood now what Hana had gone through with her lover. One moment, she would fantasize about being Mrs. Nicole Ciari, what it would be like to bear his children; she saw herself in her mother's place, keeping hearth and home while man and family lived their lives beyond its walls. And then she would look at the stars, and remember her dreams, and know the price was too high, the hunger within her too great to be denied. Perhaps there would be a time, a place—a . . . man—when it would be right and proper to give them up. But—a realization that made her cry, suddenly and quite without warning, sitting at the galley table writing a letter home—not now. Hana had seen her and offered a silent shoulder, never asking what was wrong while Nicole's tears became harsh, racking, agonized sobs. And afterward, she wondered, perversely, if Ciari cried for her.

By five weeks on, she was spending more and more time on the flight deck, deliberately isolating herself from the others, reliving in her mind the approach to the asteroid, hearing Paolo's last scream, examining every decision, looking ruthlessly for her mistakes. Wondering, in the dark moments before sleep finally released her, whether she and the others wouldn't have been better off dead along with the Rover. She knew her crew was going through the motions now, marking time, and she wondered how to pull them out of their funk. A fortnight before, in a notebook, she'd begun a long, rambling letter to her father, writing to him as if she were speaking aloud and he were present to hear her. Today, finally reading it, she could see the threads of madness weaving in and around her supposedly rational sentences. That sent a chill up her spine and she slumped forward in her chair to rest her chin on her crossed forearms, on her console, her bleak reflection gloomily looking back from the view port. *Am I that far gone,* she wondered, *so bloody near the edge? Do I fucking care?*

Another face appeared in the transparent window and she turned to discover Andrei hovering nearby, a worried expression on his face as he told her that Hana had gone EVA in a SciMod.

"She's been out every day lately, at least an hour each trip. I asked her why, but she wouldn't say."

"You want me to talk to her?"

"You are in command." Nicole's mouth twisted slightly and a rude thought flashed across her mind, checked almost immediately by the belated realization that he was right, she *was* in command. The rights, the privileges—such as they were—the responsibilities. She'd been ducking them long enough. "If there is a proper reason for her excursions," he was saying, "well and good. Though I believe she should inform us what it is. Perhaps we can be of assistance. I confess, it would be nice to have *some*thing constructive to do. But if this is a manifestation of some psychosis . . ."

"You mean, is she going stir-crazy?"

"Da."

"Aren't we all, in our own way?" He looked sharply at her, until he realized she was making a joke; his smile was as much relief as genuine amusement.

"Except the Marshal, I think."

"Are the EVAs causing any problem to *Wanderer?*" Nicole asked.

"Not yet. She cannibalized one of the Jeeps for propellant and electronics; she's running her equipment off its power-plant. But what happens when that is exhausted? We may need the other Jeep and the Rover-Three gunship. For lifeboats, if nothing else."

"Point taken. Where is she now?"

"Outside. If you look up and off to the right—say, two o'clock, two-thirty—you should see her lights."

Nicole did, and said so. "Got 'em—about a half-mile out."

"Her third SciMod EVA today." Nicole whistled. "That's why I felt the need to inform you."

She waited for Hana in the R-6 suit bay, watching through the transparent Lexan window and on the monitors as the un-gainly craft expertly settled on its extended docking cradle, nodding to herself in appreciation of her friend's skill. Hana was a natural flyer. She waved a greeting as the Rover trun-dled inside and the giant hatch closed behind it. Compartment pressurizaton took longer than usual and Nicole noted that Hana had modified the pumps to use less power.

Finally, green lights flashed on the status panel and Nicole cycled the hatch, gasping as she stepped over the threshold. Immediately, her mind flashed back to Rover-One, and the murderous cold she'd felt when Ciari opened her helmet. This was as bad. As Hana hauled herself out of the Rover, Nicole ducked back into the suit bay, sealing the hatch and turning the heaters up full in the same motion, before zipping her jacket up to the neck. Her teeth wer chattering like castanets, her entire body popped with goose bumps, a minute later when Hana joined her.

"Sorry," Hana said as she removed her helmet, the concern in her eyes belying her grin. "I wasn't expecting visitors."

"Bloody fucking *hell!*" Nicole snarled, shaking so hard she could hardly talk. She hunched her body forward, hugging herself tight as she could, and waited for the misery to pass, praying with all her heart that it wouldn't provoke a relapse of her flu, since most of their antibiotics had been on the C-2 Carousel.

"I shifted the heaters over to a manual control mode," Hana explained as she brought Nicole a heaterpak of chicken soup from the bulkhead dispenser. "I've been outside so often, it would have been a waste of power to heat the Bay after each EVA, especially when working in my insulated pressure suit isn't that much of a hassle."

"Why ? What's this all about?" Nicole asked flatly, once the blistering heat of the broth began to thaw her out.

"Hana," she said, when the other woman didn't answer, "I'm in no mood for a runaround. I want to know what's going on."

"Can it wait — just a while longer, Nicole?"

"No."

"I didn't want to tell anyone till I was sure."

"Of what?"

"I'd rather not say."

"I'd rather you did."

Hana tried a disarming grin. "Gonna shoot me if I don't, O Captain, my Captain?"

Nicole didn't respond in kind and there was a steely edge to her voice as she said, "Hana, there are four survivors on this spacecraft, and our lives are totally dependent on a collection of patchwork systems, any one of which could fail at any moment. You're using power, you're using propellant, you're using atmosphere. No matter how hard you try to divorce your operation from the rest of *Wanderer,* what you do affects us all. We're in this mess together. You haven't the right to commit us to a course of action without letting us know what it is, and giving us a chance to decide for ourselves!"

Hana sighed. "I know. It was wrong of me. I guess — " she stood silently, gazing at her thoughts before speaking further — "all this has made me a little crazy, too. You ran to the flight deck, I came here."

"Nobody's perfect."

"Part of it, maybe, is jealousy. You had the Marshal to share your strength — and your ... grief — with."

"Why didn't you say something?"

"You wouldn't have heard," Hana said bluntly, "before today. You'll have to climb into a suit," she continued brusquely, abruptly changing the subject. "My equipment is inside the Bay and the temperature is still way below freezing."

Nicole pulled a softsuit off its rack and, after changing, followed Hana over to a work table. This section of the Bay was crowded with electronics and computer modules stripped from the Jeep and this SciMod. A fresh photo cassette—the pictures Hana had taken during this latest jaunt—had been inserted into one of the computers and Hana spent some time working on it before she was finally ready. She dimmed the lights and began flashing slides across the face of a viewer.

Before a half-dozen had passed, Nicole plugged herself into the intercom and called a general crew meeting. She knew why Hana had been so hesitant about revealing her discovery, but also knew that this was something everyone aboard needed to know. Now.

"These are part of a routine STARSCAN program Paul and I started when we left Luna, as an adjunct to our main Sky-Map mission," Hana told them after everyone had gathered in the Bay. "Almost all the shots were stored in the main computer and were, of course, lost when the system crashed. For some experiments, though, we made gel slides of a few choice photos. They all cover the same basic area of the Solar System and were taken at roughly one-week intervals." She showed each of the pictures on the primary display.

"Anyone notice anything unusual?" she asked when finished, ignoring Ciari's mutter about "goddamn schoolgirl twenty questions."

"I'll run through it again," she said, "only this time, keep your eyes on this light source. . . ." She used a lightpen to indicate a medium bright dot of white in the upper right-hand corner of the screen. At the touch of a button, the dot was ringed by a red circle. As she went through the sequence, the dot moved perceptibly, shifting almost three centimeters down and to the left.

"*Boszhe moi,*" Andrei said under his breath, and then, louder, "what *is* that?!"

"Hey, babe," Hana smiled, "the best is yet to come. This next sequence is position scans I've been taking since the ambush." By the third picture, Hana had provoked a reaction from them all—Andrei gasping, even Ciari shaking his head in mixed amazement and disbelief, Nicole watching impassively. The dot was easily visible now, its glow far brighter than any of the stellar objects around it, forward motion obvious. The latest slides were slightly streaked.

"I've been taking measurements with the SciMod's telescopes, optical and radio," Hana continued, "trying to work up as much data on that object as possible. It's blue-shifted, moving towards us. I've also been able to compute a rough parallax: two months ago, that thing was fifty astronomical units distant—roughly seven and a half billion kilometers. I tried to compute one based on our position ten days ago and our position now; that bugger is close."

"How close?" asked Nicole.

Hana tapped her keypad and the dot became blindingly intense. "Taken this morning," she told them. "Its albedo is extraordinary, approximately 97%, and there seems to be no measurable fluctuation. The object has no spin; it presents the same face to the Sun."

"Ninety-seven percent," Andrei murmured. "Virtually a perfect reflecting surface. Offhand, my friends, I can think of no natural object with so high a rating."

"During my last EVA, I burned out a fuel cell on the SciMod punching a radio beam towards the object," Hana said, as the others edged closer to the screen, trying for better looks at her mysterious contact. "I got a return in less than ninety seconds."

"Thirteen and a half million kilometers," Nicole replied almost immediately.

"Right around the corner," Ciari echoed. "Wait," he went on, struck by a thought, "if that's only thirteen mega-klicks distant, we should be able to get some pretty detailed pictures of it. The SciMod carries a built-in fifty-centimeter optical telescope, and since its computers are obviously in fine working order, we can use them to enhance the shots and get far better resolution than this."

It was the moment Hana had been waiting for. She tapped a key and the display switched to her final photo.

The silence in the Bay seemed to last forever.

Ciari was the first to speak. "Fuck," he breathed, "that's a ship!"

"A ship," Andrei repeated, with a huge smile. Then, he laughed, "A *ship*," throwing his arms into the air like a cheerleader, forgetting that he was weightless. His cheer becoming

a *whoop* of surprise as he flew away from the deck. Ciari
caught him before he crashed into the ceiling. Andrei twisted
lithely in the Marshal's grasp, grabbing him in a hearty bear
hug and kissing both his cheeks.

Then he caught sight of Nicole, and his smile faded.

"What's the matter, Nicole," he asked, trying to hold on to
the joyous moment. "That is a ship, and it appears to be coming our way. All we need do is give them a tight-beam alert
on our radio and — hey-presto — we are rescued. Correct?"

"Andrei," Hana said with deliberately exaggerated patience, "what do you think I was doing with my radio beam?
I hit that ship with as loud an electronic Mayday as I could
produce, and I've been listening for a reply every since. So
far, zilch."

"If we're to do anything," Nicole said, "we'd better do it
pretty damn quickly. We're on a convergent course and at the
rate we're closing we'll be past it in a matter of hours. Why'd
you wait so bloody long to tell us, Hana; it's almost too late!"

"I waited because I didn't know what it was," Hana flared
back at her. "Its Delta-Vee profile matched that of a starship
coming out of warp; when I backtracked its course, it led
straight out of the System, nowhere near the Outer Planets or
any Station. But it's flying a ballistic trajectory, a virtual
straight line from the moment Paul and I first picked it up.
And that track doesn't take it any deeper InSystem than we
are now! I had to be sure!" She calmed a little realizing that
she'd yelled those last words. "Don't you see. I didn't want to
get your hopes up, like they are now, only to find it was all
for nothing.

"And the courses aren't convergent, Nicole — not precisely. We're traveling below its line of flight and we'll be
crossing its track about a hundred minutes after it passes us."

"Since they don't seem inclined to acknowledge our communication," Ciari asked, "can we effect a rendezvous?"

Hana looked to Andrei: "Engineering's more your department."

"It is risky," Andrei began slowly, expressive face showing
his inner doubts and questions, "but feasible. We'll have to
dump the main frame, of course, but once that's done, the
Command Module APS should provide more than sufficient
thrust to match vectors and velocity with that vessel. How-

ever, once we separate from the Service Module, we're committed, with twenty-four hours of power and environment. This is an all or nothing decision, my friends."

Nicole spoke. "I'm afraid the question isn't simply, can we rendezvous; it's also should we?"

"Of course we should," Hana told her. "Don't be absurd."

Nicole reached past Hana and tapped a command into the keyboard. The image on the main display transmoded into a computer schematic of the contact, while a secondary screen filled with relevant data.

"It's thirteen mega-klicks away," Nicole said, "yet one look was all we needed to recognize it as a spacecraft. Think about that a moment."

"Very big," Andrei mused, looking from the data screen to the schematic and back again.

"Huge, more likely. And something else besides."

"Alien," Ciari said flatly.

"Come *on,*" Hana scoffed. "That thing's over thirty times the distance from Earth to Luna, and we're using an improvised computer set-up."

"Your pictures, your set-up—no faith?"

"I know its—and my—limitations. You can't be so certain."

"Dr. Murai," he responded with finality, "I've seen or sailed or crewed just about every class of spacecraft in operation today. Take my word for it, that vessel was not designed or constructed by human hands. Humanoid, perhaps—but not Terrestrial human beings. Not from Earth, nor any colony. *Alien.*"

Again, there was silence. Nicole had imagined countless rescue and death scenarios, but First Contact with an extraterrestrial life-form was something she hadn't anticipated. Like every cadet at the Academy and officer in NASA, she'd assumed that, sooner or later, Humanity would discover that it wasn't alone in the Universe. There were simply too many stars in the sky, too many planets near the Sol system capable of supporting human life. Somewhere there had to be a culture at least as old as our own, as advanced. Or more. Or less. But it *had* to exist.

This time, Hana broke the silence. "Wherever that ship

came from, it's beautiful. The builders were as much artists as engineers."

"A criteria for civilization?" Andrei wondered.

"Define civilization," Nicole responded quietly. "Look at us, are we civilized? Hell, as a species, we're not even house-broken."

"Profound," Ciari snorted, "but not terribly helpful."

"Have you any ideas, Nicole?" Andrei asked her.

She transmoded the display back to a real image of the starship and stroked a finger along the short, sleek curve of its visible hull. So many dangers. A misstep could have horrendous consequences.

"Like it or not," she said, "we have to make contact."

"They might not be friendly," Hana said.

She shrugged. "Have we a viable alternative?"

"Nicole, we're none of us trained in making a First Contact." Hana looked to Ciari, hoping her assumption was wrong, but he shook his head.

"You suggesting we sit tight and watch it sail by?" Nicole snapped back.

"There's more here at stake than our four lives," Ciari said. "Dr. Murai is correct, we aren't trained in First Contact. We'll be improvising, Shea, running on instinct and experience, none of which may mean shit under these circumstances. A mistake here could trigger an inter-stellar war. Can we afford to take that risk?"

"Can we afford to pass it up? We're in the boonies, Ciari; we may be the only people who know the ship is even here! If we do nothing, it may keep on going, out of the Solar System, with no one else being the wiser. My original survival plan may work. We may end up rescued. We may not. If we run the cautious program, we may be throwing away an unparalleled, once-in-a-lifetime opportunity.

"NASA—even the Air Force—is more than a new breed of soldier; we're explorers. And if that"—she pointed at the display—"doesn't represent a major chunk of our reason for being—of *my* reason for being here—then I don't know what the hell does. I say, go for it!"

"That an order, Lieutenant," Ciari asked softly, "or an opinion?"

She looked from face to face, then at the deck, finally into

Ciari's eyes. "It's an order. For the record, the decision is mine alone, and the responsibility as well. But I hope you all agree. I think the gamble's worth the risk."

"So, actually, do I," he said.

Nicole turned to Andrei and Hana.

"It's scary," Hana confessed. But she nodded assent. As did Andrei. Hana held out a hand, and Nicole took it, Hana smiling, a little sadly, Nicole thought, as she gave it a gentle squeeze. Then, Nicole faced the image on the main display.

"Okay, crew," she said, "let's get to work."

nine

SHE HEARD A dull booming sound, as if someone had whacked the outer hull with a giant sledgehammer, and then the Rover was still. For a long while, no one said a word, then Nicole heard Andrei's hushed voice crackling in her earphones.

"We made it," he breathed.

Nicole nodded, suddenly too weary to even think about cheering. A rude voice within her head groused, *why bother*. There was a stimpill dispenser built into her helmet ring, but they were a last resort. True, they would give her all the energy she needed—and then some—but the effects wouldn't last long and when they finally wore off and she crashed, she'd be out for days. Instead, she contented herself with some water.

"Status, people," she said automatically as she spread the moisture over dry lips with her tongue, hoping she didn't sound as mushy, and bitter, as she felt.

Ciari tapped some switches on the main panel, tossed a quick, comprehensive look across the scanscreens, then allowed himself a thin smile. "We've established a hard dock, Nicole," he told her. "We're hull-to-hull with the Alien spacecraft, our airlock facing what seems to be one of theirs. Magnaseals are active and registering a solid contact."

Nicole craned forward in her chair, looking up through the Rover's canopy at the looming, clifflike expanse of the Alien hull. Up close, its gleaming perfection seemed to go on forever, without flaw or break to mar its unearthly beauty. But Nicole knew that was only an illusion. She couldn't forget what she, and the others, had seen as they'd matched vectors in the *Wanderer* Command Module: a hole, seventy meters long by over twenty wide, punched through the spacecraft aft. The rim of the gash was a crazy-quilt mixture of jagged, force-twisted, heat-slagged hullmetal, all too reminiscent of what their own ship had looked like as they pulled clear. It was obvious there had been a massive internal explosion.

When she saw that hole, and realized what it meant, Nicole thought her heart would break. They'd come so far, endured so much, only to discover too late that the ship on which they'd pinned their hopes was probably as much a derelict as *Wanderer*. The damage had been on the far side of the ship from their cameras, they hadn't been aware of it until their final approach, long after their separation from the Service Module. When it was too late to go back. Her orders had brought them to this, her words had condemned them.

Angrily, she yanked at the clamps on her neck ring and pushed the helmet away, covering her face with her gloved hands as the helmet caromed off the instrument panel and disappeared behind her.

Lost in her private purgatory, she didn't feel Hana's hand on her arm, wasn't aware of Ciari turning in his chair to face the others and say, "You two go aft and check the supplies, especially the airpacks and weapons. And take your time. I'll give a yell if you're needed." They took the hint and, silently, moved off the cramped flight deck.

Ciari took a moment to unseal his own helmet before reaching out to Nicole. At his touch, surprisingly gentle, she flinched.

"Nicole," he said softly. And when she didn't answer, he tried again, a faint edge to his voice, "Nicole?"

"I heard you."

"I'm glad. What's the matter, Red?" Again, Silence. "Nicole, I want to help."

She looked at him, on the brink of tears, though she made an effort to retain her self-control. And self-respect. "I know," she told him haltingly. "I ... all of a sudden, I needed some air, and the stuff in my suit wasn't good enough. Funny — "

she faked a laugh, wiping her eyes—"the moments you discover you're a closet claustrophobe." She sighed, a brusque outrush of breath. "I was looking at that ship—the Alien—and, I dunno, everything got to me."

"For instance?"

"Like, maybe, this is all for nothing. A goddamn waste of time and effort!"

"You don't know that."

Nicole snorted and turned away. "Give me a break, Ciari! You saw that ruptured hull. Add to that the fact that they *still* haven't responded to any of our signals, even when we were transmitting from a kilometer away, with every erg of power *Wanderer* could generate. We tried radios—every frequency we could think of—lasers, spotlights, flares; if you count the noise we made in docking, we've even banged on their skin. Each time, no response. Hardly cause for optimism."

"Unwarranted assumption."

"Spare me."

"The hell I will. You want to give up."

"Part of me does, yes! I'm beat, Ben, and I'm scared. I feel like I'm supposed to be holding everything together all by myself. I'm supposed to be the rock the rest of you anchor yourselves to, the prop that holds you up, strong every frigging second of every frigging day. And I'll tell you, I figure I've been doing a pretty piss-poor pathetic job of it. I want to know who takes care of me, Marshal? Who the hell am *I* supposed to turn to?!"

"Yourself."

"Terrific. I tried that, chum; there's nothing there."

"Try harder, 'chum.' In the final analysis, that's what separates the front seats from the back, and the left from the right." He grabbed her by the shoulders and made her face him, his expression as fierce and unrelenting as Nicole had ever seen. "You're Spacecraft Commander because, deep down inside, Shea, where it counts, where it fucking *matters,* you're ruthless enough to do whatever's necessary to accomplish your mission, and strong enough to live with yourself afterward. Strong enough to carry, not merely yourself, but those around you. Your crew. You can do it, Nicole. You have to."

"No. Not anymore. Not me."

"You'd rather sit here feeling sorry for yourself?"

"I figure I'm entitled."

"Bull!" She thought for an instant he was going to strike her, but he lashed out with words instead. "You're *alive*, bitch. It's Cat and Paolo and Chagay and the entire Wolfe Clan who were atomized. Cut the cards any way you like, you've had a month's more life than they'll ever have; you have chances they never will. They bought you, and me and Hana and Andrei, that time—with their lives, Lieutenant, and you have the gall to feel sorry for yourself because of it? Because the strain of living is more than you can handle?" He tried to go on, he couldn't find the words.

Nicole looked away, "You don't pull any punches, do you?" she asked, after a time.

"Damn straight."

"When I was a kid, I used to imagine myself in the Air Force, soaring through space with the greatest of ease, battling raiders, facing down dastardly space scum, saving handsome princes—the usual heroic stuff. But in your dreams, you don't think about the fear, the pain, the cost of a mistake. I've seen friends die, Ben, and I'm face to face with the possibility—the probability—that *I* may die. And I'm terrified."

"Christ, Nicole, what makes you think you're so special? You think you're the only one who feels that way? We all saw that hole; we all know what it may mean." Ciari slipped out of his chair and around until he was in front of Nicole. "Nobody's asking for miracles, darlin'; just do your best."

The hatch chimed and Andrei stuck his head in. "My apologies if I am disturbing you," he began as Nicole waved him through, "but I wondered if you might find these useful?" Cradled in his arms were Nicole's guitar and Ciari's flute, in their traveling cases.

"What the hell are they doing here?" Nicole demanded incredulously. "I said we were to bring only essential supplies."

"These do not qualify?" Andrei wondered aloud, in absolute innocence.

Nicole stroked her fingers along the molded guitar case, itching to touch the instrument inside, and grinned hugely. "Thanks," she said, with a kiss for good measure.

She pulled off her head-liner and gave her scalp a fast,

frantic rub, hopefully clearing the last cobwebs from her still addled brain, then shook her hair back into unruly place.

She keyed the intercom. "Hana," she called, "Nicole—status?"

"Like prime cannon fodder," came the immediate reply, "I sit and wait for those great minds to whom I have entrusted my fate to determine their next move."

"'Great minds'?"

"Oh, sure. I mean, if you weren't so hot, you wouldn't be boss, right?" Then, abruptly, her bantering tone ceased. "Nicole, how are you feeling?" she asked seriously. "Is everything okay?"

"Better. As good a time as any to saddle up and take a stroll."

Ciari activated the magnaseals in his boots, his feet making a solid *click* as they touched the deck, and did some stretching exercises to settle his black Marshal's armor a little more comfortably on his body. Nicole released her harness and twisted up and around until she was floating perpendicular to him at eye level. She took hold of him and kissed him, groaning deep in her throat as he pulled her as close as their bulky suits would allow. The first kiss led to another and their senses blurred, leaving them both a little giddy, hearts racing and bodies tingling.

"Damn!" Ciari fumed, in outraged discomfort.

"What is it?" Nicole asked, worried.

"Just count yourself lucky your plumbing's different."

"Oh, Jesus, oh, Ben, I'm sorry—!" Before the sentence was finished, she was laughing.

"You're all heart, Shea," he grumbled. "Fortunately, this, too, shall pass."

"How's your suit?"

"Nominal. As usual, it's the human element that's the weak link. God, Shea, you've got me going like a teenager."

"Likewise. Why is that such a tragedy?"

"I'm not a teenager."

"Life is tough. Here's your helmet." She lowered the opaque globe over his head and snapped the latches shut. Back-stroking away from him, she killed the lights. "Scanner check, Ben."

"Infrared and radar image, nominal function," he replied.

"Low-light and normal light scan, nominal. Bio-sensors, nominal. Combat systems, on-line and nominal. The brute works like a charm."

Nicole in the lead, they made their way aft through the Jeep to the single airlock.

"Before we go," Nicole said, looking at each figure in turn, "some basic ground rules. Marshal Ciari's our pathfinder. He'll enter the Alien first and once we're aboard, he'll take the point. The rest of us stay together. No matter what happens—and I *mean* this—no one does a thing, not one blessed thing, unless I give the word. Or, should something happen to me—Marshal Ciari. We'll all be armed, but no one is to *touch* their weapon, much less use it, without a specific command from me. Until proven otherwise, these Aliens will be considered non-hostile. And we'll behave the same. We aren't going to take any chances, but we're also not going looking for trouble. Any questions?"

She turned to Ciari, whose features and expressions were hidden within the ebony helmet. "Ben, you're our heavy mob. What I said for the others goes double and more for you. No shooting unless I give the word."

"Even if I'm attacked," he asked.

Nicole nodded. "In this situation, we're expendable."

"Comforting thought," muttered Hana.

"Whenever you're ready, Ben," Nicole told him. Ciari hefted his flechette rifle, the sleek weapon looking curiously toylike and insubstantial in his gauntleted hand, and stepped into the airlock. Nicole activated a compad strapped to the left forearm of her suit, its display showing her the view from Ciari's helmet camera; reception was perfect.

After a minute, Ciari's voice crackled in Nicole's ears. She fiddled slightly with the controls on her cuff below the compad until the static faded. "I'm at the Alien's outer hatch, Nicole. You getting this?"

"Five by, Ben—sound and video."

"Good. Andrei's hunch was right; I think this is an emergency airlock. I mark it as a rectangle, three meters high by four wide. These people must be very fat, or the hatch was designed for multiple ingress. *Whoops*. Here's something interesting. See it?"

"Pictograph. They look like instructions."

"You're missing the obvious; look again."

"Eh?"

Hana edged close beside Nicole, who moved her arm to give the other woman a better view of the compad, and whistled softly in amazement. "They're humanoid," she said.

"What?!"

Hana pointed at the painted silhouette as Ciari zoomed his camera in for a close-up. "That's a gross outline," she told them, "only basic features. But see what those features are: two legs, two arms, a central torso and a head. A biped that stands erect. Like us."

"The design of the hatch seems to bear that assumption out, Nicole," Ciari echoed. "The locking mechanism is built for our kind of hand. It's a snug fit. I'd hazard they're smaller than we, or wear slimmer pressure suits. But I can manipulate it, no problem. I'm following directions and opening the hatch."

He took his time, double-checking his moves every step of the way; only after he was finished, and everyone had cut loose with a collective sign of relief, did the others realize they'd been holding their breath.

"It's open," he said unnecessarily.

Nicole chuckled. "We noticed. First impressions?"

"The dimensions of the airlock match those of the hatch itself—three by four—and my Ranger says it's seven meters deep. Pretty big. Inner hatch matches the outer. Again, there are simple pictograph instructions alongside more detailed written ones. The controls are clearly marked and conveniently placed." The radio fell silent a moment. "Now, the fun beings. I'm going to cycle the outer hatch and pump some atmosphere in here."

"Whenever you're ready," Nicole said. *Be careful,* she thought.

"Here comes the hatch," Hana reported. Ciari was counting steadily upward from zero as it closed, Nicole echoing him a beat later; that way, if there was a loss of contact on either part when the lock finally sealed, they'd know it.

"Hatch closed," Ciari announced. Nicole acknowledged and told him that both audio and visual reception had deteriorated. On the compad display, the grainy image rocked back and forth fractionally as Ciari was jostled by the starship's atmosphere flooding the chamber.

"High-pressure pumps," he said, "designed to fill this place in a hurry. Well, I'll be—!"

"What?!" Nicole demanded.

"It's *air*. Within a couple of points of Earth-normal. Pressure's lower than we're used to—the equivalent, say, of living in Denver. Oxygen content is slightly richer, though; my analyzer also registers nitrogen, carbon dioxide, water vapor and noble gasses. So far, no unknown elements or organic / microbiological compounds—*shit!*"

Without warning, the image on Nicole's compad was overwhelmed by a blinding series of colored strobe lights; at the same time, audio reception disintegrated in a deafening yowl of static.

"Ciari," Nicole yelled. *"Ben!"*

"'S'all right, boss—'m'all right," came the reply as the fierce light show vanished as suddenly as it had begun. *"Whew!* That was a treat. Hang on, I need a sec to regain my bearings. I have spots big as houses in front of my eyes."

"Your helmet polarizers didn't work?"

"Happened too fast. I'm not harmed, though. There's a gas filling the lock. I think this must be some form of decontamination process. The special effects are probably meant to stop an intruder dead in its tracks. . . ."

". . . and thereby give the crew sufficient time to prepare an appropriate welcome," Nicole finished, "as well as a comparatively tractable specimen to cope with."

"Something like that. Want me to go on?"

"No choice, Ben. We sure as hell can't go back. But stay loose."

"As always. I'm trying the inner hatch. Nope. No joy, Nicole. I'm stuck until the decontamination process runs its course."

Fifteen endless, frustrating minutes later, the inner hatch hissed sideways into its bulkhead and Ciari stepped gingerly into a well-lit, antiseptically clean corridor. The hatch automatically closed behind him, both audio and video communication suffering considerably as a result.

"Ben," Nicole called, "our picture's lousy; we can hardly

see for all the snow and interference. What do things look like
to you?"

"I'm in a corridor," he replied, speaking slowly, and carefully enunciating every word. Even so, the others had to strain
to understand him. "Its width and height are the same as the
airlock's; my Ranger scans its length as fifteen meters. There
are various modules built into the vertical bulkheads, all
labeled with pictographs as well as more detailed directions, at
least, that's what I assume they are, in the Alien language.
Aha — paydirt!" he crowed. "One of them is a suit locker. I'm
opening it. Can you see what I've found?!"

"Not very well."

"Hana and I were right. They're humanoid, and smaller
than us. Their pressure suits aren't very bulky at all; ours look
like tanks by comparison. Superb engineering. I wonder how
they did it? I wonder what they use for armor?"

"Marshal...," Nicole muttered.

"I get the hint. Moving right along. The module next door
holds portable tanks, probably air. Another module holds
medical supplies, complete with gurney. Very sensible. They
assume that anyone using an emergency airlock will probably
need assistance. I wish I could take a look at their tools.
They'd tell us a lot about them. But the surgical kit is sealed.
I think I'd better leave it be. There's another hatch at the far
end of the corridor but I don't want to proceed until the rest
of you join me. The deeper on-board I go, the worse communications gets."

"I copy," Nicole told him. "We're on our way."

"Interesting set-up," Hana said. "A double 'lock system.
They can allow someone aboard, and even treat their wounds,
without violating the integrity of the rest of the spacecraft.
Want to bet, Nicole, those two compartments are lousy with
monitors?"

"Keep your money. I don't know which would be worse,
though, an empty ship or meeting a live crew. Andrei, as soon
as we're aboard, activate the MapMaker; hopefully, it'll keep
us from getting lost." The MapMaker was a portable inertial
tracking computer; already programmed with an external plot
of the starship, it would mark their progress through the vessel, showing their position both in relation to their starting
point — the airlock — and the other hull. Literally each step

they took would be recorded in its memory banks. It was said
that the MapMaker was a foolproof guarantee against getting
lost. Nicole fervently hoped it lived up to its reputation.

Their first hours aboard were slow and uneventful. Beyond
the inner compartment was another corridor, running fore and
aft for over a hundred meters in either direction. Again, this
corridor was wide and high, designed, they concluded, for
quick, easy transit through the ship.

"Courteous of them to leave their lights on," Andrei re-
marked soon after they began their explorations.

"I hate to burst your bubble, *tovarisch,*" Ciari chuckled,
"but they didn't. My sensors registered a slight power surge as
I stepped out of the airlock; that's when the place lit up. Before that, it was as dark in here as intergalactic space."

"Have you noticed," Andrei asked, almost rhetorically,
"how similar this layout is to that of our own starcraft?"

"Basic principles of spacial engineering and physics have
to be the same," replied the Marshal. "Stands to reason the
design would follow suit."

"Y'ask me," Hana grumbled with a shake of the head and a
worried twist to her mouth, "I'd feel a whole lot more secure
if the beings who built this bucket were the traditional slithery,
slimy, tentacled, bug-eyed monsters."

"Whyever so?"

"Because, Andrei, if they look like us, and build like us,
they might also think like us, and have the same instinctive,
maybe irrational, reaction to uninvited guests."

"The 'Goldilocks Syndrome'?" Nicole asked with a grin.

"Go ahead, boss, make fun. But for a supposed derelict,
this ship is in pretty good shape."

"End of the line, all," Ciari announced from up ahead.

"Found something?" Nicole queried.

"See for yourself."

A massive hatch blocked the corridor. Like everything else
they'd seen, it was marked with both the Alien written language and their basic pictographs, stenciled across the face of
the door in garish, iridescent paint. Above the hatch, bright
lights pulsed.The meaning appeared obvious: NO ADMIT-
TANCE.

"Nicole," Ciari suggested, "activate your external re-
ceiver."

She heard nothing, and told him so. "Shift your reception range up into ultrasonic levels," he directed. And she winced as a piercing, banshee wail sliced through her skull, pulsing in sync with the lights.

"Thanks a lot," she growled, after reducing the gain.

"Sorry, really. But you see what that means, don't you? This is a blunt, basic warning—'keep away'—yet the aural component of it is pitched far higher than the human ear can hear."

"Um," Nicole murmured, stepping forward to the hatch and placing her gloved hand flat against it. "The door's coated with a thin sheen of ice. I wouldn't be surprised if the far side is a hard, cold vacuum."

"Open to space?" Hana asked.

"Yah. There's a cross-corridor twenty meters back; let's head down there. I'd like to find some living quarters and control centers."

"Nicole," Andrei said, "a reminder—these are fifty kilosec airpacks. We have another fifty-pack apiece cached at the air-lock with the rest of the supplies. After that, we either breathe the local atmosphere or return to the Command Module for more."

"Hana, your responsibilities are LifeSystems; anything nasty in the air?"

"Not really my field, Nicole, and these scanners can only handle a basic analysis."

"I know that. But have you found anything to dispute Marshal Ciari's initial findings?"

Hana shook her head.

They moved forward now, their steps taking them towards the central core of the starship. As they went, they discovered that the line of sealed bulkheads moved with them, slashing diagonally across the heart of the great vessel. When they finally finished charting its progress, Andrei figured that roughly half the starcraft lay open to space.

The flight deck proved to be a surprise, a strange mixture of pragmatic design and sensual indulgence. There were seven primary control stations: four side-by-side along the forward-most lateral bulkhead, then two more set four meters behind them, flanking a massive central console built on a low dais so that it stood higher than the others. These three formed an equilateral triangle and in the space between them was a huge sphere, four meters in diameter, half its bulk above deck level, half below. It was a hologram tank, now deactivated and dark, looking for all the world like a giant fortune teller's crystal ball.

There were secondary consoles lining the rear bulkhead, on either side of the open airlock through which the four astronauts entered. Just behind what they all assumed was the Command Console—the one in the center of the bridge—was a circular opening in the deck with a fireman's pole set in the middle of it, leading down to a subordinate compartment. Ciari turned himself upside down and, rifle pointing the way, swam down to scout it out.

"Neat as my father's study," Andrei commented. No one argued the point, though Nicole thought, *too neat,* and felt a cold trickle of fear at the base of her spine.

"They can't have expected an explosion of that magnitude," she said, mostly to herself, as the three of them spread out through the compartment. Andrei unclipped his Hasselblad camera from its chest harness and began shooting pictures of everything in sight, while Hana leaned over a console, jumping back as a scanscreen flared to life, flashing a stream of incomprehensible data at her before switching off again.

"Didyouseethat," she yelped, making the sentence a single word.

"Whatever else one can say about this vessel," Andrei told Nicole gravely, "it is not dead."

"And if the ship isn't," Nicole nodded, "What right have we to assume the crew is? Everything we've seen is as tidy as if she'd just left on her maiden voyage. Look at this flight deck, for Christ's sake! Regardless of what happened, enough of the crew remained alive to clean house and ensure that the functioning on-board systems maintained perfect or near-perfect operation."

"Maybe they had cleaning robots?" Hana suggested.

"Seen any?"

"Good domestics are, by their very nature, discreet. And maybe it's their day off?"

Nicole snorted. Andrei looked at his chronometer and announced: "Fifteen kilosecs left on these airpacks, Nicole. A little over four hours. We should consider returning soon to the airlock for our reserves."

"I copy, Andrei. Ben, anything below?"

"Lots more consoles, what look like active automatic monitoring systems. Damned if I've a notion what they're monitoring, though; life support, environment, power? They must have had one helluva fire. An entire wall is scorched, together with a bank of consoles, a couple of them completely gutted."

"Okay. We'll try to puzzle out the mysteries on the flip side. Come on up. We're going back for our spares."

She wasn't expecting trouble. The starship was so huge, so empty; subconsciously, they'd all started believing that it was deserted, as much a derelict as *Wanderer*.

The first Nicole knew of anything wrong was when Ciari's hushed, overly calm and controlled voice came over the combat / scrambler circuit of her suit, for her ears only; Hana and Andrei didn't hear a thing as they kept happily poking and puttering about, more excited by their explorations than they'd dare let on.

"Nicole," Ciari hissed, "don't make a move. Not one. Freeze."

"What is it?"

"Have the others freeze. Then you pivot real, *real* slow. And whatever you do, woman, please do not make even a hint of a move towards your gun."

Nicole thought she'd felt heart and guts turn to ice before, but those sensations were nothing compared to what she experienced now as she realized what had to have occurred for Ciari to talk and act like this. She tapped her chin gently against the com control inside her helmet, activating the ALL HANDS / SCRAMBLED circuit.

"On my mark," she said, marveling at how normal she sounded, *"freeze!"* She breathed a sigh of thanks as her people did as they were told.

"What is it, Nicole?" Hana asked.

"Dunno. But I'm about to find out. Just stay loose and stay frozen—and wish me luck."

Wondering, absurdly, if her next move would get them all killed, Nicole tapped her foot gently against the casing of the Command Console. Slowly, her weightless body spun clockwise towards the rear of the flight deck. Her hands were by her sides; she left them there, painfully aware that her right hand was within centimeters of her holstered pistol.

She saw Ciari, half in, half out of the deck opening, his back to her, and then she saw what stood beyond him. For a moment, her mind refused to function, only instinct prompting her to shift her left leg slightly, snagging her boot against the console's base to brake her spin. For eight hours, they'd wandered the length and breadth of the Alien starship, wondering what its masters looked like and what had happened to them. Now, in a sense, both questions had been answered.

The Aliens lined the rear bulkhead, most of them concentrated in and around the airlock, barely two meters from Ciari. They were armed and, if looks meant anything, they were very, very angry.

ten

NICOLE'S FIRST THOUGHT was that the Aliens looked cute.

They were smaller than human norms. The bigger ones—Nicole assumed they were the males—averaged about a hundred seventy centimeters in height, the females roughly a hundred fifty. But what the males lacked in stature, they made up for in bulk. Their bodies were broad and hard, sleek muscles rippling under snug uniforms. They watched Nicole and Ciari with painful, unwavering intensity, and Nicole was certain that their strength and speed probably matched the best the astronauts had to offer.

They were a feline race, their features dominated by great, almost luminous eyes. Their faces and, Nicole presumed, their bodies underneath their clothes, were covered by a very fine layer of fur, increasing in length and thickness around their heads, much like human hair. Nicole noted patterns to the fur, subtle and distinct variations in color laid out in a myriad of designs, each unique. *Are the designs natural or artificial?* she wondered. *Perhaps they can change them the same way we get our hair styled?*

The ears were small and elegantly formed, set back and partway down the sides of the skull, their tips rising to sharp, curved points, and the fur around them was styled so that they blended in. The noses were broad, as with the Terrestrial cats Nicole had known all her life, but their faces were no more prominent in relation to those small mammals than Nicole's was in relation to her own simian forebears. Their mouths looked as mobile and expressive as Nicole's own.

With a start, she realized that, even at a casual glance, she had no trouble telling the Aliens apart; they were as distinctly individual as human beings.

One of them—a female, shorter and slighter than Hana yet possessing an innate sense of dignity and force of will that reminded Nicole of General Canfield—stepped forward. A big male caught her arm, snarling something in a low, rumbling voice and gesturing towards the astronauts; the female hissed back, breaking his grip easily as she faced Nicole and Ciari.

"Nicole," Hana called on the scrambled command circuit, "what's happening? I feel like a sitting duck here."

Nicole saw a slight stir among the Aliens, heads moving, whispers exchanged, looks flashing at her and Hana. *Christ,* she thought, *they're picking up our signals!*

"You *are* a sitting duck, dummy," Nicole replied in a hurried whisper, moving her lips as little as possible. "Make a move and we're history. We're in the middle of the 'Goldilocks Syndrome'..."

"Hei!"

"Exactly. Deep in it. Stay frozen and stay quiet—they can hear us—till I give the word. Copy?"

"Copy. Good luck, Nicole."

She allowed herself the smallest of smiles, thankful now she'd worn a transparent helmet instead of one of the opaque, gold-anodized models. The Aliens could see her as much as she could see them, which meant they had at least some idea of the physical nature of their surprise guests. And that, Nicole fervently hoped, might make them a little less suspicious and trigger-happy. *Heaven only knows,* she thought, *what they make of Ciari, all in black. Have they scanned him? Do they figure he's some robot?*

The female was looking at her. Nicole met that gaze, looking her up and down with equal intensity. Her fur was silver, high-lighted by patterns of indigo that were beautiful in their stark, pure simplicity. Her hair was longer than that of her companions, curving down her neck and back like a leonine mane. She wore a close-fitting, one-piece shipsuit of some silken material that managed to be both functional and attractive. It was short-sleeved, the indigo designs continuing down her arms to her hands. There were various patches on the suit, Nicole assuming that they corresponded to the insignia attached to her pressure suit. Like all her companions, the female had no tail; unlike them, she was unarmed.

She took a step forward and opened her arms, palms empty, held facing Nicole.

Nicole swallowed, swallowed again, and slowly stepped away from the Command Console, into the full view of the Aliens.

"Nicole?" Ciari said softly.

"Can you see me, Ben?"

"Affirmative. Be real careful how you move. The one out front looks cool, but some of the clowns in the background are very edgy."

"Thanks. They know we're talking."

"I know."

"I'm dropping my gunbelt."

First, she mimicked the female's moves, lifting her arms away from her body and opening her hands, palms facing outward. Then, with infinite care, she reached her left hand towards the buckle of her equipment belt. The Aliens reacted immediately, one of them bringing a riflelike weapon up. Nicole wanted to close her eyes, positive that in another split second, she was going to die. Ciari didn't move a muscle— even though, in his powered armor, he could have cut the opposition to pieces in the blink of an eye. The humans were the intruders here; they had to prove to the Aliens that they were friendly, and could be trusted.

Before the warrior could bring his weapon fully to bear, however, the female blocked it with a hand, using a blinding speed that brought a silent whistle of awe to Nicole's lips. The female snarled at the offending male, then turned on the others to snarl at them. Backs stiffened and fur ruffled under the obvious tongue-lashing, but when it was done, pistols returned to their holsters and rifles stayed at rest. Another command sent them off the flight deck, swimming fast, and with incredible grace, through the air, to be replaced by a trio of warriors clad in what had to be the Alien equivalent of combat armor.

"Ter*rif*ic," Nicole breathed. Her arms and hands ached with the tension of keeping them frozen in position, and she grimaced as she realized that her palms were wet. She had itches she didn't dare scratch and the more she tried not to think about how uncomfortable she felt, the worse those feelings became.

The female positioned her warriors so that their weapons could easily cover the entire compartment; simultaneously, the massive internal airlock cycled closed, sealing them inside. Then, the female turned back to Nicole, resuming her hands out, palms open stance.

Automatically, Nicole thanked her with a smile and a nod of the head. The female cocked her own head, looking at her sideways in a quizzical gesture that was pure cat; Nicole had to fight to keep her smile from exploding into a full-fledged laugh. *Be serious, idiot,* she raged silently, *be* professional! *There's too much at stake to screw up now.*

She took a breath, grateful for the Zen training given her both at the Academy Earthside and by Ciari aboard *Wanderer,* to calm herself and center her thoughts once more, and then reached towards her belt buckle. She opened it and pushed the belt free; now, she too, was unarmed. None of the four Aliens reacted.

Instead of returning her hand to her side, she reached across to the airpack controls on her right forearm; a touch of a switch closed the connections. All she had to breathe was the ambient air within her suit; in less than a minute, she'd be suffocating.

"Ben," she said, unable to keep a small quaver out of her voice, "I've shut down my airpack."

His initial reply was silence.

"I'm going to try the Alien atmosphere."

"We've only done a basic scan, remember?"

"And what do we do when our airpacks run out?"

"This breaks every quarantine rule in the book."

She chuckled, a little ruefully. "Show me the alternative, chum. But be quick about it; the air in here is getting a bit stuffy."

She rested her hands on the seal ring at the base of her helmet. The female never took her eyes off her, and Nicole sensed that she understood what was being done. One of the

warriors gestured and started forward, but the female waved
him back. Evidently, she was willing to take the same risk as
Nicole.

She yanked the latches open, then twisted the helmet off
her head. For a moment, even starved for oxygen as she was,
she couldn't help holding her breath.

The air smelt of cinnamon, a tangy, wind-blown scent that
reminded her of a summer spent camping in the Grand Tetons.
She smiled reflexively; it tasted good. The female's expression remained unchanged—serious, alert, intensely watchful.
Her attitude sobered Nicole instantly.

"Status, Nicole," Ciari demanded.

"Fine so far," she told him. She lowered her hands, leaving
her helmet to float in midair, and took a step towards the
female, who moved as well, until they stood face to face, a
meter apart. Her nostrils flared as Nicole approached. *Her
sense of smell must be more sensitive than ours,* Nicole
thought; *the ears are roughly the same size as ours, but
they're shaped so differently. Are they more sensitive, too? I
wonder how much that sensoral input influences—consciously
or subconsciously—her decision-making?*

There was an impatient *beep* from the Command Console,
the sudden sound making Nicole flinch in surprise. The female acknowledged the call from one of the subordinate consoles along the aft bulkhead and listened intently as a torrent
of indecipherable noise erupted from an unseen speaker. As
Nicole watched, the female visibly relaxed. Nicole assumed
she was hearing good news. Call finished, she pointed to Ciari
and motioned that he remove his helmet as well.

"Nicole?" he asked.

"Do it."

"May I have some help?"

"Y'know," Nicole said as she moved into position behind
Ciari, "I lay odds that call was a medical report. Our scans
told us that their atmosphere and environment was safe for us.
That lady was probably acting as a guinea pig to determine the
reverse, if we were safe for them."

"Dumb move, if she's in charge. Captains shouldn't be
cannon fodder."

"A calculated risk." Nicole's voice took on a bitter edge.
"Like Cat took over Wolfe's." She flipped the latches on

Ciari's helmet but before pulling it free, she told him: "Lay your rifle on the deck, Ben—nice and slow."

"Understood."

"Smile, m'love; we're probably on camera." Gently, Nicole removed the massive, opaque globe, the Alien female's head canting once more sideways as she shifted position for a better look at him.

Ciari smiled at her, which, after a moment's reflection, the Alien returned. Nicole wondered if it meant the same to both cultures.

The female spoke over her shoulder to the warriors. The central one objected. At least, that's what Nicole assumed, because as he spoke, the female's spine straightened perceptibly, her mane stiffening as she rounded on him, cutting loose with a short, clipped speech. There was no mistaking the exchange. She was boss and she wasn't going to tolerate insubordination from anyone. She glared furiously at the warrior until, with a stiff, disjointed motion that told Nicole and Ciari he was as angry as his commander, he turned his obedience into an eloquently silent protest, and lowered his own weapon to the deck. His companions followed suit; unlike the two Terrans, however, they didn't remove their helmets.

"You get the feeling they don't quite trust us?" Nicole hissed under her breath.

"Would you, if positions were reversed? At least we've made a beginning."

The female, again facing Nicole, hesitantly reached out towards the young woman's face. Nicole couldn't help noticing that her fingernails, thicker and heavier than their human counterparts, had been shaped and filed to a wicked point. Nasty. A hefty swipe could probably take off half her face.

Her touch so light Nicole barely felt it, the Alien stroked her smooth cheek, her lips, the lines around her eyes. Those last moments were the worst, the claws so close that Nicole couldn't focus on them. She tried to remain relaxed and unconcerned, but her mind kept flashing to all the awful schlock-horror films she'd seen as a kid.

The female sensed the conflict within her, confirmed it by momentarily laying her warm palm against Nicole's throat, to feel her pulse, and turned her attention to Ciari. She touched him the same way, comparing the difference in facial texture, stroking the bristly tips of his beard, his much longer hair, looking searchingly from one astronaut to the other, finally muttering to herself as she floated back to where she'd been. The examination, innocuous as it had turned out to be, had proved as hard on Ciari as Nicole; his face was sheened with a fine layer of sweat and his teeth were clenched, the cords of his neck stretched taut.

The female smiled at Nicole, speaking quietly in her incomprehensible language, trying to convey as much with tone of voice and expression as words. She waved a hand towards the other two, still "frozen," astronauts and mimed removing a helmet. Nicole got the message.

She tapped on the command circuit with her chin. "Heads up, troops," she told them calmly, "on my mark, unfreeze and execute a one-eighty pivot, so you're facing me. Keep your hands in full view and away from your weapons. When you've finished your turns, unseal and remove your helmets. I want no unnecessary chatter and if you don't like what you see, keep it to yourselves. At the moment, everything's fine, but we're not out of the woods yet. By a longshot. Copy?"

Both acknowledged.

"That's the spirit, me buckos," Nicole grinned. "Get ready, here it comes: three, two, one—break!"

Nothing happened. The two had resembled statues before; they did so now. Then, Andrei carefully straightened himself to his full height, waiting for Hana to follow suit before turning. She flashed a grin at Nicole, but it faded almost instantly as she saw the Aliens. Watching them, Nicole caught a sudden gleam of excitement in Andrei's eyes, reminding her of the sense of wonder she'd felt since childhood whenever she stared up at the stars. The air was clearly a delight to them, too.

Next, it was the warriors' turn. When their heads were bare, the female moved around Nicole to the Command Console, flicked a switch, said something, and all eyes went aft as the lock cycled open. The passageway beyond was more crowded than ever, the forward rank of warriors armed and armored, ready for a fight. But a sentence from the female made them put up their weapons. She faced Nicole and Ciari, smiled cautiously, and gestured that they leave the flight deck.

She started for the lock, pausing when she realized that they weren't following.

Nicole tossed her head and pushed off after her. "C'mon, people," she said. "Let's do as the lady says. I think things are going to be all right."

And so they were. The Terrans were given private quarters on one of the personnel decks and, while they were chaperoned whenever they left those quarters, almost no restrictions were placed on their movements. Nicole took full advantage of that freedom, wandering every corridor, exploring every compartment. She and the others donned their pressure suits once more, to help the Aliens stretch an airtight membrane across the hull breach—an extraordinarily resilient transparency that reminded all four astronauts of sticking plastic wrap over an open container to seal the food in and prompted its share of rude comments and hearty laughs. Nicole wondered if the Aliens wondered what the hell was happening to their "guests." Aboard, she watched maintenance teams restore atmosphere to the ruptured sections, crawled with them into cramped ductways as they checked and repaired what seemed like miles of fiber-optic cabling. Her curiosity was as inexhaustible as her energy; she had no idea how long she'd been going without food or rest until she rejoined the others and discovered she hadn't seen them in over a day. She still felt no need to rest and was satisfied by a quick bite of munchies— part of the supplies they had brought over from what was left on *Wanderer*. She was too excited, too charged up with a wild sense of wonder and discovery. No kid trapped in Santa's toy shop ever felt so happy. The others had been doing much the same and when they finally sat down to compare notes, they were surprised at how much they'd learned, simply by observation, coupled with an improvised pidgin sign language.

A day after their arrival, they transhipped the remainder of their salvagable equipment and personal effects over from *Wanderer* and cast the Command Module loose, using the last of its fuel to send it curving away from the starship. Nicole stood by the Command Console, next to the Alien female —who, for convenience, she'd begun thinking of as "Captain"—watching on a display till it was out of sight. She wasn't even aware of any tears until Ciari offered a handkerchief and she flushed with embarrassment. She was the Captain's equivalent for *Wanderer* and here she was, bawling like a baby. Some impression she was making. Hopefully, the others were doing better.

"Incredible," Andrei exclaimed over dinner after a tour of the starship's engineering levels. "Absolutely incredible." He was so caught up in his enthusiasm that he lapsed into rapid-fire Russian.

"Enjoyed yourself, did you, *tovarisch?*" Ciari asked him, in the same tongue.

"*Da.*" He shifted back to English. "If I were religious, I might say I had died and gone to heaven."

"We all feel pretty much the same, pal," Nicole said with a chuckle. "What did you find?"

"Their primary power source — it is a faster-than-light system that appears analogous to our own Baumier Drive.

"I must say," he continued, "that membrane is incredible! They had a sample piece and I couldn't cut it — couldn't even scratch it. Though I do not see how it could possibly withstand the stresses of a WarpSpace transition..."

"Forget the membrane," Nicole told him between bites of a sandwich. "Tell us about the drive. You say it resembles Baumier's?"

"I'd stake my life on it."

"That's not saying much."

"Belt up, Hana," Nicole snapped, her expression belying her tone. "This is serious. Go on, Andrei."

"It isn't a one-to-one match, of course, any more than are engines and airframes constructed by different companies, with different design philosophies. But just as those different designs are derived from the same basic set of physical principles, so this alien FTL powersystem derives from the same principles and givens as our own Baumier Drive."

"Stands to reason," Ciari added. "The Baumier Drive is a remarkably efficient means of flitting about the galaxy. It's also surprisingly simple. If we could do it, why not someone else?"

"Why not, indeed," Nicole agreed. "Can we help them in any way," she asked Andrei, "any more than we already have?"

The Russian shrugged. "Fitting the membrane was — if you'll pardon me — an idiot procedure, a simple matter of directing and applying brute force, bodies with muscles, few brains required. To do more, we need to be able to talk with them. Our pidgin is a beginning but it's far too imprecise. So, regrettably, until we truly learn each other's language—the details of meaning, the critical nuances—we'd be whistling in the wind. Control procedures, circuitry, fuel feed systems, computers, converter assembly, take your pick. I can tell you what should happen when the right buttons are pressed, I just don't know the right buttons."

"It's worse than a Westerner trying to learn Chinese or Japanese." Hana sighed, stretching full-length in midair with a sinuous grace that reminded Nicole of the Captain. "Not merely a matter of learning new words, but a completely different set of sounds that the human throat may not even be capable of reproducing. I'm not saying we shouldn't try, but we might as well accept that in the end it's going to take the best linguistics computer available and probably months of work, at the very least, to make sense out of their gobbledygook."

"What about a common basis in mathematics?"

"I think I've got them to the point of comprehending our basic numerical structure, and I may be getting a handle on theirs. But it's a real misery when their simplest sentences sound like a godawful cat fight."

Laughter rippled around the room as the others sympathized with Hana's lament.

"I like their outfits, though," she said, sliding her hands down the sides of her shipsuit. "Smooth as silk, comfy as cotton, you lot should give it a try."

"You're the adventurous one."

Hana flipped a wing of hair off Nicole's forehead, a casual unexpectedly intimate gesture. "And you need a haircut." She pushed for the door. "I'm for another tour on the flight deck before I crash. Maybe my colleagues and I will make a quantum jump to multiplication. See ya!"

Nicole found the two men looking at her. "What's going on?" she demanded.

"Nothing," Andrei said hurriedly.

"Not a thing," Ciari echoed.

"Minds in the goddamn gutter," Nicole muttered furiously.

"If you say so."

"What's that supposed to mean? What the hell's your problem, Ciari?"

"Nothi . . . ," he began, then thought better of it. "You want to know my problem, Shea. It's that nothing has changed. Yes, we're on a live ship, but it's got warp engines it doesn't dare use and sub-light systems that are so much freeform slag. We're stuck on a ballistic trajectory that's taken us as deeply In-System as it's going to and for safety's sake we can't risk broadcasting for at least a month, the same situation we faced on *Wanderer.* Our felinoid friends—assuming they really are friends, which is not as foregone a conclusion as we'd like to believe—may have heavy weaponry on this bucket but it won't do much good because they can't maneuver."

"You think we will need it, Marshal?" Andrei asked him.

"If we could spot this starship with the jury-rigged, piss-poor systems aboard *Wanderer,* others can, too."

"Like the raiders."

Ciari nodded. "When I'm feeling fanciful, Nicole, I say 'like Space Command.' U.S. or Russian. I guess I've gotten too old for fancy."

There was a deliberate double meaning to his last words and Nicole sensed it was directed at her.

"Reason?" she asked.

"Those bastards who nailed us are too good. No way they'd pass up a plum like this. I sure as hell wouldn't. If for no other reason than to make up for the loss of Wolfe's claim." As Ciari spoke, Nicole felt herself grow still and cold inside —not with fear, the icy tension she'd felt on the Alien flight deck or during the approach to the derelict *Rockhound* so many weeks ago, but rage. And her face took on a grim, indomitable cast that caught even Ciari's attention. It was something he'd sensed, and nurtured, but never seen before. The wolf. The lion. The eagle. The huntress. As he was a hunter.

"An hour doesn't pass when I don't think of what happened, you know that," she said. "I've gone over every detail of that engagement, picking them apart, analyzing what we did right, and wrong, searching for a reason why. I have answers. But the more the pieces fit together, the more terrible it becomes."

"Care to share?"

"That ambush was no accident, Ben," she said softly. "We were set up."

"Explain."

"We come across Phillip Wolfe's derelict spacecraft. Surface evaluation indicates an accident but with a little digging we discover indications of something more sinister. So we decide to check out his mining claim. Logical course of action, especially considering that he and Major Garcia are old friends. We show up at said claim, along with another vessel that knows not only Air Force recognition codes but intimate details about Cat as well. Boom—we're hit. And if Cat and Paolo and the Bear hadn't sacrificed themselves, we'd have bought the farm, right then and there.

"Rockhound's the key. If we hadn't found Wolfe's trashed ship, we'd have continued blithely on to Pluto, leaving the raiders free to strip Wolfe's rock to the core and skip clean with none of us the wiser."

"As you say, Nicole, *Rockhound* is the key. Could it not have been an accident?"

"Not a chance, Andrei. Stands to reason, if the raiders wanted Wolfe's claim, they'd eliminate him. But why, in the process, go to so much trouble to create such a plausible wreck? Why not simply atomize *Rockhound*? That's their most sensible course of action. I mean, why make unnecessary trouble for yourself?" She looked to Ciari for confirmation. He nodded.

"That's the standard MO, Andrei," he said.

"Conclusion—they *wanted* us at Wolfe's asteroid. With a suspicion of something wrong but insufficient hard evidence to justify summoning a legit backup. And why? To destroy us. Nothing else makes sense."

"That makes no sense," Andrei protested. "Why go to such trouble and expense for us? A milkrun, a training flight. Being caught up in a situation—a shootout—that, I understand. But deliberate murder—of *us?!* Absurd!"

"I agree. That's what's been driving me nutso." Her voice broke off as Ciari lunged for the door, shoving Andrei violently aside, and wrenched it open. The others piled into the corridor after him in time to see a slightly built female Alien disappear around a T-junction down the passage with Ciari close behind.

"Damn, they're fast," he growled a minute later as he rejoined them.

"What the hell was that all about," Nicole demanded.

"Every time I turn around lately, there seems to be a cat standing close by with some kind of portable hand-held module pointing in my direction. And the moment they realize they've been spotted, they scoot. Or disappear into a crowd. I grant you, maybe they're naturally nervous. Or shy. They're certainly curious. Those critters could be taking pictures, just like we did when we came aboard. Unfortunately, cops are naturally paranoid. While you were talking, I noticed the door was open a fraction. Except that I recalled closing it after Hana left. Sure enough, right outside was that Alien, with a module."

"I've noticed that, too," Nicole nodded, "though they hadn't made anywhere near as great an impression on me."

"Remote scans for their data banks?" Andrei suggested.

"Anything's possible."

"If they're up to no good, Ben, there isn't a helluva lot we can do about it."

"Dynamite legend for our tombstones, Shea. Right up there with Cat's 'take care, y'all.' "

"On occasion, Marshal, you're a righteous prick."

"I'm alive. I'd like us all to stay that way."

Their dead-end corridor ended in a T-junction with a wider, longer hall and as they turned back to their door, Hana poked her head around the corner and called excitedly to them.

"You pass an Alien?" Ciari asked her, adding a detailed description of the one he'd seen only for a moment.

"About a hundred meters along," she replied, "heading UpShip. Why?"

Nicole told her and with that slight prodding, Hana too realized she'd been under surveillance. She wasn't surprised and even less bothered, noting that she'd probably do no less were circumstances reversed.

She led them to a large, mostly open room. In its center was the biggest hologram field Nicole had ever seen and that first look made her gasp in astonishment. There was no sense that she was looking at an image; for the seconds it existed, the projection was another reality, so complete she tried once to touch it, to convince herself it *was* illusion. The three-dimensionality was perfect. The first picture was a beach scene and as she floated around it, the perspective changed, so that she moved into the surf, looking down the beach towards a cliff-lined horizon that faded naturally into daylight haze, flinching instinctively as a large wave crested past her. Then, she was out in the open ocean, grinning in delight at the sight of her friends standing on what appeared to be a splendid white sand beach. She looked up, and had to cover her eyes with her hands, squinting her lids almost completely shut, to protect herself from the glare of a star significantly brighter than Earth's Sol. Hotter, too—there was an environmental sub-routine operating within the holo field—and she felt sweat prickle her skin, heard strange cries as even stranger birds circled overhead, smelled the familiar salt tang of the sea. That, at least, these two worlds had in common. The only thing missing was the physical feel of water, and for that she was supremely grateful, considering she was probably in way over her head. At which point the ocean hissed and boiled nearby and something huge broke surface with a nerve-shattering roar, baring a mouth that was easily big enough to swallow her whole and jagged teeth well able to rip her to shreds. Reflex action threw Nicole backward head over heels, pinwheeling through air—and holo field—her spin dunking her head underwater, for an equally terrifying sight of an iridescent body ten times her size, with giant flukes and wickedly barbed spines. Then, Nicole spun into the air again, flailing like an idiot in a vain attempt to regain her equilibrium. By her next spin, she'd reached the land, which did her no good at all, because that solid ground was as much an illusion as the ocean and she spun through it just as easily, a few seconds of absolute darkness before she popped into bright sunlight again and, finally, into Ciari's arms. Her heart was thundering, but not loudly enough to drown the sound of laughter from her crew.

Indeed, once she'd calmed a little, she couldn't help but join in at the memory of how she'd looked coming ashore. Ciari, bless him, held her close, letting her draw what strength and comfort she needed. She thanked him with a slight nuzzle of lips against the hollow of his throat and a slighter kiss, acknowledged with an equally slight tightening of his embrace.

"Godalmighty," she said, her voice still shaky, "did you *see* that monster."

"Not too shabby," Hana commented.

"They have sharks," Ciari said, releasing Nicole, who took a moment to restore herself to a semblance of normality.

Hana made a disparaging noise; obviously, she disagreed. "Or Orcas," she said thoughtfully. "Killer whales."

"Intelligence?" Ciari asked, understanding her reference.

"Impossible to say, Marshal, but that was the most expressive face I've ever seen on any sea-faring creature."

"You're anthropomorphizing."

"Maybe. Be fun to find out, though."

The scene changed, to a stark mountain range, snow-capped peaks glittering diamondlike in the dawn sun, the air shivering with the rumble of a distant avalanche. Next was a forest, plants with wild, incredible shapes and colors that took their collective breaths away. Trees—or what passed for them —towered overhead, branches blocking the sun and reducing the ground to a perpetual twilight. They sensed a multitude of fragrances, not all of them pleasant, but saw no signs of animal life. Nicole kicked herself off the deck, but she hit the roof of the compartment before she'd passed through the bottommost tier of branches. While still in the forest, the seasons changed. Leaves burned bright with autumn's colors—a variety and intensity that put Nicole's New England home to shame—and the ground was buried in snow higher than the astronaut's heads. Even with the trees stripped to their bare branches, they could barely see the sky. They found themselves in a wild, empty land, and then before a waterfall plunging what appeared to be miles from the crest of a magnificent escarpment. They saw polar caps and an island covered with equatorial jungle. Even Ciari was caught up in the wonder of discovery, this unparalleled opportunity to explore a completely new world, and they lost all track of time as they explored each projection, calling out their observations and excitedly comparing notes.

"A wondrous travelogue," Andrei noted, while a howling blizzard made them instinctively huddle together, even though they felt only the barest hint of its fury.

"Okay, sourpuss," Hana grumped back at him, "we're seeing what they want us to see, does that really matter? We're still learning."

"Oh, they're certainly being very free with views of their world," Andrei agreed. "But don't forget, Hana, I am the child of a society that views the control of information by the State as paramount. As a consequence, we become quite adept at reading 'between the lines.'

"What have we seen," he asked, "really? Wild lands. For all we know, parks. And never on a clear night, when we could see their sky and thereby get a sense of where their planet is. We have never seen their Moon. Do they have one? Two? Any? Where do these people live, and how? Are there cities, technological centers, manufacturing ones? We have been given a sense of their world, not their society."

"Not completely," Nicole said. "assuming they're feeding us accurate data, the air is clean. We've seen very little unnatural haze, which we would if they were extensively burning fossil fuels for power, and it's sweeter than anything I can remember on Earth."

"The question is, why are they doing this?" Andrei wondered.

"Test."

"How do you mean, Ben?"

"You've brought four strangers aboard, representatives of a presumably unknown, but technologically equivalent, culture. You want a sense of what kind of people they are. So, you turn them loose in a sort of playground. How do they respond to the situations they're thrown into, how do they interact? Are they a strict hierarchy, or loose and relaxed? Give them an opportunity to play and sufficient time to allow them to drop their guard, so we can see them as they really are. If they don't drop their guard, that's an answer, too."

"Wonder how we scored?" Nicole asked, mostly to herself.

The room changed again, returning to a beach scene, though not the one that had been manifested originally. The sun hung low in the offshore sky, which they arbitrarily christened "west," painting it with reds and oranges and purples and a wild streak of green. The atmosphere wasn't as blue as Earth's, there was just the barest hint of color to it when the sun was high. The beach, and land beyond, stretched away flat to the south, but rose steeply in the other direction to a

towering, rocky bluff that loomed like a minor mountain over
their heads. All of them noted a winding path etched into its
side, rising to the top, which they could clearly see but which
they were equally convinced would turn out to be above the
ceiling, just like the roof of the forest. From nowhere, a
cheery bonfire materialized on the sand, in the lee of a small
bluff that protected them from the evening breeze, and they
hunkered down around it, enjoying the phantom warmth, Nicole smiling in appreciation as Hana waxed eloquent about the
capabilities of this projection system. She caught Ciari's eyes,
gave him a silent signal, and he left them, to return minutes
later with their instruments.

"The fire, the sun, the sea," she told the others as she tuned
her guitar, "it's too good an opportunity to waste." They responded with grins and arranged themselves comfortably
against soft stools scattered around the room, that, disguised
by the holo field, appeared to be hummocks and drifts on the
beach. Hana snuggled close to Nicole while Ciari kept his
distance, facing her an arm's length away. Andrei stretched
full-length on the far side of the flames, gazing up at the
darkening sky.

Ciari started with Bach's Partita Number 3, and Nicole
quickly joined in. They segued smoothly to Mozart and then
Nicole broke the mood by launching into the wildest, raun-
chiest rock-and-roll song she could remember. Hana was on
her feet instantly, dancing up a storm, madcap poetry in motion as she boogied weightlessly over to Andrei and pulled
him up to join her. The sun touched the horizon, atmospheric
parallax trebling its size, clouds scudding across the ocean, far
out to sea, suddenly rimmed with fire. So much of the moment, the setting, was illusion, that Nicole didn't blink an eye
as Paul appeared laughing before her, applauding her performance with a wryly mocking tilt to his eyebrows that
warned her not to let this acclaim go to her head. Her con-
science, as she'd been his. He loved the ocean as much as she,
but always lamented the fact that American beaches, and the
women who roamed them, were so much tamer than those of
his birthplace, Rio de Janeiro. Just last year, his father had
been named Ambassador to Brazil and the pair of them had
gone to visit during their post-graduation leave. *How, oh how,
am I going to tell him Paolo's dead*, Nicole thought and at-

tacked her tears, this resurgence of a grief she knew would never completely pass, with another Lila song. Paul had introduced her to all his favorite haunts and by the end of their two-week stay she'd become as relaxed and uninhibited as any *carioca*—a transformation that amazed them both, because neither thought she had it in her.

Now, it was Ciari's turn to break the mood, by playing a quiet, rueful folk song, a Newfoundland sailor's lament about being far from home in a strange sea, bound for an unknown port, a yearning both for these undiscovered harbors and for the loved ones left behind. Andrei knew the words and filled the air with them, his perfect voice sending chills up Nicole's spine. The sun was gone, the sky a velvet dome above their heads. For the first time, she beheld the stars of the Aliens' home. There were dual shadows on the sand—those cast by the firelight combined with a fainter one going the other direction, thrown by the full moon that had just risen in the East. It appeared bigger than Earth's satellite, though Nicole had no way of telling whether it was due to actual size or its being closer than the Moon is to its primary, and she knew that it would mean horrendous tides. Her eyes drifted down from the pock-marked face of the Alien moon, and found shadows that hadn't been there before. Aliens, at least a score, a fair chunk of the surviving crew, lined along the wall, some standing, some crouched or sitting, some together as couples or trios, an occasional quartet, very few alone. They were watching the four Terrans and, Nicole noticed, listening to their impromptu concert. When Ciari paused, she came in with an old Scots Christmas carol called *Wassail,* probably the most riotously joyous, good-humored and just plain silly song she knew. As she'd hoped, it finished raggedly, in four different keys, with all of them laughing like idiots.

Then, suddenly, a deep, resonant tone rolled through the room and Nicole and the others looked upward at the crest of the bluff, where the sound had originated. The scene changed, beach gave way to a flat expanse of naked rock, and they all knew they were atop the bluff. Their bonfire had vanished, but when Nicole cast a glance over the edge of the precipice, she could see it cheerily burning on the sand far below. She breathed a faint whistle of amazement at the genius programming this fantastic simulation. And the raw technology needed to pull it off.

The Alien Captain strode past them to a meter-high cairn set in the center of the small plateau. She faced the horizon, lifting her arms high and wide apart, and unleashed a high, ululating cry that echoed and re-echoed around them. A moment later, her crew did the same, although their collective voice was much deeper. They'd arranged themselves in a rough semi-circle before the cairn, with the astronauts off to one side, between them and their Captain, and each time their Captain spoke, the crew offered a response.

"A ceremony," Hana whispered.

"Memorial service, most likely," Ciari said.

"Should we be here?" Andrei wondered, casting a nervous eye towards a doorway he could no longer see.

"I think we're meant to be," Nicole told them all. "There was nothing to prevent them shunting us back to our quarters before starting. For whatever reason, they want us involved. Better hush now," she finished, even more quietly, noting a couple of obviously angry glares from the Aliens nearest them and remembering how acute their hearing was. "We don't want to disturb things any more than we already have."

They heard a skirl of what could have been bagpipes on another world, which gave way to a softer, more melodious sound, underlaid by a strongly rhythmic drumbeat. The Captain brought her arms together above her head, then lowered her barely touching palms to breast height, assuming an almost human attitude of prayer. An arm was thrown sharply back and to the side, the momentum pulling her weightless body off the ground, into the air, and Nicole couldn't repress a gasp of awe as she began to dance. The Captain moved in three dimensions, each gesture of such poetic eloquence that the finest dancers on Earth were put to shame. There was simply no comparison.

A faint mist blurred the air, giving the plateau an unreal, faery aspect. The drumsound grew louder, an insistent beat that brought the crew forward to begin their own dance and stirred resonances within Nicole herself. Five of the Aliens had been wrapped from neck to toe in brilliantly colored gowns, and as they moved through the assemblage, hands reached for them, gently peeling away the cloth in strips—each panel a different color—until they reached the cairn clothed only in simple shifts of pure white. Then, as the Captain danced above them, they matched her moves, perfect mirror-images, one by one pushing away from the ground to rise past her through the air and disappear into the ebony darkness overhead.

"Those who died, rising to Heaven," Ciari noted, pitching his voice so only Nicole would hear.

The music picked up its tempo and before anyone could stop her, Nicole was among the dancers. There was another minor crescendo and the other three found themselves impelled by physical urges that would not be denied. Each was partnered with one of the Aliens, but, impossibly, before their eyes, that partner slowly transformed into one of their lost companions. Hana danced with Paul DaCuhna, Ciari with Cat Garcia, Andrei with Chagay, each of the dead clad in the same robes the Aliens had worn. Only Nicole danced alone, making her way to the cairn, to take the Captain's place in the air above it. And, as before, hands reached out to strip the avatars. The three humans tried to follow as their friends approached the cairn but they were held back in gentle grips that could not be broken. Their eyes went to Nicole as she repeated the Captain's dance, a flawless performance, her moves and manner becoming less human, more Alien, as it progressed. As before, the avatars matched her, but then, Nicole came down to the plateau, to circle among them, taking a moment to partner each, much more than a moment with the one representing Paul, bidding this last farewell. And they were gone. And the drums were louder, the music more elemental and demanding, the mist a fraction thicker, burning the throat and lungs as vintage whiskey does when swallowed too much, too quickly. Nicole sensed, in that rapidly dwindling part of her consciousness still taking notes, they'd been drugged, but she didn't care. Her heart had been ripped from her once more, her grief and shame laid bare for all to see, and the only solace was in yielding totally to the music and the dance, to sear away the pain with exhaustion. She faced the Captain, and then Hana as the Captain spun away towards Ciari. She found herself torn in two, gripped with an eerie double vision, experiencing the moment fully while simultaneously observing it Godlike from outside. The Captain returned to her, and a smile lighted Nicole's face with joy. Throughout the evening, save for the briefest of turns with Hana and Andrei, the Captain danced with none save Nicole and Ciari. And as time passed, it was more and more often with Nicole. Whenever she was gone, her place was taken by Hana. They never touched, but the space between them seemed to crackle with energy, the forging of a bond neither had anticipated yet neither refused. Nicole looked at Ciari, wondering why he stayed apart from her, and her mouth formed a perfect O of astonishment as she saw his features fade under an overlay of an Alien face and body. *Was this illusion,* she wondered, *a trick of the hologram?* He was as tall as the tallest male and though not so broad, his body rippled with a power and indomitable will that would give the strongest of them pause. *A tiger,* she thought, *my tiger!* And knew, even as she thought it, that was a lie. He was—and would forever remain—no one's but his own.

Her eyes burned with this new insight, new pain, and she abandoned herself to the dance. The Captain was with her, and would not leave again. And with that strange double vision, Nicole saw herself cast off her flight jacket, and then the jumpsuit beneath, until she was naked, skin glistening with sweat, eyes bright with joy, teeth gleaming as she laughed. She saw round pupils elongate into slits, and the eyes themselves tilt impossibly upward, the very shape of her face subtly change until it matched the Aliens'. Skin disappeared beneath a fine pelt of russet fur, decorated with indigo patterns reminiscent of those on the Captain's body, her hair transformed into a fiery mane. She grew claws and fangs and was as one with the Aliens and, moreover, with their Captain. She was home, among family and friends, she was happy.

She woke with a start, taking a deep, reflexive breath through her nose, as if to convince herself she was alive. She lay on her belly in the large common room, its lights dimmed, providing enough to see while not disturbing any who slept. Ciari was by her side. Otherwise, they were alone. The room was bare—its natural state—and clothes and instruments lay close at hand. Both she and Ciari were naked. She shook her head to clear it, then snuggled close to the man, gently raking her nails along the length of his back while kissing his throat where it joined the shoulder. Eyes still closed, he returned the kiss, the embrace. There was no thought, no conscious decision, merely desire that both acted to slake. His groans of hunger and anticipation matched hers; there was nothing she would not, could not, do for him, nor he for her. She'd never felt such an irresistible, primal need, nor, when they were done, such magnificent satisfaction.

Neither spoke for the longest time.

Ciari broke the silence, his voice quiet, containing a resonance Nicole had never heard. "The Irish," he said, "now have competition in the Wake department."

"Really," she agreed, and recognized a similar resonance to her own words. "What the hell happened?" she wondered.

"Damned if I know, apart from one helluva hallucination."

"I wish I could remember. But it's like a dream, the bits and pieces fade as I focus on them."

"You were never more beautiful."

"Then why didn't you come say so? Hana did, what kept you away?"

"I don't know." But he did, and so did she.

Another deep breath brought an awareness of a very empty stomach. "I'm hungry," she announced, and reached for the nearest piece of clothing—her flight jacket. "Better look up the others, while we're at it. Christ, what they must think about all this." She aimlessly waved a hand, to indicate their impromptu boudoir. "What those Aliens must think!"

"Hell, I figure it's mostly their fault. Probably another test." He picked up his flute to pack it away.

"Oh God," Nicole moaned, "were they watching?" And she flushed crimson.

Then, they heard Hana's yell.

They were out the door in a flash, Andrei rounding the corner from their own corridor a split second later, not even batting an eye at their appearance, Ciari still naked, Nicole wearing only her jacket. All of them saw Hana racing their way as fast as she could, far faster than was safe, scrambling for purchase on the slick hall surfaces. She cried out as they appeared, but that was all she got to say. A bolt of energy caught her in the back, outlining her body in a scarlet corona; they heard a *whoulff*-sound, like the sharp exhalation that comes with being punched in the gut, and then she crumpled, her limp form skidding to rest at their feet.

As she fell, a warrior stepped into view, hand weapon leveled at the three Terrans. Ciari exploded out of the shelter of the doorway, deliberately drawing the Alien's attention. It looked like an easy shot, but the warrior, like so many others before him, tragically underestimated the Marshal's speed and agility. An instant before he fired, Ciari heaved his flute down the hall like a spear, before caroming off the wall after it. The warrior instinctively ducked out of the way and his shot went wild; then, Ciari was on him. Two brutally expert karate blows later, the warrior was unconscious and Ciari had his gun.

An alarm sounded, felt more than heard, the ultrasonic vibrations giving them all instant headaches, and Ciari flattened himself against the wall as scarlet energy beams sizzled down the main corridor; the warrior hadn't come alone.

"We've got to get out of here," he yelled. "You two scramble. I'll cover you!"

Andrei scooped Hana up and slung her over his shoulders in a fireman's carry. "Marvelous suggestion," he said, "but where do we go?"

Nicole never had a chance to answer. One of the scarlet beams hit Andrei as he stood up, its force sending him pinwheeling towards Ciari. With a cry of fury, Nicole charged the Aliens who'd struck at them from behind. She knew it was a hopeless gesture—they were too far away—but she made it anyway, part of her wondering if it would hurt when they shot her.

Only they didn't fire. A roared command over the loudspeakers—from the Captain, Nicole recognized her voice—made them hesitate, and that was all the opening Nicole needed. In midair, she rolled into a tight ball, erupting out of it to deadly effect, thankful now for all the hours of training and all the bruises she'd endured at Ciari's hands.

She heard a cry and spun around to see Ciari kneeling over Andrei's body, calmly firing his hand gun down the main corridor. Nicole had one foe left to deal with. She braced herself against the deck and hurled both feet into the warrior's face with all her strength; as her feet struck home, Nicole used the force of the blow, plus her hands on the floor, pulling as hard as she could, to propel herself towards Ciari. She could see energy beams flashing all around him; it was merely a matter of time before he was hit. Events rushed by with terrifying speed, but Nicole experienced them with an eerie double vision; reactions and moves that actually were measured in split seconds seemed to her to be taking forever. She grabbed Ciari's arm and dug her bare feet into the deck, hissing as friction burned them, pushing them off the way she'd come. She had no real plan of action, simply a mindless, atavistic need to flee.

They didn't get very far.

Nicole felt something snag her feet; then, she and Ciari were both sent spinning like tops as some kind of living net gathered them up and reeled them in. Before she knew it, she was immobilized, legs bound together, arms pinned to her side, wrapped mummy-style head to toe, and the harder she struggled, the tighter the net became. Ciari was trussed just as effectively.

Facing them was a crowd of Aliens, led by the Captain. Nicole sneered as she saw that the Captain's shipsuit had been torn and there was a nasty bruise on one cheek. Hana had done some damage before she ran to warn them.

"Why," she cried as they were hauled erect and left floating. "God damn you, *why?!* We came to you as friends. What happened to make you change like this? *Tell me!*"

The female who'd been lurking outside their compartment spoke up, holding her module out to the Captain. She took it, pointed it at Nicole, then Ciari, then Nicole again and finally, for a much longer time, at the Marshal. Nicole caught a glimpse of the device's face. It was a scanner, some controls framing a display, and on the screen were computer silhouettes of herself and Ciari. Both were outlined in gold, but his was tinged with red.

The Captain snapped an order, and two non-warrior males took hold of Ciari and hauled him away.

Nicole called out to him, her voice cracking with rage and fear, his voice choked off in midreply, his words indistinct so she didn't know what he'd said. Nicole went berserk, twisting and clawing at her own webbing like a wild animal in a mad, futile attempt to free herself. With each movement, however, the web pulled tighter and tighter—crushing her, strangling her, killing her.

It was an act of mercy when the Captain took a pistol from one of her warriors and shot Nicole in the head.

eleven

SHE KNEW SHE wasn't dead, because she dreamed. But after a while, after the dreams gathered her up and swept her away, she wished she was.

Again and again and again, she watched helplessly as Rover-Two vectored towards the raider's anti-matter missile. She found herself actually on board, sitting by Paolo—she wept to see him, so handsome, so brave—Cat and the Bear. Paolo was sobbing as he locked the gunship's lasers on target; Cat had a wild look in her eye, a crazy gunfighter grin on her face; the Bear prayed, taking this, as he did everything, utterly in stride. Energy spat away from the Rover's belly—and reality went white as the warhead detonated. Events passed in exquisitely slow motion. Nicole could actually see the fireball grow towards them, taking a perceptible amount of time to vaporize the ceramic steel hull and the three people within. Death must have been instantaneous. Yet, to Nicole, it took forever.

The light faded, the dream ended. And then, like a tape rigged to a moebius loop, it began again.

With each replay, Nicole felt herself spinning faster and deeper into a maelstrom of madness so intense she knew she'd never escape. She wondered if that was really so bad a thing. No worries, no pressures, no responsibility, no grief—the ultimate escape. Tempting. But then, another presence made itself known. Ciari was with her. She had no idea what brought him, and didn't care, her heart leapt to see him. She reached out but he wouldn't take her hand. He looked sad, vulnerable in a way she'd never seen, as if he'd lost something uniquely precious, that he could never hope to regain. Nicole called his name, but her voice made no sound. She stretched her arms, reaching along the entire length of her body, and he responded, his fingers brushing the tips of hers. Suddenly, though, his body spasmed in agony, the impetus of that violent move sending him into a forward roll. When Nicole saw his face again, it had changed.

It was human, but another image was superimposed over his familiar features—the cat-face of the Aliens! As Nicole watched, as helpless to aid or protect him as she'd been to save the Rover, Ciari's face faded away, while the Alien mask became more and more distinct.

Nicole lunged for him, frantic to touch Ciari, to stop this transformation, but he started moving away from her, quickly disappearing into the infinite darkness that surrounded her.

She felt the dream begin once more. This time, it was more than she could endure.

She awoke with the echo of her scream ringing in her ears.

She was lying on a metallic slab, in a pool of blinding light. She was shaking—the seizure triggered by a mixture of cold and fear, plus a purely physical reaction to the Alien drugs administered to her. She wasn't alone. The table was ringed by Aliens. She was naked, but that realization didn't sink in very deeply; she was more impressed by the fact that she was alive.

Then, memories flooded her mind and the raw, elemental fury in them sent a surge of adrenaline racing through her system, galvanizing her into instant, murderous action.

She lashed out wildly and the Aliens immediately fell back in disarray—clearly Nicole's onslaught had taken them completely by surprise, and they were unsure of how to deal with it. She pressed her advantage, pushing off the table and bouncing around the large compartment like a ricochetting bullet. She kept in the shadows and moved as fast as she could, hitting and running, never staying in one place long enough for anyone to get a decent shot at her. But nobody seemed to be trying.

There was a squall of rage from the far side of the room. Nicole recognized the voice, the Alien Captain. At her command, the Aliens evacuated the compartment, to be replaced by an armored warrior whose massive bulk filled the doorway. He carried a rifle and looked ready and willing to use it. Nicole moved into the deepest shadows but had no illusions about being hidden there from him. That suit had to contain infrared, radar and biological scanners that could track her no matter where she hid. She knew her time had just about run out, and wondered what would come next.

The Captain spoke again and, surprisingly, the warrior stepped back out the doorway, closing the hatch as he went.

Nicole didn't move, didn't speak. She was calmer now. Her berserker rage had gone as quickly as it had come, leaving her drained, and more than a little unnerved by her capacity for violence; she thought she knew herself better than that.

The Captain remained silent, it was Ciari who spoke.

"Nicole?" For a moment, she was too stunned to reply. "Nicole," he called again, a fraction louder. "It really is me, scout's honor."

"Step into the light," she told him.

Nicole found herself remembering her dream, and what she'd seen happen to the Marshal, and she felt ice clutch her heart.

At first, from a distance, he looked unchanged. Same figure, same face, with that slightest of shy smiles he reserved for her. He was wearing one of the Alien shipsuits, its silken material doing his lean, powerful physique almost indecent justice.

But he wasn't the same. His hair was thicker, an echo of the Captain's mane, framing his head majestically. His pupils were pointed ovals, like cat's eyes—like the Aliens' eyes. And he moved with an inhuman—feline—grace that put his old self to shame and turned even the simplest of gestures into an exercise in visual poetry.

He met her gaze without flinching, as direct and sure of himself as ever, prepared to deal with any reaction.

"Oh Jesus, Ben," she breathed, the very softness of her voice revealing the depths of her pain far more completely than any cry of anguish, "what have they done to you?"

"Come on, Red," he said, with an achingly familiar toss of the head. "Let's talk."

After Nicole donned one of the Alien shipsuits, the professional side of her brain noting automatically that the garment felt as good as it looked, gently molding itself to the contours of her body while permitting total freedom of movement, Ciari escorted her to a conference/briefing room. The Captain was waiting for them.

Warily, Nicole perched herself across the table from her, while Ciari moved to a food dispenser set into one wall. He set a steaming cup of dark liquid in front of Nicole, sipping some out of a cup of his own as he took a position between Nicole and the Alien.

"What's this?" Nicole asked.

Ciari grinned. "Taste."

She did, looked confused a moment, sipped again. "Cocoa?"

"Gold star for you, girl," he answered with a nod. "That's precisely what it is. The Halyan't'a seem to have as voracious a sweet tooth as we and, since their synthesizers had trouble managing programs for coffee and tea, I went for the next best thing."

"We can metabolize their food?"

"Within fairly broad parameters, yes. The Halyan't'a . . . ."

"Halyan't'a?" Nicole queried, stumbling a little over the pronunciation. Ciari said the word with a swallowed growl she couldn't match.

"That's what they call themselves, Nicole. *Halyan't'a*— the Chosen. Their homeworld orbits a main sequence G-type star farther down the spiral arm, about thirty-odd lights beyond Faraway. Their race seems as old as ours, their technology a bit more sophisticated; they also seem to have been aware of us, as a fellow intelligent species, for a considerable while. The reason for that seems to be that, while both Earth and their world, which they call s'N'dare, put out tremendous amounts of electromagnetic energy, their transmissions are seen against the incredibly crowded stellar background of the galactic core. For all the quantity and power of their output, by the time it reaches us, it's effectively drowned out by 'static.' Whereas, Earth, from their perspective, is seen against the vast emptiness of intergalactic space."

Nicole nodded. "Effectively the difference between spotting a particular tree in the middle of a forest and spotting the same tree out on the open prairie."

"Precisely." Ciari gestured towards the Captain, who looked utterly relaxed, with her own drink. The pose was an act, Nicole knew; she'd been watching her intently since she entered the room. Nicole had been doing the same.

"This is Shavrin," Ciari said, the Captain inclining her head in greeting. Nicole nodded back.

"The closest English equivalent for her title is Clan Matriarch," Ciari continued, "but that's only a rough approximation. The rank indicates social, political and economic status, plus emotional and physical standing. It would be analogous to Cat Garcia—as part and parcel of her position as Mission Commander—being a Princess of the planetary nobility, a member of the planetary government, a member of the elite economic class and biological mother to the crew."

"Sounds crazy."

"To part of me, it does, too. Again, the translation leaves a lot to be desired. We have nothing in Terrestrial experience to compare with the Halyan't'a social system, so any terms we apply to it are inherently limited and imprecise, even with the simplest of words. To us, for example, a tree is a tree. A specific, literal meaning. But to the Halyan't'a, a tree is home and sanctuary and amusement park and hunting ground—and on and on—it means a dozen different things to them, each with its own distinct, unique term."

"But *you* understand."

Ciari nodded.

"I can guess how. Tell me why?"

"Shavrin and this ship are the Halyan't'a equivalent of NASA Pathfinders. Her mission was to approach us—Humanity, the Earth—make contact, and, if possible, establish peaceful diplomatic relations."

Nicole tried to keep an emotionless poker face, but the implications of Ciari's words were too staggering.

"Do they have any idea what they're getting into?"

"For the Halyan't'a—and maybe us as well—it's a matter of survival. As I said, they've been aware of us for a number of years. They know a lot about us. They respect us, because they see in Humanity a slightly distorted reflection of them-

selves. S'N'dare and Halyan't'a-controlled space are between
us and Galactic Center; if we keep expanding, sooner or later,
we'll run into their territory. As if that wasn't problem
enough, the Halyan't'a have discovered evidence of other intelligent, space-faring races."

Something in his tone made her ask, "Hostile?"

"Very. Thus far, there've only been skirmishes—singleship encounters—both sides seem to be feeling each other
out. But the Halyan't'a have concluded they're facing a nu-
merically and technologically superior opponent. They don't
like admitting it—they're as butt-headedly proud as we—but
they're scared. Especially with Earth moving up behind them.
Under the circumstances, they'd prefer us as friends and
allies."

"Can't fault that analysis. So what happened to this ship?"

Ciari took a breath, his eyes suddenly haunted as he looked
around the sleek, sparsely furnished room. Nicole wondered
whose memories he was reliving. "Shavrin isn't sure. Possibly
a malfunction, a major systems failure. Or enemy action. Or
sabotage. Not everyone at home is thrilled by this embassy.
Why bring Earth in as equal partners when we can effectively
colonize the place?" Nicole's eyes flashed at his use of "we"
to describe the Halyan't'a.

"As the Europeans did India and the Third World."

"Yup. Fortunately for us, Shavrin's party prevailed."

"Anyway, the incident occurred when *Range Guide*—this
vessel—was in warp space, well away from s'N'dare. A
glitch developed in their cryogenic fuel network, a repair crew
went to work on it, and there was an explosion. The blast
killed all the duty engineering staff and voided the atmosphere
through two-thirds of the ship before the automatic bulkheads
closed. They lost seventy percent of the crew. Including the
Speaker," he finished.

"That's you," Nicole said flatly. Ciari looked sharply at
her, then quickly translated what she'd said to Shavrin. Nicole
tried to distinguish individual words in his speech, but found it
impossible; there were no breaks in the phrasing, merely shifts
in harmonic tones and intensity, and in the shape of the sound
itself. He was singing—and how he sang seemed as important
as what he sang.

"Correct," he said at last, in English. "That's me.

"A *Speaker*," he continued, "is probably one of the most crucial members of an embassy, and, I think, of Halyan't'a society as a whole. They're very rare; a handful each generation is considered extraordinarily good fortune. To have one as a member of your family — I suppose it's akin to having a relative elected Pope. Honor without parallel.

"The name describes the function: a *Speaker* is one who communicates. In his or her brain is contained the sum total of Halyan't'a experience and knowledge, tied in with total recall. That complete awareness, combined with a highly sensitive telempathic talent, makes them invaluable as mediators. They can see both sides of a dispute, in immediate and long-range terms, how that dispute and its resolution will affect not only the parties involved, but society as a whole. Simultaneously, they're conditioned to remain above the conflict — dispassionate and uninvolved — the ultimate arbiter, whose decisions are invariably accepted without question or argument because all involved know that decision was made impartially, without malice or prejudice.

"The *Speaker* aboard *Range Guide* had been briefed with every scrap of data the Halyan't'a had amassed about Earth and its peoples. He spoke English, he understood us about as well as any Halyan't'a could. With his telempathic talent, he could have told Shavrin not only what our representatives were saying, but the social and political context of the words, and the emotions behind them. Without him, she was hunting blind, deaf, and dumb."

"Why didn't she head home for repairs, then, and a replacement?"

"She couldn't. They managed to cope with the damage while staying in warp space. Miraculously, the explosion left their stardrive untouched. But the integral structure of *Range Guide* itself was badly damaged. She wasn't sure the ship could survive the downshift transition into normal space, let alone an upshift back into Warp. She decided there was more risk in going back than coming on."

"Would there have been a political cost to her returning in failure?"

A silence, then, "Yes."

"Which would have changed the balance in favor of the other party?"

"Possibly. They'd also lost a critical amount of life-support—food, water, air—to conserve what remained, Shavrin placed the ship under computer control and ordered her crew into stasis. That's why we found no signs of life when we came aboard; everyone was in suspended animation."

"And the computer woke them up as soon as you opened the airlock."

"Actually, it woke Shavrin when Hana bounced her radio beam off the hull. She observed our approach from a shielded compartment. We were left alone till we reached the flight deck because she wanted to see what kinds of beings we were, how we'd treat their ship."

"I assume she liked what she saw."

Ciari looked up at the deliberate shade of irony in Nicole's voice. "She nearly had a seizure when you took off your helmet," he said.

"Worried about Terrestrial diseases . . . ?"

He shook his head. "Nope. From that aspect, they'd medi-scanned us pretty thoroughly and were fairly certain we were safe. It's that, to Shavrin, you . . . stank. Still do. That's why she's wearing nose filters."

Nicole remembered her own supposition about the Ha-lyan't'a sense of smell and was pleased to see it borne out, although mildly chagrined at Shavrin's reaction. "Okay, Ben, they needed a *Speaker* and they chose you. The modules," she asked, "that's what those were about?" He nodded. "What about Andrei and Hana? I've been assuming that if I'm all right, so are they, but I wouldn't mind some reassurance."

"They're fine, Nicole. They're in stasis." He touched a button on the table top and a holo-image appeared in the air. It was a view of the chamber where Nicole had awoken, only now she could see that one long wall was marked off into transparent squares. Most were empty, but within the two central in the image, she could make out Hana's and Andrei's faces. She couldn't tell if they were alive or dead and, though she tried, she couldn't repress an instinctive shudder of revulsion. The place reminded her too much of a morgue.

Ciari pressed another button and the image vanished.

"Why am I awake and not them?" Nicole demanded.

"They'll be revived as soon as we've finished this talk.

I . . ." Ciari shrugged, trying to come to grips with emotions that were solid as steel one instant, elusive as quicksilver the next. "I couldn't forget your face as the warriors dragged me away. I . . ." He searched for words, Nicole's eyes narrowing at this uncharacteristic hesitancy in Ciari's manner, where before had been sure self-confidence. "I wanted to stop the hurting inside you. To show you *I* was all right."

"You cared," she said flatly.

A nervous smile. "I always cared. Now, it meant something—important—to let you see. Also, I needed to explain what had happened, and why. Aside from the fact that you were Spacecraft Commander, I trust your judgment more than Andrei's or Hana's. The Halyan't'a aren't our enemies, Nicole, and they aren't by nature cruel. By doing to me what she did, Shavrin violated every ethical canon she's ever been taught. Her people may forgive her, especially if she succeeds in this mission, but I doubt she'll ever forgive herself. She felt she had no alternative. She was right."

"Perhaps," Nicole said, reaching across the table to Ciari. Hesitantly, she touched his hair, his cheek, unconsciously repeating the gestures Shavrin had made when they first met. The textures weren't what she remembered; he was the same, yet . . . *Alien*. "They used a genetic virus, correct? The modules were to determine which of us was the most compatible with the process."

"Impressive."

"It wasn't all that hard to figure out, Ciari. The only way your body could manifest such subtle, yet fundamental, changes is if someone's been fooling about with the basic DNA structure of your cells."

"You're angry."

"I suppose I am."

Shavrin growled a low phrase, her voice touching rumbling basso levels no human could match. Ciari answered in kind.

"Shavrin understands," he told Nicole, after the exchange, "but she also believes that, were you in her position, you would have done the same."

Nicole made no reply, but knew Shavrin had hit the mark. That realization was, in fact, the reason for her fury.

"They began scanning us the moment we boarded. Shavrin had no plans then to transform any of us, but she would have been remiss in her duties if she didn't at least explore the possibility."

"Is it rough, Ben?"

"You have no concept," he told her. "Most of the time— now, for instance—I can handle myself fairly well. But then . . .

"Christ, Nicole, having another head inside your own is frightening enough, but this is like having billions and billions of heads all crammed together; every so often, I'm overwhelmed by sheer weight of numbers. Usually, y'see, potential *Speakers* are tagged at birth. They have a unique genetic matrix, and they undergo conditioning through childhood to enable them, physically and psychologically, to accept the virus. With me, not only do I not have any of that conditioning, I'm an alien species to boot. I'm lucky I'm not crazier than I am."

"Is the effect permanent?"

"No, thank the Maker. But the more time that passes before I take the antidote, the less effective it'll be."

"Why'd she do it!" As she asked the question, Nicole rounded on Shavrin, the pain and rage in her heart lashing out like a whip. *"Why?"*

"The raider, of course," Ciari answered simply.

Nicole faced him, anger transformed instantly to shock. "What!" she stammered, trying to regain her mental equilibrium.

"The raider. I'm afraid I hit that one on the nose. *Range Guide* was too big a plum to pass up. It showed up on the Halyan't'a scanners while Hana was on the flight deck; she recognized it instantly. It's the same cruiser that ambushed *Wanderer*.

"Shavrin had no intention of using the *Speaker* virus before then. She didn't know whether or not we represented any of Earth's governments, but she liked us and, strange as it may seem, trusted us. We gave off good vibes and the Halyan't'a responded to them. That impromptu concert we gave worked wonders, as did our collective responses to their holographic Rorschach. They were why we were permitted to participate in their Memorial Service. When Hana saw the raider, and reacted with such primal emotions, that suddenly made establishing effective communications between us imperative. And the only way to do that was the *Speaker* virus. Shavrin decided to go with her instincts. She had you and the others stunned and locked in stasis because she knew you wouldn't understand and, not understanding, would resist. Try to rescue me. Also, the stasis chamber is completely shielded against sensor probes, so that, when the raiders scanned *Range Guide,* all they'd register would be Halyan't'a."

Something about Ciari's manner prompted Nicole to mention, "I saw a scanner just before I was clobbered; you and I registered about the same."

"Actually, you were more psi-sensitive."

"Then why'd they choose you?"

"You remember the Service?"

"I try. That was another examination?"

"In part. You're lucky, in a way; I remember it all, like watching a film inside my head."

"I saw you change, as if you'd put on a tiger's mask."

"True. I wore a mask, but *you* were the one who *changed.* You're more like them—more like Shavrin—than you know; if they'd administered the *Speaker* virus, you'd never have found your way back. You'd be Halyan't'a in a human body. For the rest of your life. Maybe it's my age, or my experiences. Among other things, flying singleships builds a helluva sense of self-possession. Maybe I'm just stubborn; whatever, I seem able to hold on to my *self.* Barely. You couldn't."

"I see. And when did all this occur?"

"Ten days ago."

"Jesus."

"The virus took about six hundred kilosecs—a week, Standard—to completely take effect. Most of the time I spent hanging on to my sanity by my fingernails. This morning, we arrived at the raider base. It's an asteroid, a couple of klicks in diameter, part of a large mid-Belt cluster. This is a big operation, Nicole, very professional, probably with Corporate backing. We spotted three other spacecraft on our way in— two strike units and a refinery—and Shavrin's Tactical Officer suspects there are others docked on the rock's farside. Our escort's the biggest of the lot, but that other pair pack a respectable punch, easily *Wanderer*'s match."

"Go on."

"We're hard-docked against the asteroid, with transfer tunnels connected to our main portside airlocks. Shavrin's opinion is that, regardless of whether or not she cooperates with these people, her crew is doomed if they stay here."

"I agree."

"So do I. Got any suggestions?"

"You're the cop, isn't this your territory?"

"I'm—" he flashed his rare old grin—"not myself."

"Okay. Crack Hana and Andrei out of the icebox and we'll see what we can do."

twelve

"ANY BRIGHT IDEAS?" Nicole asked no one in particular.

Andrei spoke first. "We could always surrender."

"Hey," Hana squawked, "that was *my* line!"

Nicole sighed and rubbed her eyes. *Thanks a lot, Lord,* she thought, *it's going to be one of* those *days.* "I did say *bright* ideas, guys."

"Can we see that exterior scan again, Nicole?" Hana asked.

Nicole nodded and carefully tapped the touch-sensitive computer keyboard inlaid on the surface of the briefing room table. She took her time, working the controls as Ciari had taught her. She knew she was doing it right, but still couldn't contain a grin of triumph as the airspace over the table *blinked* into a three-dimensional portrait of the view outside *Range Guide.* She swung the camera towards the asteroid.

"Hold it!" Hana snapped. Nicole took her hand off the panel as the other woman levered herself up from her chair to hover right beside the image. "See these?" She indicated various points on the rock's hulking, irregular surface. "Nicole, can you lock on to one and focus the lens as tightly as possible?"

When she'd done so, they had the illusion that they were standing outside the bunker, so close—the picture was that clear—they could almost touch it. The sense of reality was unnerving. Someone whistled.

"Missile launchers," Andrei noted quietly.

"And particle beam weapons," Nicole added. "Pure murder at short range. This rock's easily got sufficient firepower to deal with any single cruiser that tries to take it on. And perhaps even a whole squadron."

"Could the bunkers be eliminated, or crippled somehow?" Andrei wondered.

"If they have a common energy source and/or See-cubed link," Nicole answered. "Then, if we zapped that central control, they'd be helpless. Unfortunately—" she shifted focus slightly—"the bunker has its own radar tracking system. They probably have triple redundancy and better, plus independent power. If central command goes off-line, they simply switch to their individual command and control systems and keep on shooting."

"We wouldn't need more than a few minutes' grace, Nicole," Andrei said. "Just sufficient time to sever all physical connections with the asteroid and gain ourselves a small amount of clearance."

"And then what," Hana demanded, sarcasm obvious. "We simply disappear?"

"Something like that." Andrei smiled. "We turn on the stardrive."

For a moment, no one said a word, stunned by the terrible simplicity of Andrei's suggestion.

"That's right," Nicole murmured, when she'd found her voice. "It's fully functional, isn't it? But I thought *Range Guide* couldn't withstand the strain of Warp transition."

"We need keep the drive active for at most a couple of seconds—on, beat, beat, *off!* I think the hull can endure that level of stress. The critical maneuver will be establishing our proper flight attitude, so we don't accidentally plow into a planet or the Sun when we DownShift."

"Andrei," Nicole asked incredulously, "how the hell far is this jaunt going to take us?"

"Based on a flight time of three seconds—here are my rough figures, Hana, can you work it out?"

She scratched at her pad a moment, chewed the end of her pen, then let out a low whistle.

"It should take us across the System. We'll probably end up a little outside Pluto's orbit."

"Forty astronomical units," Nicole said, "over six billion kilometers—in *three seconds?!*"

"From a standing start," Andrei nodded. "The Halyan't'a stardrive is slightly more efficient than our own."

"No foolin'. If the raiders find this out, all bets are off; Shavrin and her crew are history."

The door hissed open and Ciari entered. Nicole saw him first and his unearthly beauty—that was the word that fit best, though he was inescapably male—took her breath away.

He wore the full, formal robes of a *Speaker*—a floor-length, long-sleeved gown worn under a floor-length, sleeveless vest. The gown was a very dark green, the vest black, highlighted with intricate runes etched in silver thread that flashed fire with every move he made. The vest hung open, revealing two pieces of jewelry: a silver and turquoise belt buckled around his waist, and a chain of office around his neck. Someone had styled his hair and made up his face to subtly accent the aspects of his physiognomy that had become more Halyan't'a than human. The end result was magnificent, civilized, yet hearkening back to a passionate, barbaric past. And it was unhuman.

"Wow," was all Nicole could say.

Ciari managed to maintain his impassive, Alien mien for a few more seconds before his face dissolved into an unrestrained, totally human grin. He held out his arms and did a slow pirouette—no mean feat, considering the Velcro-like gripsoles keeping his sandled feet stuck to the deck in the starship's zero gravity.

"Like it?" he asked them all, with a momentary sideways glance that focused the question exclusively at Nicole.

Again, all she could say was, "Wow." And she asked him how he felt.

"So far, so good." He chuckled. "I feel alive, I feel excited, I feel terrified. I feel speedy and high. I'm dancing on clouds and racing along a tightrope stretched a million kilometers above the ground. I'm babbling."

"Yeah." Nicole took his hands and led him away from the others, dropping her voice so that he alone could hear. As they moved, Ciari's grip suddenly tightened around her wrists and she winced at the unexpected pain. She didn't try to break his hold; she wasn't even sure she could. "It's harder than you thought, isn't it, Ben? Holding on to yourself."

He took a long, shuddering breath, eyes flicking anywhere but at her. "The difficulty comes, Red, when you can't keep straight which 'self' is really and truly yours. I look in a mirror and think I'm ugly, because I'm tall and gangly and graceless and my body isn't covered in fur. Or I think I'm crippled because I can't smell or hear or see half as well as the Halyan't'a around me. I look at you . . . and sometimes it takes a conscious effort to remember who you are and what you mean to me. Funny how important that is—crucial, even— you, me, us—the bind that ties. And I was the one who wanted to keep my distance."

"It's not working, Ben. Tell Shavrin to administer the antidote!"

"No."

"Listen to yourself, goddamn it, you're tearing yourself apart!"

"No!"

"This masquerade isn't necessary. Andrei may have come up with a way out of this mess, for all of us." In a few words, she told him Andrei's plan. "By the time these assholes know what we've done, we'll be on the other side of the System, leaving an energy wake so broad and unmistakeable that Space Command will be falling over itself in its haste to check us out. We'll be intercepted in no time. Tell Shavrin, see what she thinks."

After a fast, growling exchange over the intercom, Ciari said, "It's feasible. Shavrin agrees that *Range Guide* should survive so brief a trip. But the drive's completely shut down. She estimates it'll take her people three or four kilosecs to cycle it up to Ignition. And there's no way that process can be hidden from external sensors. You can bet, Nicole, that the moment the raiders spot anything like that, they'll be over here with every combat trooper they can muster."

"What about a cold start?" Andrei suggested.

"Shavrin says she likes your style," Ciari told him, translating the Matriarch's response. "She also wouldn't want to be within a couple of mega-klicks of this ship should anything go wrong. Cold starting a Matter/Anti-Matter drive is a frighteningly delicate procedure; the slightest miscalculation could turn

Range Guide into a pint-sized supernova. Wolfe's asteroid *redux*."

"I am aware of the risks, Marshal. And the alternative."

"Shavrin's engineering crew was killed, Andrei; can you handle the MAM intermix?"

"I know the theory, Nicole, and I've run simulations. I will, however, require someone to brief me on the controls and sensor telltales."

"I can do that," Ciari said. "But we'll have to move fast."

"Why? What's up?"

"We got a call from the raiders. They're sending a delegation, headed by their top people. They want to talk to Shavrin. And they'll probably insist on access to *Range Guide* for their scientific and security teams."

"Can you stall 'em?"

"What d'you think I've *been* doing?"

"How long have we got?"

"Three, four kilosecs. Maybe an hour. Enough time to show Andrei the ropes in Engineering, but that's about all."

Hana spoke up. "Nicole, even a cold start will create a blivet on the raiders' sensors."

"By the time we're ready to roll," she said, "those bastards will have more trouble than they'll know what to do with. That, Hana,"—her smile held neither warmth nor friendliness, and in her eyes was the fierce gleam of a predator on the prowl—"is our job."

"Only one flaw that I can see," Hana groaned later, after she and Nicole had examined every square centimeter of the rock facing *Range Guide*.

"Well?"

She pointed at the holo field above the table, now showing a medium close-up of the entire asteroid, taken during the starship's final approach. "There are weaponry bunkers spaced across the whole surface, with multiple, interlocking fields of fire."

"We've been over this, Hana. Tell me something new."

She tapped the tabletop keyboard and the image shifted from reality to a computer-generated schematic. Hana played with the computer a few seconds more and looked up in time to see lines of brilliantly colored light streak away from the bunkers, creating an impenetrable protective cocoon around the rock. Then, she rolled the image until they were looking at a bows-on shot of *Range Guide* on its docking cradle. There was a visible space between the starship's hull and the bunkers' fields of fire.

"What's the scale?" Nicole asked as she moved closer, concentration plain on her face. "How much room do we have to maneuver?"

"A hundred meters, if we're lucky. Mind you, this just applies to energy weapons; fire and forget missiles are a whole different story."

"Still, so long as we stay close to our cradle, those bunkers can't touch us."

"Hai."

The communicator beeped. Andrei, on audio link from Engineering.

"Status," Nicole asked him.

"Splendid, assuming one is fond of speaking pidgin sign language. I shouldn't complain, though; considering the time he had, Marshal Ciari did a superb job. At least now, my Halyan't'a counterpart and I can make ourselves understood. More often than not."

"Can you handle the cold start?"

"Dear lady, that you never know until you try. It's not something done out of choice, and I'm told, the event never occurs precisely the same way twice."

"Ter*rif*ic. I gather Ciari's not there?"

"Summoned to the flight deck. Evidently, the raider delegation is on its way over."

"Here they come," Hana announced. She'd switched images in the holo field to a view of the midships transit tunnel. They were looking past two unarmed, unarmored Halyan't'a warriors, the smallest and least-assuming Nicole had seen. She wondered if that was a deliberate ploy on Shavrin's part, to make the raiders underestimate the Aliens. A small crowd of humans was approaching. Something in that crowd caught her eye and the image zoomed at her with frightening speed as Hana suddenly refined the focus.

"Nicole," she cried, *"look!"*

Filling the field was a face they'd seen before: handsome, with wheat-colored hair and emerald eyes and the smile of a rogue. He'd been drunk when last they'd seen him—or so they'd thought—but even then, Nicole had recognized the man's charisma. It was far more evident now that he was in his element. He wore a simple, unadorned shipsuit, without insignia or badges of rank, but there was no mistaking that he alone was in command.

Major Daniel Morgan, United States Air Force, Space Command, retired. Holder of the Congressional Medal of Honor.

Pirate.

Nicole sprang forward, forgetting all she'd ever learned about moving in zero-gravity. Hana managed to snag hold of her legs and stop her before she did a front flip through the holo field. "Nicole," she yelled, "what the hell are you doing?!"

"Ciari!" she roared back, fingers stabbing at the intercom. "Morgan knows him. They faced off in the Oak Room, remember? Christ, he knows us *all!* If he recognizes Ciari—or, just as bad, the Marshal recognizes him, and shows it—we're finished!"

"Too late!"

Nicole twisted in Hana's grasp, pulling the other woman into the air as she backed up the image to provide a panoramic shot of the airlock and the Halyan't'a reception committee. Ciari and Morgan were barely ten meters apart; yet, if either recognized the other, they made no sign. Ciari's face remained impassive, almost remote, as if mind and soul existed on a higher plane of reality than those around him.

The raiders entered the airlock and stopped, Morgan stepping forward, hands outheld in friendship. His gaze swept the assemblage, pausing momentarily on Shavrin, resplendent in her own formal robes, before fixing on Ciari. Only a few seconds passed before he spoke, but to Nicole it was time without end.

"He's spotted him," Hana said, voice breaking a little, and she clutched Nicole's arm tighter.

Nicole shook her head. "He isn't sure."

"Greetings, star-farers," Morgan was saying. "In the name of the people of Earth, I welcome you to the Sol System. . . ."

"Arrogant fuck!"

"Hush up, Hana," Nicole growled. "I want to hear this."

"I am pleased that this commercial operation was able to provide assistance in your hour of need."

Ciari, face still expressionless, turned slightly towards Shavrin and translated Morgan's speech. The Matriarch's speech was brief, her tone soft, almost deferential.

"In the name of the Halyan't'a—the Chosen—greetings are returned," Ciari said, giving the words a lilt and sibilance Nicole had never heard from him before; she understood at once that he was speaking English as a true Halyan't'a might, with inflections and tonalities no human could easily match. Morgan must have realized that, too, because Ciari's speech seemed to throw him slightly off balance.

"And thanks are given for your aid," Ciari continued, "though, in truth, such aid was unnecessary. We planned to establish electronic communications with your homeworld, and our LifeSystems were more than adequate to sustain us until planetfall."

"Perhaps, Speaker, assuming a peaceful journey. But there are those who would view your spacecraft as no more than a valuable prize. A target, ripe for the taking."

"Ah. You spoke in the name of the people of your world, but said nothing of the government which rules them."

"There is no government that rules the entire planet."

"How . . . anarchic. This means, therefore, you represent no political entity?"

"As I said, we're a commercial operation. Our politics are profit."

"I see."

"You have nothing to fear from us, Speaker."

Ciari merely smiled.

"We've transmitted a full report of our encounter to our central office," Morgan went on, "who have by now, I am sure, informed the requisite authorities. Until we hear from them, however, it might be better for all concerned if you and your Captain"—he indicated Shavrin—"were to join me on the asteroid as my guests. Suitable accommodations have been prepared; you'll lack for nothing."

"Save freedom?"

"This is for your protection, Speaker. I must also insist on access to your spacecraft for my scientific and security personnel."

"Could we keep them out, even if we wished to?"

"Our relations thus far have been amicable; I'd like to keep them so."

After a brief conference with Shavrin and her senior officers, Ciari faced Morgan once more. Both men were matched physically, but suddenly Ciari seemed much taller, imbued with an inner strength that dwarfed those around him. There and then, *he* was the force to be reckoned with, not Shavrin, nor the unseen Halyan't'a warriors, nor even the starship itself. Morgan recognized that reality and tried to match it, but couldn't even come close. He wasn't pleased, and didn't care if it showed.

"It is agreeable," Ciari said.

"If you'll follow my people . . ." Morgan held out a hand and Ciari followed Shavrin down the tunnel and into the asteroid. Immediately, a squad of raiders moved towards the airlock. The Halyan't'a let them troop aboard.

Inside the briefing room, Hana was hunched over the computer keyboard, trying to refine audio and video focus on the holo field as it responded to a tight-beam broadcast from within the asteroid. The image that finally appeared was upside-down, and showed mostly a vast expanse of deck plating. Hana compensated as best she could, and slowly, in the distance, two men came into view. One was Morgan.

"It worked," she announced in cheery triumph, giving Nicole a thumbs-up, "Ciari planted a 'bug.' "

"Morgan," they heard the smaller man say, his voice crackling slightly, the picture breaking up, forcing the two women to strain for every word, "what the hell is wrong? Regardless of how this turns out, we've pulled off the coup of the century, possibly the millennium!"

"Have we?"

"I thought so, until you stepped off that ramp looking like you'd seen a ghost."

"I had."

"Make sense, man!"

"Lal, that man—the Speaker, the Alien translator—the moment I laid eyes on him, I'd have taken any odds he was no more Alien than I am. He's the near twin of a Federal Marshal named Ciari that I met at DaVinci."

"So?"

"He was assigned as Law Officer to the DSV *Wanderer.*"

"Oh."

" 'Oh,' " Morgan mimicked viciously, mocking the Indian's accent. "I love your sense of understatement, Rajmansoor."

"You believe the Speaker to be a human man?"

"Off a vessel I thought I destroyed weeks ago. I truly do not know. I don't know what I believe about him anymore. But can we afford to take that chance?"

"I don't see where it matters, really, since we have no intention of releasing them."

"If that is Ciari, others could have survived, and that could jeopardize my cover." Lal nodded agreement. "I want the Speaker run through a complete medical exam. Check everything, right down to basic chromosome and DNA structure. Then cross-reference the results with Ciari's file."

"It will take time to procure those records."

"The Halyan't'a aren't going anywhere."

"This could be coincidence."

"Perhaps."

"It is your own damned fault, Morgan! The problem would not exist were it not for your obsession for vengeance!"

"You don't understand, Lal."

"No, I do *not!* You jeopardize a multi-billion dollar operation, simply to destroy a NASA space vessel that was on a *training* flight, for mercy's sake!"

"It wasn't the flight—or the ship—it was the woman commanding it! Cat Garcia. We went through hell together. Sixty-one people, in a lifeboat designed to hold twenty. I sailed it across the face of the Solar System, Lal, I brought fifty-three home alive. I was a hero. The finest officer the Air Force had ever seen! But they retired me! *Retired me!* Medically unfit, they said. Even Canfield, the bitch. Who the hell is she to talk, with most of her body made of plasteel! I had no idea how much I could hate, until I heard the Review Board's findings.

"I was dumped. Cat wasn't. I asked her to come with me, to stand by me. To remain as true as she had in the boat. But she didn't.

"Seven officers sat on that Board. I've killed three. And now Cat. I'm saving Canfield for last."

Lal was visibly unnerved by Morgan's outburst and he spoke with a faint tremor. "Suppose, when we've compared bio-stats between Ciari and the Speaker, some readings match and others don't?"

"If I'm to err, it'll be on the side of caution. We know who was in the Command Module, we start looking for them. Hard. And pass a contract through the System, shoot on sight."

"That's messy. And far from foolproof. Our employers will not approve."

"Would they rather see this"—Morgan waved an arm to encompass the rock around them—"shut down?" The other man's silence was the reply he'd expected. "Hurry up on the file, Lal. The longer the delay, the greater the possiblity of something going wrong."

The two men went their separate ways and, after staring at the empty corridor junction for a long time, Nicole finally snapped off the holo field.

"Fucking *bastard!*" Hana screamed, blinking back tears of mingled grief and rage. Nicole tried to comfort her, but was waved away. For now, Hana wanted, needed, to be alone with her pain. Nicole understood, but stayed close at hand, ready to respond if needed.

She called Andrei on a secure intercom channel.

"Big trouble," she told him. "Can you be ready to Ignite on a moment's notice?"

She heard Andrei take a deep breath and wiped her own face with a sleeve while waiting for his reply. It was, "Perhaps."

"No good," she said wearily. "Do it."

She closed the channel.

"What was that all about?" Hana asked.

"You heard. The longer we wait, the worse our chances become. So we strike now. We free Ciari and Shavrin, and we take Morgan—to stand trial for piracy and murder—and we skip."

"Tall order."

Nicole smiled. There was death in her eyes.

thirteen

THERE WERE SEVEN, all told, in the party they were after: three armored troopers and four technicians. The raiders moved easily through the starship—troopers cocksure of their ability to crush any resistance, technos confident of the troopers' ability to protect them.

Nicole, lying prone on the deck just around the corner, about fifteen meters ahead of them, with a Halyan't'a warrior crouched above her, felt a faint tingling as a sensor web swept over them. Nothing happened, though; a Halyan't'a electronic "cloak" kept them hidden from its prying beams. Other Halyan't'a warriors were spaced along the maintenance crawlway above the corridor ceiling, ready to drop through the panels on command.

Hana was by herself, in one of the locked compartments lining the passage. She would spring their trap.

Nicole whispered into her boom microphone: "On your mark, Hana—they're moving past—get ready, set, *go!*"

There was the faint hiss of a door sliding open, then Hana cheerfully saying, "Hiya, fellas, how's tricks?" The plan was for Hana to literally pop out of her compartment, wearing a Halyan't'a shipsuit and lugging a respectable load of files and tape cassettes, looking as normal as could be. She greeted the raiders and then moved casually, briskly on her way.

"Hold it, Miss," a trooper barked, and his partner, in a harsher tone, ordered, *"Halt!"*

"Hit 'em!" Nicole roared, and she kicked off the wall, Halyan't'a crossbow cocked and ready to fire. Their ruse had worked perfectly; all raider eyes were on a very startled, very confused-looking Hana. Nicole sighted on the back of the nearest trooper and, possessed by a preternatural, icy calm, pulled the trigger. Beside her, the Halyan't'a did the same. In that same moment, Hana hurled the clutter in her arms at the unarmored technos before diving headlong into their midst, flailing in every direction with hands and feet. And the rest of the assault team struck from above.

In barely a dozen seconds, it was over. Of the seven raiders, the three troopers and one of the technicians were dead, the rest unconscious. Neither humans nor Halyan't'a had pulled their punches and Nicole thought the surviving raiders should consider themselves lucky to be alive. She looked at the man who'd taken her first bolt, sprawled against the bulkhead where the arrow's impact had thrown him, and then her eyes fell to the crossbow nestled in the crook of her arm.

"You okay?" Hana asked. Her eyes were strangely bright, wide with mingled excitement and stark terror, and faint tremors shook the surface of her skin as her adrenaline rush began to fade.

Nicole slowly shook her head. "What's scary is how easy it is. Bang—he's dead. No hesitation. No second thoughts."

"I hesitated a little. Hell, I almost didn't come out that damn door. But then—I thought of Paolo and Cat and the Bear. I told myself these might have been the ones responsible for murdering them. And I did what I had to do."

Nicole looked at her friend and saw her own mixed-up emotions of pain, grief, fear, hate and exultation mirrored in Hana's eyes. Impulsively, she pulled the smaller woman into a tight embrace.

"I may only be a civilian, Nicole," she heard Hana say in a choked voice, "but I won't let you down. Not ever."

They moved apart with surprising reluctance. "Come on, partner," Nicole said, "let's help clear the hall, and then get ourselves changed and out of here before these clowns are missed and someone comes looking."

The technos' coveralls weren't the greatest fit, but the two women managed to make themselves presentable. None of this party were Oriental so they used a baseball cap pulled low, plus Hana's own eyeglasses, to hide her face.

As they turned to go, Hana slung a crossbow over her shoulder. Nicole stopped her. "Leave it," she said.

"*Hm?*"

"I'd like to take 'em, too, but we can't. We have to leave *Range Guide* carrying the same equipment the technos had when they entered. No more, no less. Replacing their side-arms with these Halyan't'a hand weapons is already pushing our luck as far as we dare."

"Right. Sorry."

With that, they left their Halyan't'a comrades and made their way towards the midships transit tunnel, mixing in with another party of technos *en route*. By the time they reached the airlock, they were in the midst of a fair-sized crowd, and Nicole noticed a lot of nervous looks on the faces around her. As the technicians were rushed through the tunnel, and into a holding area at the far end, where they were strip-searched and identiscanned, they were replaced by troopers, many carrying heavy weapons.

"What's up?" someone asked in annoyance.

"Haven't you heard?" another replied, not bothering to disguise the quaver of apprehension in his voice as he kept looking over his shoulder, as if expecting to be attacked and massacred at any moment. "Command lost bioscan downlink to one of our scout teams. They figure an ambush. They're pulling everyone out until this ship's secured."

"Shit, they should'a done that right off. Effing furballs give me the creeps. I say, space 'em all."

"Shut up, both of you," Nicole snapped, turning to face *Range Guide*'s interior and noisily sniffing the air. "You!" she jabbed a finger at the nearest trooper. "D'you have atmospheric samplers in that suit?" Without letting him reply, she rushed on, "use 'em—fast! And tell me what you find!"

"Yessir," the man stammered, taken aback, but responding instantly to the force of command in Nicole's voice.

"Rafe, something wrong?" a guard called from the tunnel.

"Fire," Nicole's trooper cried, "Jesus, Mary and Joseph— *fire!* Inside the alien ship! There's a fire!"

Immediately, klaxons erupted from the asteroid, the skull-piercing wail of the fire alarm, a noise deliberately calculated to wake the dead. Aboard *Range Guide,* status lights began flashing insanely on hatch-side and bulkhead panels and Nicole winced as the Halyan't'a alarm, its pitch deliberately lowered enough to be exquisitely painful to the human ear, kicked her in the head.

Pandemonium reigned, as technos evacuating the starship in sudden, growing panic clashed with troopers trying to force their way inside to combat the blaze. The massive confusion was made to order for the two women and they crossed over to the rock without being challenged.

Once there, they ducked out of sight. Loudspeakers blared a steady stream of orders, while troopers worked to quell the panic. It quickly became evident that there was a major fire aboard *Range Guide.* Intense heat combined with huge amounts of choking, black smoke, burning fiercely out of control.

Nicole plugged a minicom into her ear. "Andrei," she called, "do you copy? Andrei, acknowledge, please, over? Andrei?"

"Receiving you five-by-five, Nicole. Are you well?"

"The fire stunt is magnificent. From this side, it sounds like you're about to lose the entire ship."

"Appearances, fortunately, are deceiving. The only compartments being sacrificed are peripheral and currently unused. They were the quarters of the Halyan't'a who were killed. This new damage shouldn't affect our planned minijump. And even without it, there's no way *Range Guide* could even try to return to s'N'dare without major dockyard work."

"A small army of troopers is heading InShip; is that a problem?"

"From the way the Halyan't'a are acting, the impression I have is: the more, the merrier. You needn't worry about the steelbacks."

"And the fire?"

"We cut off its fuel and void the compartments. Out in seconds."

"Great work, Andrei. We're inside the rock. On my mark, you initiate a thirty-minute countdown. At zero, whether we're back aboard or not, you get the hell out, copy?"

"That isn't much time."

"It's too much time, against opposition like Morgan."

"Nicole—*look out!*" Hana cried, stiff-arming her in the chest and leaping across the corridor towards a man who'd just emerged from a vertical DropShaft. It was hard tackle, and Hana pivoted as the two bodies slammed together, throwing the man over her hip in a perfect judo throw that bounced him off the wall. She hauled him over to Nicole, her prisoner groggy and helpless in her grasp, and they faded into a shadowed alcove.

It was Lal, the man they'd seen talking to Morgan.

"Keep a look-out, Hana," Nicole said. "Let me know if we've any more company."

"Copy. I shouldn't worry about it, though; our playmates here seem a bit preoccupied with the fire."

"Let's hope they stay that way." Nicole slapped Lal's face lightly once, twice, to bring the man around. As his eyes opened, Hana tucked the barrel of her hander in his ear.

"So," he said quietly, "Morgan's suspicions were correct. The Speaker is human."

"We want information," Nicole said.

"No."

"Then you're dead," Nicole told him. Hearing the flat finality in Nicole's voice, Hana looked at her in surprise, certain she was bluffing. The expression on Nicole's face, in her eyes, told her otherwise. Lal saw that, too.

"Wait!" the raider cried.

"Why?"

"You haven't a chance, you must know that. Two of you against hundreds. And we're as well-equipped—if not better —as your precious Air Force."

"Lal, if we've no chance, then your only chance is to cooperate. Tell us what we want to know, lead us where we want to go, and pray you don't get caught in the crossfire. Otherwise, you're a dead man. That's a certainty. Make your choice, I won't ask again."

"I . . . I shall help you."

"Keep him covered, Hana. He even twitches, cut him in half."

"Getting a bit blood-thirsty, aren't we?" Hana whispered as Nicole passed her.

"Merely doing what comes naturally." Nicole meant it as a joke, but was starting to suspect it was true.

Just then, a squad of men in anti-fire suits floated up the DropShaft from a level below.

"Where's the fire?" their leader snapped.

Nicole pointed towards the entrance to the transit tunnel; the air there was thick with haze, despite the efforts of the cyclers to keep the asteroid's atmosphere from being contaminated.

"Thanks," the man said. "Evacuate this section, we're going to seal it off. Follow me, men!"

Only when they'd disappeared into the smoke did Nicole relax, glancing back at her friend with a wide grin. "Oh my heart," she mock-groaned. "Frights like that, I can do without." But Hana didn't react and Nicole reverted to business. "Take a look at this," she said, indicating a large plastic rectangle mounted at head height next to the DropShaft.

"What is it?" Hana asked, marching Lal over with her.

"A map," he said. It combined a schematic diagram of the asteroid with a detailed plan of this level, major compartments neatly labeled, either in full or indecipherable acronyms.

Nicole realized that the man's hair was sticky with blood over the right ear.

"He tried to get rambunctious when he saw the firemen," Hana explained. "I had to slug him."

"Nice work," Nicole said.

"It's a compliment I can do without."

"I'd leave you out of this if I could! I know you're not military, I know this isn't your job, but there's no one else! I can't do it alone, I *need* you! And I need to trust you."

Hana nodded. "I know. I guess," slight pause, a sigh, "it's that I'm finding it easier than *I* ever dreamed to do things I always abhorred. Learning to be a killer was never part of my program."

"I'll take Lal and try to find Ciari and Shavrin. And Morgan. Your target's the central life-support station. Give me fifteen minutes and then blow everything in sight with your hander; if feasible, blow their powersystems as well. Anything to create as much chaos as humanly possible."

"You don't ask for much."

"Afterward, hotfoot it back to *Range Guide*. Don't forget,

once I cue Andrei, we'll have exactly a half-hour. If we're not home by then, we'll be left behind. Clear?"

"As crystal."

"It only sounds impossible."

Hana managed a derisive snort.

"Andrei—?"

"Yes, Nicole," she heard in her earjack.

"Sorry for the delay, we've had some slight problems. Here it comes, then: three, two, one—*mark!*"

"I copy," he acknowledged. "Launch minus eighteen hundred seconds and counting. Get a rush on, you two—and good luck."

"Go!" Nicole snapped, shoving Hana towards the Drop-Shaft. Then, she hauled Lal to his feet. "Morgan ordered a medical exam for the prisoners—are they still there?" She tucked her hander tight under the small man's chin, her tone demanding an immediate, truthful reply.

"Y-yes."

A glance at the map board told her where the infirmary was and she frog-marched Lal along the silent, deserted corridors, telling the one raider they passed that Lal had been injured in the fire. The man offered to help but Nicole told him to assist at the fire scene instead, there were bound to be more casualties. Lal said nothing; the muzzle of Nicole's gun, snug against his side, hidden by the bulk of his own body, kept his mouth shut.

Two troopers stood guard outside the infirmary. Nicole called out that she had a wounded man here, could they give her a hand, please? She gave them a moment to relax and react and then she shoved Lal as hard as she could into the arms of the nearer one, diving over the woman's head to fire her hander at full power at the helmet of the other. The needle-thin energy beam seared through the faceplate as if it didn't exist and the trooper crumpled. Nicole gasped, she'd never imagined the weapon held such power.

Almost too late, she remembered the other trooper. She spun in place, in time to see Lal punched aside as the woman brought up her shotgun and fired from the hip. In that same instant, Nicole kicked the wall, throwing herself below the line of fire, crying out reflexively as pellets clipped her side. Nicole pulled the trigger as she fell, scything her beam fan-wise across the corridor, and the trooper shrieked in horrible agony as she was cut in two. There was no blood, save Nicole's own. The heat of the beam instantly cauterized its wounds. But the stench of charred meat made her want to vomit. Lal did, before curling into a sobbing ball, cringing away from the carnage.

The infirmary door flew open and an unarmored officer, flechette pistol in hand, stepped into view. It was an easy shot, but Nicole didn't take it.

Instead, she called out to the man, "Freeze!" He had sense, and did as he was told. "Toss the gun away," she ordered, and when he had, "Now, hands on top of your head and move back into the room—slowly!"

Nicole followed him inside, using him for cover. She looked swiftly around the room. It wasn't very crowded; the officer and Morgan were the only non-medicos present. Shavrin was tied to a chair and, from the appearance of some of the medicos, Nicole could guess why. To the Halyan't'a, Ciari had told her, the person of the Speaker was sacrosanct, to be defended at any cost. Ciari was strapped naked to an examining table; he'd evidently resisted as well, and been hurt for his trouble. There was a nasty pattern of bruises along his ribs and he wore a beaut of a black eye.

"Don't move," Nicole told the raiders. She spotted a medico at the opposite end of the room edging towards a desk, and swung the barrel of her hander fractionally in his direction; he took the hint.

"You," she tapped the officer on his shoulder, "release the Speaker." The man hesitated.

"Do it, Wallis," Morgan said calmly. "The young lady means business."

As Wallis moved, Nicole moved with him, always giving herself a clear field of fire. The bulk of her concentration was focused on Morgan. He was the most dangerous man in the room, and probably on the entire rock, no matter how blasé and relaxed he might appear. Nicole knew that, if there was trouble, he'd be the one to start it. And, if given half a chance, finish it as well.

Ciari came off the table slowly, rubbing life back into stiff, sore limbs.

"You okay?" Nicole asked, sliding over, her tone con-

cerned; she hadn't anticipated him or Shavrin being too badly
hurt to travel unassisted.

"I'll live." He managed a grim smile. "Don't fret, Nicole. I
ache in all sorts of nasty places, but I can still function."

"Glad to hear it. You want to release the Matriarch, and
collect these bozos' weapons, before any of them get any
ideas?" As he did so, Nicole stole a glance at her watch. Time
was racing by; they had to get moving.

She was turning as the dart hit. That's what saved her,
making a fatal shot through the heart a wicked shoulder
wound instead. At first, she wasn't even aware she'd been hit.
But although her brain hadn't yet gotten the full message, her
body knew what was happening and reacted instinctively. The
shot came from behind, which meant the sniper had to be in
the doorway, so Nicole kept turning, kicking herself down and
to the side, dropping to cover behind the examination table.
Her consciousness still hadn't quite caught up with events.
They seemed to be passing in an eerie sort of slow motion, as
they had aboard *Wanderer* during those last terrible minutes
over Wolfe's asteroid.

Nicole registered a belated warning from Ciari as she
brought up her hander. Another dart struck the table and exploded, but she ignored it. She didn't bother aiming, she simply flipped the selector to the Halyan't'a ideograph
representing broad beam, pointed the gun in the right general
direction, and pulled the trigger.

She took a necessary split second to check her target. The
door's steel frame was buckled and both it and the rock wall
across the corridor were badly charred, graphic testimony
to the raw power of Nicole's weapon. She thought of the
Halyan't'a rifles and shuddered at the idea of what they could
do. Of the sniper, there was no sign. As she ducked back
under cover, a bullet clipped the base of the table, centimeters
from her head.

"Ciari," she called.

"Shavrin and I are fine, Nicole. We're both armed and we
have good cover. I think Morgan's the one who fired."

"Who else," she grumped to herself. She tried moving her
wounded arm and immediately regretted it. Then, louder,
"Major, how about giving up, before this gets nasty?"

"It's already quite nasty enough for my taste, Lieutenant.

But why should I? You're in the heart of my turf, outnumbered and outgunned, even in this room. If anyone should surrender, it's you."

"You've seen what my hander can do. All I have to do is hose your side of the compartment. You and your people might get lucky, but I wouldn't count on it. Dump your weapons, or I'll fire—copy?"

Silence.

"I'm losing patience, Major!"

"Here's my weapon, Ms. Shea." A pistol floated into view.

Morgan rose to his feet behind a doctor's desk, hands visible. Nicole stayed as low as she could, gritting her teeth against the pain that slashed across her torso, from wounded side to torn shoulder, with even the slightest move. She wondered why she hadn't yet slipped into shock and then concluded, absurdly, that she had and hadn't yet realized it. She deliberately flexed her arm, using the pain to sweep away her muzzy-headedness.

"Marshal, cover the Major. If anything pops, drop him." She heard his acknowledgment as she kept talking. "I'll handle the others. Right—the lot of you—on your feet! No fast moves—no moves at all unless I give the word—and keep your hands where I can see them. I spot a gun, I'll burn you all."

Nicole was about to gather them together and tie them up when a low, rolling rumble shook the entire asteroid. The lights flickered once, then went out.

In the room, only two people reacted before everything went black. Nicole and Morgan moved simultaneously with the sound of the explosion, Morgan diving sideways, out of sight, while Nicole headed for Ciari and Shavrin. She fired as she fell, but all she did was slash a jagged line across the bulkhead above her elusive target, exposing the bedrock underneath.

Nicole's outstretched hand found the edge of another examining table and she hauled herself up and over as fast as she could, assuming that Morgan was going for a gun. She was right, and a dart hissed past her. She fired blind back at him and heard a scream. She cursed. The voice was wrong. She'd hit one of the other raiders.

"Ciari!" she called in a frantic, raw-voiced whisper.

"Here," he replied beside her. She jumped. "What in the Seven Hells was *that?*"

She thought of asking what "Seven Hells" were, but decided her curiosity could keep. "Hana," she replied hoarsely, nodding in admiration. "I told her to bust up the rock's life-support control system and as much of their powersystem as possible. She did better than I expected."

"For you, she would. Pity we're stuck in this hole."

"That's the least of our troubles. We've got fifteen minutes to reach *Range Guide* before Andrei warps her out of here."

"How do we find our way in the dark?"

Nicole pulled a MapMaker out of a thigh pocket of her coveralls and flicked it on. The plasma display was a welcome glow.

"Very nice, Nicole. All we have to do now is get out of the infirmary in one piece."

"Yah." Nicole returned the beam setting to narrow focus and snapped off a random, unaimed shot in the general direction of the opposition; a couple of raiders immediately answered in kind, scattering their shots off the table and overhead. They ceased fire after that single volley. Careful to make no sound, Nicole stretched flat just above the floor, edging into the open, using the hander's infrared scanner to sweep the room. The raiders had decent cover, but nothing that would protect them for long against her hander.

Suddenly, there was a faint *clink* of metal from the opposite end of Nicole's table. Instantly, every armed raider sprang into view and cut loose, their concentrated fire ripping chunks of material from deck and table, sending ricochets buzzing throughout the room. Nicole swept her energy beam across the deck directly in front of them, trying to scare more than hurt, but ready to kill if her ploy didn't work.

As the raiders fell back in disarray, some crying out to her not to shoot, that they surrendered, Nicole grabbed Ciari's hand. She told him to catch hold of Shavrin, and then headed for the door. She let go as she cleared the entrance, twisting in midair to use her sneakered feet to rebound off the still hot bulkhead across the way. She landed in a combat crouch, braking herself with a hand and both feet while she scanned the passage ahead with her hander's infrared. The corridor was empty.

"Ciari," she whispered, "you still with me?"

"Here, Nicole." His voice placed him a meter or so behind and above her. "I have Shavrin."

"Clear the door. Carefully. Let's not give some glory-hunting asshole in there any ideas. Are you near the cool bulkhead?"

"Affirmative."

"Move towards my voice, then, until we make contact." Moments passed, while Nicole spread-eagled herself against the wall, an eye glued to the scanner, the gun covering the infirmary door. No one inside, it seemed, was eager to play hero. Good; she'd had her fill of slaughter.

She felt a feather-light stir of air across the outstretched fingers of her bad arm as Ciari's hand just missed hers, then he had her. The jolt was excruciating and she tasted blood, cursing to herself for biting the inside of her cheek. For a couple of breaths, all she could do was stand stock-still, hand in hand, not daring to move, holding onto Ciari and consciousness for dear life.

"You're hurt," he exclaimed.

She nodded, forgetting that he couldn't see, then said, "It's not serious," hoping he'd believe the lie. "I'll keep."

"How much time," he asked.

"Damned if I know; my watch got smashed in the scuffle. None to waste, that's certain. You have a weapon?"

"Shotgun, off a trooper."

"Then you're rearguard. Keep the doorway covered; I don't want any more surprises from that quarter."

"What's wrong?"

"When you or Shavrin drew the raider's fire—by the way, I thank you for that, should have thought of it myself—"

"No one's perfect, Red."

"—anyway, when those fucks popped up, I got a pretty good look at them through my IR scanner. I didn't see Morgan."

"Maybe he didn't 'pop.' "

"I think he ran. Probably the moment the lights blew, after taking those shots at me. If he did, we can bank on his being somewhere up ahead. Between us and *Range Guide*. And this time, when we run into him, he won't be armed with a lousy little darter."

"You're sure?"

"It's what I'd do in his place."

"Can we follow a different route to the dock?"

"We're committed to the route recorded on the MapMaker. Besides, Morgan probably knows every cubic centimeter of this base by heart; he can find us no matter which way we go. Getting ourselves lost in the process will only make it easier for him. Nothing else for it but to be careful and keep our fingers crossed."

The air swirled and eddied slightly as bodies moved in the darkness, and his hand in hers was replaced by Shavrin's. It was warmer than human and her claws pricked Nicole's skin. The Matriarch gave a squeeze, which Nicole decided meant that Ciari was in position, and the three of them started down the corridor.

At the first junction, Nicole checked every direction before they moved into the open, only to find the way clear. A few levels above them as they crossed, they could see the jiggling beams of portable work lamps—a repair crew, struggling to restore the collapsed systems—but they were too far away to be any sort of threat.

"Any action?" she asked Ciari.

"All quiet behind."

"The same ahead, so far. I wish that was good news."

"Shall I take the point?"

"I'm fine."

"You don't sound it."

"Neither do you, chum."

"Which way, then?"

"Down two levels, then left."

"Nicole, there are bound to be emergency flashlights or lamps somewhere along these corridors; why don't we take some? We'll be able to move faster."

"We'll also be a helluva lot better target. Or they'll draw the attention of everyone else in this rock, thinking we're a rescue or repair team, like the one we just passed. I'm surprised at you, Ciari; I thought you'd know better than that."

"You're right. I should. I do."

"As you said, you're not yourself. A Speaker is logical, not a hunter."

"Hunters, Red, are what Halyan't'a *are*."

She pushed herself down the DropShaft, finding the correct level by touch, and then waited for the others to join her. There was a noticeable tinge of smoke in the air. With the LifeSystems inoperative, smoke from *Range Guide*'s fire was quickly spreading throughout the complex. *They must not have gotten the emergency bulkheads closed,* Nicole thought, *lucky for us.*

Every now and then, despite her care, Nicole made a wrong turn and they lost valuable seconds retracing their steps until the MapMaker's warning beeper finally fell silent. It was a laborious, drawn-out, nerve-wracking process, and the geometrically increasing tension soon took its toll. Though they'd covered barely a few hundred meters since leaving the infirmary, Nicole felt as if she's run a marathon. Her left arm was virtually useless and she'd long since passed the hander back to Shavrin and while the pellet wounds on her side were superficial, they bled freely, making her that much weaker.

The smoke was very thick when they reached the final DropShaft, making them cough almost constantly. Shavrin was most affected by the bad air; Nicole was half-carrying her. They were crawling now, a simple matter in zero-gravity, staying as close to the floor as possible, where the air was cleanest. As they neared the transit tunnel, they found evidence of the savage battle that had erupted after Nicole had left the ship. Most of the bodies were raiders, some in armor, most in coveralls, but, occasionally, they came across a Halyan't'a casualty. Each time, Shavrin growled deep in her throat, the noise ringing all sorts of primordial bells at the base of Nicole's brain. A squall of mingled rage and grief that was echoed louder by Ciari.

As yet, they'd had no contact with Morgan.

Nicole knew that was about to change.

She stopped Ciari, faced him in the dark, touched him with her right hand. His skin was hot to the touch, and he was making unconscious *chirrup*-growls that reminded Nicole of the noises her family's cats made when they were hunting. With a start, she realized he was wearing steel finger-claws that mimicked the natural claws possessed by Shavrin and the Halyan't'a. He'd taken her good arm in both his hands and was gently, absently flexing his fingers, digging the claws into her forearm. It frightened her to realize how little she really knew him now.

"Ben," she said softly, "listen to me. We're nearly there—up this shaft a level, then straight ahead through the exit, follow the corridor around to the reception area and we're home. This is where Morgan's going to make his move."

"I know. I can smell him. I want him, Nicole; he's mine."

Smell him, she thought, astounded, *through this smoke?!*

"No," she told him, putting all her strength of command into her voice. "Do you hear me, Marshal. *No!*"

He snarled with anger, claws drawing blood. "He's *mine,* Nicole. He killed Cat and Paolo and Chagay. He's slain Halyan't'a. It's my right to claim his life in return."

"I'm in command," Nicole said slowly, spacing her words. "Until that changes, you'll do as I say, when I say it. You have one responsibility, Marshal, and that's to return Shavrin safely to her vessel."

"She's going to help me; she wants Morgan dead, too!"

"Does she? Ask her. She'll tell you what I'm telling you. She's needed to command *Range Guide;* you're needed to help her communicate with Andrei and Hana and the ships that find you. Without you both, this Embassy is over, and all the lives lost thus far will have been sacrificed in vain. That comes first, not your personal desire for vengeance, no matter how imperative it may seem. *Do you understand?!*"

The Speaker discipline etched in Ciari's genes by the Halyan't'a virus forced him to relay Nicole's question to Shavrin, and repeat the answer to Nicole. Shavrin indeed understood how her "little brother" felt. But Nicole was correct. Duty must take precedence over desire.

Ciari roared, a feline/human outcry that echoed and re-echoed through the still corridors.

Well, Nicole thought with a grim amusement, *if Morgan had any doubts about our location, that took care of 'em.*

"What do you want me to do?" Ciari asked, his voice dull.

"Wait. Here. Shavrin has the hander and I'm leaving you the MapMaker."

"You're going up against Morgan unarmed—?!"

"Don't be absurd. I took this off a corpse." She laid a Halyan't'a crossbow across her lap. Ciari caressed it lightly, pausing when his hand touched hers.

"Only one quarrel?" he asked after a while, his hand still resting on hers.

"No. I've a quiver as well. I'm good for a half-dozen shots. I'll go first, to draw his fire; you two wait till the fireworks start. I'll try to lead Morgan away from the transit tunnel, to give you a clear run."

"Suppose he doesn't fall for it?"

Nicole shrugged. "Calculated risk."

"Let me help, Nicole; we could work together."

She was tempted. *If only you were in your right mind, Ben,* she thought, *if I were sure I could trust you, even a little...*

"No," she said. "Stay with Shavrin. Her safety is your primary responsibility."

"Usually," he joked, "where Speakers are concerned, it's the other way 'round." And he pulled his hand away, the tips of his claws raking through her sleeve to leave parallel trails of blood along the inside of her arm.

Nicole told herself these weren't really Ciari's reactions, but those of a Halyan't'a, courtesy of the goddamned Speaker virus, his own natural passion being twisted and accentuated by the equally fierce emotions of that feline, predator race, the vicious rip-tide of feelings somehow breaking down both the rational restraints of his own mind and character and those imposed on him by the Speaker as well. He was being torn to shreds inside, a state of ongoing insanity that was growing progressively worse, as more and more of his human personality was submerged beneath the Halyan't'a facade. Nicole had no idea how to stop it. All she had in her favor was whatever ties of love and respect bound the two of them, combined with her own force of character. Slender threads on which to hang three lives.

"Don't fold on me, Ben," she breathed. "I'm counting on you."

She tried her radio a final time. If she could contact Andrei or Hana, they might be able to hit Morgan from the rear and either capture the renegade or drive him off. But all she heard was ragged static. Reception had disintegrated the moment Hana's bombs had gone off, making Nicole's attempts to call for re-enforcements, and learn how the others were faring, a waste of effort. For all she knew, their cause was lost, her crew dead, *Range Guide* full to the brim with raiders.

She wondered how much time they had before Andrei fired the drive. Not much, probably. She shook her head in grim amusement—it would be too ironic for words to make it to the tunnel the instant after Ignition.

With that cheerful thought in mind, Nicole had to force herself to move slowly, cautiously, through the pitch-black maze. Every sense, every fiber of her being, felt strained to the breaking point—alert for the slightest sound, stir in the air, smell, anything. Even though she couldn't see her hand in front of her face, maddeningly intrusive ghost images kept bursting across her mind's eye—memory flashes of what she'd seen coming this way barely a half-hour before. She had no idea how accurate the pictures were, so she ignored them, tried to shut them out of her awareness.

She checked the IR scanner on her bow; the DropShaft was clear in both directions. She was about to push off when her foot slipped on something wet on the deck. She didn't fall—impossible in zero-gravity, at least in the traditional sense of falling *down*—but she did sprawl inelegantly in midair until she managed to brake herself with a hand on the entrance to the DropShaft.

Underneath her was a body in battle armor. Inspired, she slung her bow across her back and hooked her good arm under the shoulders of the dead raider, heaving him into the shaft with an effort that left her sweating and nauseous. But she couldn't afford the seconds needed to rest and recover her strength. Instead, she gritted her teeth and shoved the body upward as hard as she could.

The suit went up fast, as it would have done were the raider wearing it still alive and heading into a firefight. Nicole was right behind it.

As the head and shoulders of the suit cleared the deck above, a rifle blaster fired on needle-beam, scoring a direct hit on the helmet. The rifle fired again, this time at the torso—a perfect shot through the heart. By then, Nicole had cleared the shaft and spotted where the shots were coming from. She paused long enough to snap off a quarrel, then sped around a corner and down a tangential passage. She made it to the first junction with all of a split second to spare—*Morgan*, she thought, heart pounding like a sledgehammer, *it has to be Morgan, and the slimy fuck has a blaster, one of the big ones, must have stripped it off a Halyan't'a; oh Christ oh God I'm dead I can't outgun that what am I saying, the prick missed, I conned him, he made a mistake!* Behind her, the sniper slapped his beam setting to broad and scythed his rifle across the compartment, lighting it and the surrounding corridors with a lambent red glow. The gentle light was deceptive, however; what Morgan created in those few seconds was a holocaust, an instant vision of Hell.

He did tremendous damage, but missed Nicole completely. Morgan was pivoting clockwise—unaware that Nicole had cut away to her right. So, she merely waited until the deadly lance of energy moved away from her before stepping out of hiding and letting fly a second bolt.

She heard a sharp cry and the rifle stopped firing. She didn't stay where she was. The wound might be superficial, or she might not have even hit the man at all; Morgan might well be putting on an act. She turned quickly down the next corridor she came to.

The faint scrape of metal on metal told her that Morgan was following.

Almost instantly, Nicole knew she'd made a fatally wrong turn. She was swimming as fast as she could—without making any noise—and though she figured she'd gone a ways, she hadn't found any side passages. She must have turned into a main Trunk corridor—a direct, express, limited-access route from the docking bay to deep within the asteroid. She couldn't be certain, of course. In the darkness, a junction could be right in front of her, how was she to know? But if she acted on that assumption and was proved wrong, she was dead. She was well within the effective range of Morgan's rifle, without shielding or any place to hide.

She checked her scanner. The image was miserable. The background heat generated by Morgan's barrage severely distorted its reception. Nicole prayed his scanner was having similar trouble. She turned back the way she'd come, leapfrogging from surface to surface—floor to wall to ceiling. Her only chance was to catch the man by surprise, to get in close where the rifle wouldn't be effective and try to take him hand to hand.

With a rotten shoulder.

Nicole had almost reached the junction when she heard the

snap of the rifle firing, and saw the entrance to a far corridor fill with light. Morgan was spraying each passage in turn, counter-clockwise this time. Nicole had two shots before it was her turn.

She exploded out of the tunnel like an Olympic sprinter. Morgan spotted her immediately and held his trigger finger down as he swung the blaster to bear. But the advantage was Nicole's. She had a marginal head start and her random pattern through the air kept her foe fractionally off balance, just enough to make the difference.

She caromed into him, the rifle beam scorching her cheek. She smashed at Morgan like a crazy woman as she tried to wrest the gun from his grasp. Somehow, she managed, sending it looping through the air, out of reach. She tried to pin the man, only to discover that the cry of pain she'd heard *had* been a ruse. The bastard was unhurt! And while luck had saved Nicole till now, it was little use against Morgan's decades of training and experience. She struck out with hands and feet, denying the pain in her left arm, forcing it to function, but he parried the blows easily, holding on to Nicole with one hand while the other hammered at her body. There was no elegance to this roughhouse fight, and each knew it would probably end with a death.

Morgan had Nicole on her back, his hands tight around her throat, pressing against the carotid artery. If she couldn't break free, she'd be unconscious in seconds. Her right arm was tangled in the slings of her crossbow and quiver, pretty much useless. As a red haze closed over her mind, she twisted desperately, bitterly aware that she was at the end of her strength, while Morgan seemed at the peak of his. In the last, brutal flurry of punches, he'd thrown three to Nicole's one, and that one hadn't bothered him a bit.

Suddenly, the slings slipped off her shoulder, giving the arm a bit more play. Nicole was running on instinct, her subconscious dredging up every dirty trick taught at the Academy and, more importantly, by Ciari. She groped for the bow. The safety was on, but that was all right, she had no intention of firing yet—and jabbed it straight upward into Morgan's body.

This time, the raider's *whoulff* of surprise and pain was no sham. He released Nicole's neck and pushed away, trying to get clear before she could pull the trigger. Nicole snagged his leg with the bow, yanking him down, and got a foot in the face for her trouble. Morgan bounced off the deck like a jack-in-the-box, moving faster than Nicole could follow, over her head and towards the junction.

Nicole rolled into a sitting position, freeing the safety as she brought the bow to her shoulder. She tried to raise her left arm to steady the bow, but it refused to move, so she rested the weapon on her upraised knees. She put her eye to the sight in time to see Morgan sweep across the deck towards his rifle, visible in the glow of the fires he had set. Nicole was trembling but there was no time for any Zen meditations; she had this single shot, it had to be good.

Nicole held her breath, centered the cross hairs. Morgan found the rifle and rolled flat to the deck, to present as small a target as possible as he brought it to bear. She pulled the trigger.

The quarrel took him full in the chest, and threw him back and away from the gun; he didn't stop until he struck the wall.

By then, Nicole was staggering in the opposite direction, down the passage to the reception stage and the transit tunnel beyond. She'd gone all of a dozen steps when, without any warning, the lights came on.

She cried out, throwing her good hand in front of her flash-blinded eyes. The smoke was so thick that, even at full power, the illumination was little better than a foggy twilight on Earth, but it was more than sufficient to dazzle eyes with fully dilated pupils.

Still, Nicole pushed on, desperate not to be left behind. Out of the smog, she heard her name. She tried to reply, but could manage no more than a strangled croak that *she* could barely hear and which instantly sent her into a spasm of vicious, hacking coughs.

Again, her name was called, cried by a man's electronically amplified voice.

"Here," she managed, or thought she did. She opened her eyes, but that was of marginal use. Even if there was anything to see, her vision was blocked by a huge shimmery purple and blueish-green ball, with smaller dots made up of weirder colors dancing around its rim. Eyelids open or closed, it made no difference; the spots wouldn't go away.

She collapsed to the floor, dragging herself along, feeling her way by touch. No matter how hard she tried, she couldn't draw a decent breath, her chest hurt so, everything hurt, she couldn't get a purchase on the slippery plating, a nail tore on a deck seam, she tried pushing with her toes, cheered inside as her body stirred. *Try again*, she thought, *do it again, nothing to it, push push PUSH!*

A shape emerged from the shadows, wearing an airpack and carrying a spare for her.

Ciari!

He knelt beside Nicole and fitted the pack over her face. She wanted simply to sit where she was forever and gulp down the cool, fresh air, even though her initial reaction was total nausea, but Ciari tugged her up, half-carrying her to the ramp.

"Time . . .," croaked Nicole.

"None," Ciari told her. "Our fifteen minutes ran out seven minutes ago. Shavrin and Andrei have been holding the ship till we found you."

"Goddamn it, I—*why?!*—told you . . . not to . . ."

"Peace, woman. Save your strength."

A Halyan't'a in full armor—looking like she'd seen some action—awaited them at the transit tunnel. Strangely, as they neared *Range Guide,* the atmosphere became much clearer. Nicole could feel a definite draft washing across her body, as the smoke was flushed OutShip, into the asteroid, adding to the pressure on the raiders' LifeSystem.

"Others . . .?"

"Fine. Hana came home via the aft tunnel. That's been blown, as have all mooring lines and umbilicals. This tunnel's our sole link with the rock. Did you nail Morgan?" he asked without missing a beat.

"Think so. Hit him . . . with a bolt."

"You didn't make sure?"

"Ben, all I cared . . . was getting out . . . intact . . ."

Ciari stopped, snapping a command to the sentry before reaching for Nicole's bow. She tightened her grip and refused to let go.

"What—?!" she demanded.

"Honor demands life for life, Nicole. I don't expect you to understand."

Desperation made her find her full voice. "I do understand. But this isn't the time! We have to go!"

"I have to finish Morgan!"

"That's crazy!"

Ciari spat another command, but the warrior never lived to obey as a volley of rocket darts ripped her apart. Nicole reacted faster than she thought possible, kicking Ciari's legs out from under him and hauling him to the deck. She wrenched the sentry's rifle from her hand, dimly registering that there was blood everywhere, how incongruously messy this death was, and returned fire. The response was a second volley of HiPower warheads that shattered plating and sprayed shrapnel all around them. Nicole heard the shrill whistle of escaping air and knew the tunnel had been breached.

She hooked her hand onto Ciari's airpack and heaved him towards the open airlock. He bellowed in fury, trying to grab hold of something to brake his flight, but Nicole had deliberately sent him down the center of the tunnel; he'd be hard pressed stopping before he reached the lock's inner hatch. She cut loose into the smoke again, a broad beam blast to keep the oppositions' heads down, and followed hot on Ciari's heels, a final surge of adrenaline giving her the strength required for this idiot stunt. She snagged the hatch controls and yanked hard.

Ciari was on her as the massive door cycled shut. She ducked his claws and grabbed him by the waist, shoving the pair of them up above the mass of the hatch, trying to keep Ciari as far as she could from the opening.

Close, please, dammit, she thought desperately. *Close!*

"Let me go," he raged. "Let me *go!*"

"Stop it, Ben! Get hold of yourself. You can't go out there! Remember who you *are!*"

"Morgan's out there! I have to kill him! The dead cry out for vengeance! If I don't, their souls will drift forever in *Maenaes't'whct'y'a*—the void *between*—without honor, without Name!"

"That isn't Morgan! It's a squad of raiders, in full armor,

and if we don't get our act together they're going to blast their way in here! Ciari, please—!"

He didn't hear, or didn't want to hear. Her words had no effect, except perhaps to make him even madder. Fortunately, he'd forgotten virtually all he'd ever known about fighting, or Nicole wouldn't have lasted seconds. He was trying to kill her as a Halyan't'a would, but his body couldn't obey the commands given by his brain. His timing was off. He kept missing, giving Nicole openings she couldn't ignore. She couldn't match his power. He was too big, for all his unaccustomed clumsiness, and she was death warmed over, so she went the sneaky route, ducking under a roundhouse slash of his claws to climb onto his back like a leech, legs around his waist to lock herself in place, arm tight around the throat. Then, before he could dislodge her, she did to him what Morgan had tried with her—pressed down on his carotid artery until he blacked out.

The wallcom beeped and she heard Hana's frantic voice: "Nicole! What's happening in there, we don't have video? Are you all right? Nicole! *Nicole!*"

"Alive, Hanako, both of us. He went kind of bonkers, had to deck him. Tell Andrei—fire the engines!"

"As soon as you're clear . . ."

"Now! There's a battle squad of raiders knocking at the door; we can't afford to wait any longer! If you're ready, Andrei, do it! Forget about us—*just get* Range Guide *the hell out of here!"*

Nicole heard a hiss and, for a split second, thought they'd been holed. Then, giant cushions ballooned outward from the bulkheads to fill the compartment. While she was able, Nicole scrambled to Ciari's side, casting about for the airpacks, but they were out of reach and the cushions were growing so quickly she had no time to get to one.

As the bags flowed over her, Nicole realized they weren't fabric at all, but some sort of gelatin. Instinctively, she held her breath, but the goo, warm and slightly cinnamon tasting, like the Halyan't'a atmosphere, forced its way down her throat and into her lungs. A numbness spread outward from her chest and Nicole was astounded to discover that, though she'd ceased breathing, she was in no way starved for oxygen. The gel was keeping her alive.

She felt a massive, basso vibration—a majestic *thrumm* that shook her inside and out, as it did the starship—

—and then she was crushed against the rear bulkhead by an acceleration so monstrous that, despite the gel, she was smashed into instant oblivion.

═══════ fourteen ═══════

SHE HEARD A musical chime, and then a soft, female voice inquired, "Destination, please?"

"Challenger Plaza," she replied.

"Stand by, please."

The computer announced, "A car is available. Do not enter the car until it has come to a complete stop and the access hatch is fully open, and watch your step crossing the sill."

She winced slightly as she settled herself into the seat nearest the door, stretching her right leg beside her cane and rubbing it. The leg was less than a fortnight out of its cast and, after months in zero and low-gravity hospital wards, even the Moon took some getting used to. She wasn't looking forward to her trip Earthside next week.

She dozed as the tiny Rapitrans car raced through the labyrinthine tunnels beneath DaVinci Base, outbound for Grissom Starport. She still tired easily, and today's award ceremony had taken her very nearly to the end of her string. She wanted a nice, firm bed and about a year's uninterrupted rest. But those luxuries would have to wait.

The gentle shift in the car's Delta-Vee that indicated its deceleration into a station woke her, and she stretched. As she did, she caught sight of herself in a polycrystal advertising poster, and grinned. She looked much the same as she had when she left the Moon aboard *Wanderer*. True, there were lines across her foreheard and around her eyes that hadn't been there fifteen months ago, but they weren't all that noticeable. Her physical injuries were healing nicely. There was no permanent damage, and in time, the medicos assured her, she'd be as good as new. The only permanent scars were inside her skull.

An obvious difference was the medal worn beneath the pilot's wings on her left breast. A simple silver cross, with a flaming golden Sun at the intersection—the Solar Cross.

Paolo and Cat had received the Congressional Medal of Honor, posthumously.

The wallcom chimed, the disembodied female voice spoke: "Arrival at your requested destination will be in one minute. Please remain seated until the vehicle has come to a full stop."

As the door swung open, she pushed herself clumsily to her feet, wondering, as she heard herself make a noise somewhere between a sigh and a groan, if this was what it was like to be old, and automatically slid her IdentiCard into the car's charge slot.

"Thank you for riding Lunar Rapitrans, Lieutenant Shea," the voice told her. "Have a pleasant day, and congratulations on your award."

She smiled incredulously as she turned back to the car. Whoever programmed the Rapitrans computer had a truly wacko sense of propriety. She loved it. "Thank you," she replied, "very much."

"You're quite welcome," the computer said as the hatch closed.

Nicole was laughing as she made her way up the ramp to Challenger Plaza.

Her mood changed as she crossed the broad promenade to the man-high cenotaph in its exact center. The monument wasn't really much to look at, just a pillar of rough-hewn, haphazardly stuck together stone, but the rocks that formed it were gathered from every planet and moon known to Humankind: Earth, Luna, Mars, Venus, Mercury, Pluto, the Jovian and Saturnian moons, all the big asteroids, and many of the small ones—the Outer Planets and their moons, plus the Out-System colonies of Faraway, Last Chance, Paradise and NieuwHome. The year didn't pass without some new chunk of rock, from some previously uncharted celestial body, being added.

Outside of Tranquility Base—where Neil Armstrong and "Buzz" Aldrin had become the first men to set foot on the Moon—this was the most famous memorial anywhere in Human Space.

One face of the cenotaph had been smoothed and polished. There was an etching of a Type 1 Rockwell STS—the original Shuttle—a second after Ignition, as the massive spacecraft was just lifting clear of the gantry. And below, a plaque. It bore no legend, only a list of names, but Nicole knew what it represented. She wouldn't be surprised if every child in the Global Village did. And you certainly didn't spend an hour inside the Air Force—and especially NASA—without learning of this memorial, and what it meant.

These were the names of those who'd died in the exploration of space. Gus Grissom, Ed White and Roger Chaffee of *Apollo 1*. The Russian, Vladimir Komarov. The crew of *Challenger*, in whose honor the plaza was named. So many names. With three new ones at the bottom: Catherine Garcia, Paul DaCuhna, Chagay Shomron.

As she looked at them, Nicole's fatigue finally caught up with her and she hunched forward, putting her weight on the cane. She reached up with a hand to wipe eyes suddenly blurred with tears and, for a while, stood motionless, crying, letting her grief carry her along.

"There's an old saying," a familiar voice said. " 'We fly, and we die.' "

Nicole automatically straightened to attention and saluted General Canfield, who shook her head. "No ceremony here, Nicole. No rank. Merely two astronauts—colleagues, young and," a slight pause, a slighter smile, "older, paying their respects to those who've gone before and paid the price."

Canfield held out a handkerchief and Nicole took it, wiped her eyes, blew her nose; the General tactfully motioned for her to keep it. They were dressed the same, in formal Air Force blues, Canfield's stars gleaming on her shoulder boards, medals striking multi-colored fire on her breast.

"I was thinking of the plaque at Chaffee," Nicole said, "listing the recipients of the Congressional. I wanted to claw Morgan's name off it. It was scary, to feel such hate after all this time, but to see him sharing space with the likes of Cat and Paolo, I thought it obscene."

"What Daniel became in no way diminishes what he was. Therein, I suppose, lies the tragedy of his life."

Nicole looked around the Plaza, following the vaulted columns up to their apex. The roof was a giant back-lit transparency of the galaxy that shifted in concert to the natural movement of the Moon, Earth and Sol, creating the illusion that one was outside, on the surface, gazing at the actual stars.

"I had a lot of time in hospital," she said. "I did a lot of reading." Now she looked Canfield in the eye. "I know."

"What"—Canfield placed the faintest emphasis on that word—"do you know?"

"My father was a junior member of the firm that handled your appeal; he got no credit, but I know his style. It's obvious he wrote the briefs."

"So?"

"What was he to you? And what am I?"

"A friend. And a somewhat smart-assed shavetail."

Nicole shook her head. "It was more. Too many people react as if my being here has something to do with you, that there's some sort of link between us, old business. Morgan wasn't simply coming after Cat when he ambushed *Wanderer;* I was part of it, two birds with one stone, a chance for Morgan to twist the knife into your guts, to hurt you for the sheer joy of it, before he finished the job. That does not bespeak a casual link."

"Your father and I were involved."

"Lovers?"

"In love. Very much so."

"But you wouldn't stay. And he couldn't go."

"What he was then—what we had—in no way diminishes what exists today. He loves your mother very much, I see that in you."

"What else?"

Canfield smiled, then chuckled. "A mirror," she said.

"I never asked for any special favors."

"What you got, young lady—good and bad—you earned. That won't change. It isn't your supposed connection to me that marks you. Though, on occasion, it will no doubt make life difficult. It's your own skill. You set your standard, Nicole; I, and my staff, merely mean to hold you to it."

"Lucky me."

"You look uncomfortable. Is your leg acting up?"

"A little. But mostly, it's this damn uniform. Haven't worn one in so long. I feel like I'm in a straight jacket. I'd give almost anything to dump it for some cut-offs, a sweatshirt, sneaks and my flight jacket."

"In time." She looked past Nicole. "Good morning, Marshal."

"General," Ciari replied.

"If you'll both excuse me," she said, "I suppose the Embassy awaits." And she strode purposefully away.

Ciari gathered Nicole into his arms and she couldn't help a wince as he swept her off the floor. Immediately, but gently, he set her down, eyeing her with concern.

"I'm okay," she assured him. "Really."

"Well," he confessed, certain he'd been conned, "you seemed fine last night."

"I was inspired. In retrospect, I was also crazy. I am paying the price."

A laugh rumbled out of him and she gave his hand a squeeze, thinking how nice it was to feel the smooth tips of his fingers again, instead of Halyan't'a fighting claws. Looking at him, she compared images. Shavrin had fed him the antidote to the Speaker virus as soon as rescue parties pulled them from the airlock. Nicole had seen the video tapes; even thinking about it, months later, made her queasy. The gel had saved them from certain death, but only by the barest of margins. Hana and Andrei, working with the Halyan't'a medical staff, had stablized them as best they could and then shoved them into stasis until they could be conveyed to a decent hospital facility. At that, for the first couple of weeks, it had been touch and go. Nicole almost hadn't made it.

Today, however, both were on the road to full recovery. Physically, Ciari's eyes were normal, though their perceptive range had expanded closer to Halyan't'a norms, and his hair would always possess a texture more Alien than human. He'd retained much of his ability to speak their language, while losing the vast majority of the racial memories that had briefly driven him insane. He was more graceful than he'd ever been, yet far less so than a Speaker; in bed, he'd complained bitterly of feeling like a "lump" whenever he moved.

"The moon for your thoughts," he asked her.

"I'll miss you," she said simply.

She wanted to say more — so much more — yet found herself confined by simple language. The words available to her weren't appropriate to what she wanted to say.

"I'll miss you, too," he said. "Walk with me?"

She let him lead, then cried out in mock-anguish: "My shit-for-brains memory's going, along with my manners. Have I congratulated you, Ben, on your appointment to our Embassy to the Halyan't'a?"

He smiled, nodded. "Often."

"See. I rest my case. Senile before thirty. Official translator, though — quite a responsibility."

"More than most suspect. I'm de facto number two to Ambassador Kimandre. His sole conduit to the Confederacy and theirs to him. Until they roll up another Speaker."

Nicole shook her head. "I doubt I could handle that kind of pressure. I'm always too tempted to go my own way."

"I wasn't much different. But I've changed."

"I envy you." She paused, buying herself time to gather her thoughts by gazing around the vast concourse. "You see the final report on Morgan's asteroid?" she asked, taking refuge in shop talk.

"Of course. I translated it for Shavrin."

"Of course." There was nothing left. The rock, all the ships within a thousand klick radius, simply vaporized — *poof* — when *Range Guide* warped away, leaving no clues as to who, or what, was backing the raiders, other than Lal's reference to some Corporation.

"They were a big outfit; the loss'll be noticed."

"Until the next big outfit takes its place."

"That's why we're here, Red, to help keep the buggers in their place." he glanced at his watch.

"Want to head for the boarding lounge?"

"Not particularly. But I suppose we must. Shavrin tells me I'm one of a kind; it'll be years before another Speaker — or a human — achieves my degree of knowledge, and especially comprehension."

"You'll be gone awhile."

"Awhile," he agreed, and the years yawned like an abyss between them.

He had a strangely rueful cast to his face and he turned, searching her eyes for the meanings behind her words. "I don't want this to end, Nicole. I know what I said, but we've built something special, you and I. If I go..."

"But you must. There's too much at stake not to."

"Cold solace."

"You have my heart, my love; what more can I offer?"

"Commitment?"

"God, I haven't felt so awkward since I was in junior high, leaving my first serious crush for two months of godawful summer camp. I was eleven. I thought I was going to die."

"What happened?"

"When I got home, everything had changed. We still liked each other, but the ol' *va-va-voom* had *va-va-voom'd* right out of our life."

"The wheel turns."

"True. You taught me that, Ben." She thought of a line from one of her Gran's favorite stories, that she delighted in reading to Nicole before bedtime a lifetime ago. "Where did you get so young and me so old, all of a sudden? The Speaker you imprinted must have been a baby?"

"Everything changes. Sometimes, for the better."

He leaned over and kissed her lightly on the lips, and her heart leapt as she felt the primal electricity as strong and vital as it had been at the start. She wrapped her arms around his back and pulled him as close to her as she could in a fierce, passionate embrace that put a fitting *coda* to all their stumbling words.

They didn't break contact until they had to, at the sound of the PA system's prefix-chime.

"Attention, please," a female voice, close cousin to the one on Lunar Rapitrans, announced, "this is the first call for all personnel assigned to the StarShip *Enterprise*. Will all personnel please report to Boarding Gate One, for scheduled lift-off at one-eight-zero-zero hours, Lunar Mean Time. Current time is one-seven-zero-zero hours, LMT.

"Marshal Benjamin Ciari and Lieutenant Nicole Shea, please report to Boarding Gate One, immediately."

There was a second chime and the voice began again, in

French, *"Faites attention, faites attention, mesdames et messieurs..."* The litany would be repeated in all the major Terran trading languages, and by then it would be time for the second warning.

A *mrrwowling* cry stopped them at the door to the VIP lounge. Shavrin, resplendent in formal dress. In the background, Nicole spotted General Canfield in conference with Ambassador Kimandre and two holo-figures she recognized as the President and the Soviet Premier, on a real-time video link from Earth. Her jaw dropped, aghast, at the expense involved in such a set-up.

Shavrin greeted them both, laying a gentle hand on Nicole's breast, over her heart. Ciari listened intently until she paused, then translated: "Shavrin apologizes for not being present during your convalescence and hopes you both understand why that was not possible and forgive the transgression."

"Of course," Nicole tried to say, but Ciari was still speaking.

"She further hopes you, Nicole, comprehend why she did what she did... to me. If words will not suffice—now that her mission has been substantially accomplished—she is prepared to offer her life in atonement. It is called *alach'n'yn*—blood price."

Nicole was stunned. From the volumes of notes of his debriefings Ciari had sent her, she had an idea of the implications of what he'd just said. Impulsively, she pulled Shavrin to her and held her close, hoping body language might convey what words could not. Shavrin was stiff at first, but then Nicole felt her relax, clawed fingers lightly stroking the young woman's neck. There was a softly rumbling resonance, vaguely akin to a purr, deep within Shavrin's chest that made Nicole feel safe and warm and cherished and tears suddenly stung her eyes, without Nicole knowing quite why. When they disengaged, Shavrin gave her that familiar, quizzical, sideways look and growled at Ciari.

"Have I transgressed?" Nicole asked.

"Quite the contrary."

"Ben, please. Tell Shavrin I could never demand this *alach'n'yn* of her. It's not for me to demand, even if I wanted it. Which I don't. If I was hurt by her actions, it was indirectly. You were the one who was transformed; if you can understand and accept—and, I don't know, forgive, if that's appropriate—then what right do I have to bear a grudge?"

Ciari smiled. "I always knew you had potential. Nice to see it realized so well." She flushed in pleased surprise. "By the way, Red, that was nice pronunciation."

"I've been working with those language tapes you sent me."

"I'll make more, then. Something to remember me by."

"Don't make fun, not of that."

The Lounge was bustling with dignitaries—all of whom were discretely ogling Shavrin and the others of her Command Staff, while a few spared somewhat less discreet glances at Nicole and Ciari. She was painfully conscious of the prying eyes. It was hard enough being paraded before your fellow officers, but to be the center of attention among total strangers, even for only a few minutes . . .

"Attention please—this is final call for all personnel assigned to the StarShip *Enterprise* . . ."

There was a polite cough behind them, indicating an interruption that could not be denied, Jomo Kimandre of the East African Union, former Secretary-General of the United Nations, now Ambassador Extraordinary of the planet Earth to the Halyan't'a Confederacy.

"Your pardon, Leftenant." He spoke with a faintly cultured English accent, legacy of study at OxBridge and later exile in London. "Marshal, but we must be on our way. Time, tide, and evidently the stars, wait for no one."

"We'll be along, sir," Ciari told him.

"Certainly." He held out a hand to Nicole and she automatically took it. "May I say, Leftenant, how much this world of ours is in your debt. Few know of the service you have done but it is something that will never, I think, be forgotten."

Her ears burned. "It was my duty, sir. No more, no less."

He smiled, the way her father did when he knew the Secret and no one else, and nodded.

"Farewell. I hope, someday, we meet again." He kissed her hand and strode up the transit tunnel leading out to the shuttle craft that would take his party up to the *Enterprise*, in her parking orbit high overhead. Nicole and Ciari followed at a much slower pace, with Shavrin, hand in hand while she watched. They spoke little.

At the crest of the ramp, Shavrin removed a chain from her neck and placed it around Nicole's. As she did, the young woman had a flash of memory, of the Memorial Service aboard *Range Guide* and her wild changeling dance with Shavrin. The Halyan't'a Captain had been wearing the chain that night.

" 'Of my house,' " Ciari repeated formally, word for word, " 'art thou become, of my flesh art thou made; thou art to me as a kit from mine own womb, bearing rights, titles, honors and assigns as do pertain thereof. Blood hast thou shed on my behalf, blood have we shared to bind our spirits forever.

" 'Fare thee well, daughter.' "

And she was gone. Slowly, Nicole released a breath she hadn't been aware she was holding.

"I'm going to cry again, dammit," she grumbled.

"Good," Ciari said. "I hate solos." And she saw that his eyes were unnaturally bright.

They kissed. And he left her.

And she knew it was over.

She stood motionless, facing the mural-covered wall as the hatch silently closed, waiting for the jolt that would signify the docking cradle moving out to launch position. Eventually, it came, and, a minute after that, the status board above the reception desk notified all concerned of a successful lift-off.

In her mind's eye, she watched the shuttle climb away from DaVinci, towards its rendezvous with the great, gleaming starship that would soon be taking Shavrin home and Ciari to a magnificent adventure. But then, in Nicole's imagination, the details melted into something else. The shuttle wasn't heading for *Enterprise*, but *Wanderer*; and aboard weren't statesmen, pathfinders and Aliens, but two young officers, a quartet of Mission Specialists and their skipper. For Nicole, for those moments, it was over a year ago, when life was cleaner, simpler, happier. So much had happened in so little time; so much had been learned, about others, but mostly about herself. And much of that, she didn't like.

And the most important thing, she realized now, was that she'd hardly learned anything at all.

Her leg ached as she started down the ramp from the Lounge

to the Plaza below; the docs said it would ache for a while. Damage that extensive took time and care to heal, and madcap indulgences like the previous night were most assuredly not part of that therapeutic program. So, if she hurt, it was her own damn fault. She didn't care.

The Lounge was almost deserted, but had it been jammed full of people, she still would have felt alone.

"Hi," Hana said shyly, approaching her quietly.

"Hi yourself. Where have you been hiding? I looked for you at the ceremony."

"I was there, but you left like a shot as soon as it was done; and once I caught up to you, I . . . really didn't want to intrude. Like your new look."

Nicole made a shy, smiling face as a hand went reflexively to her hair. The day after her release from the hospital, she'd trekked over to Andrei's flat outside Gagarin and let him work some wonders. He'd trimmed her hair close on the sides, leaving it fuller on top, clipping it at the collar, without any sort of tail—not quite as extreme a style as Hana's mohawk, but dramatically insouciant in its own way. Nicole had drawn more than her share of glances.

"Thanks. But I didn't have the guts to go all the way."

"You military-types have higher responsibilities."

"And standards, I'm told, with appropriate frowns."

"Any plans?"

Nicole looked around at the Lounge and transit tunnel beyond, her throat suddenly thick with emotion: "Yeah, I want to go," she said.

"Because of Ciari?"

"I wish. Be easier to handle." She shook her head. "No, it's that I want to *go,* Hana! There's a culture out there the likes of which we've never seen! A people, a civilization! And that's only the beginning! There are other races as well! I want to see 'em, I want to learn, I want to *go!*"

"You think you're ready?"

"You mean, aside from not being able to walk?"

"You know what I mean."

"No. I'm a hero, but I'm not ready. I've been told that, too."

"Such bitterness ill-becomes you, Shea." Both young women reacted to Canfield's appearance. She'd been sitting on one of the meditation benches that ringed the Plaza, almost invisible in the shadows. As they turned, she rose to her feet and stepped out to join them.

"Any fool can be a hero," she continued quietly. "It requires no more than being in the right place at the right time. And that happy confluence has been duly noted by your peers. What it comes down to is that these...." she touched the Solar Cross on Nicole's tunic, "...are won. This..." she tapped the Command Astronaut wings on her own, "...is *earned*.

"You've made your First Flight, Nicole. And done better than anyone had even a right to expect. You have potential. But also a long, long way to go before that potential is fully realized. Anything less and you're short-changing yourself. Is that what you want?" Nicole shook her head. "It won't be easy. But nothing truly worthwhile is."

Hana was looking at the cenotaph.

"So many names, General, and ours came so close to joining them."

"Perhaps they will yet, Dr. Murai. Ours is a hard profession. But they believed in what they were doing. They had a dream. Much like yours, Nicole. Space is our 'Final Frontier,' the ultimate challenge. To them, the risk was justified, and the price. Think of it, a century ago, we—the human species—were totally earthbound. There's no comparison between what we do today and what we did then. And yet, in essential terms, really nothing has changed. Our ships are better, our knowledge vaster. But at the same time, we've also discovered how infinitely much more there is *to* learn. Amused, Shea?"

"Serendipity, ma'am. I was thinking something like that myself, not long ago."

"You're heirs to an extraordinary legacy, whose value is expressed in the cheapest, yet most precious, of resources: human lives. Your challenge is to prove yourselves worthy of it."

"You mean us both?" Hana said, her voice lilting upward at the last moment to turn her statement into a question.

"This isn't a closed shop, Doctor. I wear a civilian hat as well. Are you saying your dream isn't the same as Nicole's?

That you wouldn't jump at the chance to join the *Enterprise* mission?"

"How high?"

They laughed.

"Patience, both of you. You'll get your chance, I promise. In the meantime, would you care to join me in my quarters for dinner? Dr. Elias will be there, and my Chief of Staff, Colonel Genda, Dr. Zhimyanov and his lover. We'd—*I* would—like very much to hear the story of your flight from your own lips."

"Thank you, ma'am," Nicole said, "it'll be our pleasure."

"Shall we, then?" And she motioned them towards the Rapitrans station.

Canfield hung back a step to watch them, Nicole trying her best to disguise her hobble and make it appear she could walk normally, while Hana stayed close by, seeming to hesitate—as if nervous about being rebuffed—before slipping her arm through Nicole's. There was a moment of mutual stiffness, then the two women's tension drained from their bodies and Nicole let herself sag ever so lightly against her friend, while Hana took the extra weight with obvious joy. They had both loved and both been torn from that love by duty—only to find, to their surprise, a stronger, truer, more lasting bond. Canfield envied them that, as she did their youth. She had set the stage, done her best to help the Earth take its first hesitant steps into the stars, but they were the ones who would lead the way. *What wonders they will see,* she thought, *what adventures they will have.*

She smiled at the romance in that phrase, in her soul. No less now than the morning of her own First Flight, as blue sky beyond her Shuttle's canopy darkened to indigo and she watched with irrepressible delight as the stars came out. She'd been there and back and lived to tell the tale; now, it was their turn.

She stood a last, reverent moment before the cenotaph, and bid farewell to the ghosts with a salute, before following the new generation down the ramp.

STEVEN BRUST

__PHOENIX 0-441-66225-0/$4.50

In the return of Vlad Taltos, sorcerer and assassin, the Demon Goddess comes to his rescue, answering a most heartfelt prayer. How strange she should even give a thought to Vlad, considering he's an *assassin*. But when a patron deity saves your skin, it's always in your best interest to do whatever she wants . . .

__JHEREG 0-441-38554-0/$4.99

There are many ways for a young man with quick wits and a quick sword to advance in the world. Vlad Taltos chose the route of the assassin and the constant companionship of a young jhereg.

__YENDI 0-441-94460-4/$4.99

Vlad Taltos and his jhereg companion learn how the love of a good woman can turn a cold-blooded killer into a real mean S.O.B...

__TECKLA 0-441-79977-9/$4.99

The Teckla were revolting. Vlad Taltos always knew they were lazy, stupid, cowardly peasants...revolting. But now they were revolting against the empire. No joke.

__TALTOS 0-441-18200/$4.99

Journey to the land of the dead. All expenses paid! Not Vlad Taltos' idea of an ideal vacation, but this was work. After all, even an assassin has to earn a living.

__COWBOY FENG'S SPACE BAR AND GRILLE
0-441-11816-X/$3.95

Cowboy Feng's is a great place to visit, but it tends to move around a bit — from Earth to the Moon to Mars to another solar system — and always just one step ahead of whatever mysterious conspiracy is reducing whole worlds to radioactive ash.
